W9-BFT-122

A Delicious Wager

"Care to wager on it?" he asked.

"Wager on what?"

"On your ability to ride the beast, of course. Or perhaps"—his eyebrows quirked insolently—"we should better your odds by making it on your ability to capture him?"

"I have never wagered in my life."

"Are you unsure, Mrs. Lovering, of your abilities?"

She looked at him for a long moment. "What would I win?"

He smiled. "More importantly, what would you lose?"

They paused for a moment, each thinking as quickly as possible. The earl closed the gap between them. "A kiss. If you lose, that is," he said.

"No," she said.

"A kiss if you win, then, if you prefer."

"No," she said again.

"Then we are back to if you lose."

She knew he expected her to refuse again, stomp off and refer to her reputation and the like. What could she counter it with to wipe the smug expression off his face and end this entire wagering business?

"All right," she said slowly. "But if I stay on the brute, you'll marry me." Really, she only wanted to see him unsettled. Titled gentlemen were so sure of themselves, this one in the extreme. And she knew she could unseat herself if she did manage to ride the beast. She could tell by his strained expression that she had outmaneuvered him.

"Mrs. Lovering, your wager is very tempting."

SIGNET

REGENCY ROMANCE
COMING IN MARCH 2004

Castaway Hearts
by Nancy Butler

Miss Lydia Peartree's afternoon cruise turns out to be
a disaster at sea, and she only has the scruffy captain
to count on. But when she finds that he's a handsome
spy in disguise, she realizes she may have passed
judgement too quickly.

0-451-21181-2

Tabitha's Tangle
by Emily Hendrickson

Lord Latham has resigned himself to a loveless
marriage with an earl's daughter. But when he hires
Tabith Herbert to catalogue his library, he finds that
falling in love is a delightfully novel idea...

0-451-21164-2

Kiss of the Highwayman
by Jenna Mindel

Artemis Rothwell is on her way to London for her
coming out, but she is robbed by highwaymen who
steal her precious ring. When one thief kisses her and
promises to return the ring, Artemis finds herself
longing for the masked man to fulfill his promise.

0-451-21034-4

Available wherever books are sold, or
to order call: 1-800-788-6262

A Secret Passion

Sophia Nash

A SIGNET BOOK

SIGNET
Published by New American Library, a division of
Penguin Group (USA) Inc., 375 Hudson Street,
New York, New York 10014, U.S.A.
Penguin Books Ltd, 80 Strand, London WC2R 0RL, England
Penguin Books Australia Ltd, 250 Camberwell Road,
Camberwell, Victoria 3124, Australia
Penguin Books Canada Ltd, 10 Alcorn Avenue,
Toronto, Ontario, Canada M4V 3B2
Penguin Books (N.Z.) Ltd, Cnr Rosedale and Airborne Roads,
Albany, Auckland 1310, New Zealand

Penguin Books Ltd, Registered Offices:
80 Strand, London WC2R 0RL, England

First published by Signet, an imprint of New American Library,
a division of Penguin Group (USA) Inc.

First Printing, February 2004
10 9 8 7 6 5 4 3 2 1

Copyright © Sophia Nash Ours, 2004
All rights reserved

Ⓟ REGISTERED TRADEMARK—MARCA REGISTRADA

Printed in the United States of America

Without limiting the rights under copyright reserved above, no part of this pub-
lication may be reproduced, stored in or introduced into a retrieval system, or
transmitted, in any form, or by any means (electronic, mechanical, photocopy-
ing, recording, or otherwise), without the prior written permission of both the
copyright owner and the above publisher of this book.

PUBLISHER'S NOTE
This is a work of fiction. Names, characters, places, and incidents either are the
product of the author's imagination or are used fictitiously, and any resemblance
to actual persons, living or dead, business establishments, events, or locales is
entirely coincidental.

BOOKS ARE AVAILABLE AT QUANTITY DISCOUNTS WHEN USED TO PROMOTE PRODUCTS
OR SERVICES. FOR INFORMATION PLEASE WRITE TO PREMIUM MARKETING DIVISION,
PENGUIN GROUP (USA) INC., 375 HUDSON STREET, NEW YORK, NEW YORK 10014.

If you purchased this book without a cover you should be aware that this book
is stolen property. It was reported as "unsold and destroyed" to the publisher and
neither the author nor the publisher has received any payment for this "stripped
book."

The scanning, uploading, and distribution of this book via the Internet or via any
other means without the permission of the publisher is illegal and punishable by
law. Please purchase only authorized electronic editions, and do not participate
in or encourage electronic piracy of copyrighted materials. Your support of the
author's rights is appreciated.

In memory of Richard N. H. Nash,
my mentor, my father
1923–2000

ACKNOWLEDGMENTS

I would like to express my thanks to all who helped me complete this book: to my husband, G. Ralph Ours III; my mother, Marie-Solange Howard, and my two children for providing loving support; to my editor, Hilary Ross, at Signet/NAL and my agent, Jenny Bent, at Harvey Klinger, Inc., for their enthusiasm and belief in the book as well as judicious improvements; to Kathy Caskie for her incomparable generosity, friendship, and vast knowledge of the intricacies of the writing world; to Jessica Benson, Diane Perkins, Hope Tarr, Meredith Bond, and Tim Bentler-Jungr for their encouragement, critiques, guidance, and fellowship; and finally to Mary Balogh and Mary Jo Putney for creating books that inspired me to start writing.

Chapter One

"It is exceedingly important to look for the same qualities one would search for in a wife when choosing a prime piece of horseflesh," Mr. Billingsley advised his acquaintances.

"In what way, may I ask?" inquired Rolfe Fitzhugh St. James, the seventh Earl of Graystock.

The young gentleman paused for effect. "Well, of course one must find perfect breeding, good bones, intelligence in the eye, an excellent disposition, with a willingness to obey. You understand the idea."

Graystock found it difficult to take Billingsley seriously given his high shirt points and overblown airs.

"Why, Billingsley, we were afraid you would suggest it necessary to have talent for playing the pianoforte or doing excellent needlework," replied Sir Thomas Gooding.

"And what about a soft rump and good teeth?" Mr. Compton added. A round of laughter greeted his remark.

"Graystock, what say you to these ideas?" Mr. Billingsley asked.

Rolfe paused until the laughter gave way to silence. "I say you have forgotten the essential ingredients: those of spirit and courage. For without those, you have quite an ordinary creature."

The group of young bucks parried his comment with sidelong, smirking glances amongst themselves.

"The countess was quite a spirited creature, I daresay," countered a smug, mocking voice from the group now fallen behind him.

Hands clenched, Rolfe whipped around to confront the audacious fop. But to his disgust the coward and the rest of the dandified group had peeled off to blend into the dark sea of top hats all moving toward the five large gates of Tattersalls.

Gooding was the only gentleman who remained in the earl's company. "Sir, take no notice of the riffraff. Those perfumed bob tails cannot even claim to be of our sex," he said.

Rolfe was silent. He stopped on the threshold, where the pungent odor of fresh manure mixed with pipe tobacco and the serious discussion of all things equine was the order of the day. He could feel the familiar muscle in his jaw beating a military tattoo as he walked past the throngs of gentlemen, many of whom refused to nod and acknowledge his presence. He should be used to it by now. Even the *ton*'s greedy mothers had shielded their daughters from his gaze during the past season. While his supposed wealth was tempting, speculation was rife that an alliance with the Earl of Graystock was not desirable. No, he would have to agree he was not the most enticing possible son-in-law.

"Let us hope you have more luck today, sir—finding a mount to replace Caesar," said Gooding in an attempt to change the subject. "Although I know he really is irreplaceable."

Rolfe watched as stable hands led in a parade of immaculately groomed animals. "You are right, Gooding," he said with a sigh. "And I am tiring of this fruitless quest. I would give a pocket full of gold for a warm-blooded cavalry horse over the whole lot of these fine-boned bundles of nerves any day," he said as they watched a mare whose handler could barely restrain her. Rolfe sat down with his former second in command in the seats reserved for the peerage in the viewing stand.

"I'm of the same mind, sir," Gooding agreed.

Rolfe turned to look down the long hallway leading from the

stables where private business and sales were being conducted between reputable and not so reputable breeders. Suddenly, above the deep bellowing of the auctioneer, Rolfe heard a faint, short scream from a horse in the distance. The sound shot scalding blood throughout his body as he was reminded of the sounds of dying horses on a battlefield. Without thinking, he rose from his cramped seat and made his way to the decaying lower stables. His footsteps gave way to a run as he searched for the source of the sound of whip on flesh.

Around a far corner stall, a huge black animal reared as it tried to paw a man wielding a cat-o'-nine-tails. The small man swore as he approached again with a whip and a leather halter. The horse's bloodied sides were heaving, and its eyes were crazed. It screamed again.

"Give me your pistol, man," Rolfe ordered. The man jumped back and turned.

"I suppose yer right, Guv'na. Shoot the beast, afore he 'urts another bloke," said the skinny, loose-toothed horse trader with fear in his slit eyes. A wiry young stableboy fished a pistol out of the medicinal trunk and handed it to Graystock. Rolfe turned and pointed the weapon at the horse trader and cocked the trigger. The man gulped and stammered. "Now see 'ere, whyever are ye pointin' that at me? This 'ere animal is crazy. Cost me a stable 'and and stitches on another. I didn't do more than it deserved."

"What's his price?" Rolfe demanded as he kept one eye on the man and appraised the animal behind the dealer.

The grimy little man's eyes gleamed with greed as he spit in the corner. "Well, Guv'na, a hundred guineas be the price," he crowed, smelling a sale.

Rolfe narrowed his eyes and stared into the man's face as he tossed him some coins. "That's half. Which is more than you deserve. It is clear this horse has not been properly fed or watered in a long time."

The dealer replied, "Now, looky 'ere, I gots the stitchin' doctor to pay, and the box stall, and sumpin' for me trouble." Rolfe remained silent and raised the pistol to eye level. The breeder backed away. "I'll 'ave the authorities, I will. This 'ere's property."

"Yes, do get the authorities, my good man, so I may have a word with them. However, if I don't see your return in five minutes, I'll understand the sale to be complete."

As the breeder scuttled away, Rolfe lowered the pistol and uncocked the trigger. He returned it to the nervous stableboy, then took a handful of grain from a nearby bin and walked over to the front of the stall. He looked the huge, big-boned stallion in the eye. Yes, there was a definite insane look, but it might well be temporary, due to the conditions. He offered the grain in a slow movement. The animal pawed and blew on the ground, scattering meager tufts of straw and dust in the dank stall. Rolfe stood motionless for all of ten minutes before the horse rolled his head several times and whinnied. For every stumble forward there were the requisite number of steps back, accompanied by head tossing. Finally, the horse grabbed the grain in a swift movement, his long neck stretched to the limit. "That's it, old boy," Rolfe said in a low tone.

"Ah, there you are," Gooding called out as he appeared from the gloom and made his way to the corner stall. "Ho, ho, don't tell me you finally found the one!" he continued. They both stood back and looked at the animal as it snorted and pawed the ground. "Looks like it will play the pianoforte quite nicely," Gooding added with a laugh.

Rolfe, unable to suppress a rare smile, answered, "Yes, perhaps Billingsley would be interested."

Jane Lovering entered the maze of lanes leading to the town of Littlefield at dusk. She closed her eyes as she angled her face to the breeze. A few wisps of hair, shaken loose on her long ride, blew across her cheek. She pushed them back and breathed deeply. She always knew when she was close to the sea, and this was somehow calming.

Even though she was dog-tired, a small part of her wanted to urge her mount even further, all the way home to Pembroke in Land's End, Cornwall, where the sand always seemed to end up in her short boots and the sea air left its traces of salt on her skin. Moreover, home was where Harry was, along with everything else that brought joy to her life. She longed for the comforting presence of Pembroke and her beloved horses. Her mind wandered to former days of trapping butterflies with Harry, and mad gallops across the beaches. But that was a long time ago—six years ago, to be precise, before Harry had left for university and she had married.

She looked down at her dirty gauntlet gloves and the thick layer of dust on her dark blue riding habit and realized that going any further was out of the question. She should count her blessings that she had got this far without mishap. She shivered as the cool breeze touched her plain white lawn collar, dampened by perspiration.

She rode to the end of the main road before finding the smithy's shack. Dismounting, she tied the reins to the railing and moved inside a bit awkwardly. The muscles in her legs and back were cramped and painful.

"Excuse me, boy. Where may I find the blacksmith?" she asked a wiry lad while leaning against the doorjamb.

"He's me, fer now leastaways," the red-haired boy said in his slight Scottish drawl. "Me Da went to fetch some new tools in Blackhaven."

"Well, I was wondering if we could come to some sort of arrangement regarding my horse, as I see the inn's outer buildings have been destroyed. I will be staying with Miss Fairchild."

"Well, Missus, we dinna have night stabling, but ye could try the inn in Blackhaven."

She pondered the dilemma for several seconds. "Could I take the stall your father's horse had until he returns?"

The young boy hesitated. "If ye be a friend of Miss Fairchild, then I'm thinking it could be so. Ye'll have to talk to me Da when he comes back day after tomorrow."

"I will, young man. And thank you," she said. Jane exhaled and unsaddled her mare, refusing the child's offer to care for her horse. After seeing to the animal's feed and water, she walked through the back of the stable and beyond the budding apple trees away from the small cluster of houses on the road.

Within a short distance lay her beloved aunt's cottage. As the last bit of light left the evening sky, the scent of honeysuckle growing wild over the fence posts overwhelmed her senses, and tears burned the back of her eyes. The intense, sweet smell reminded her of home and the craggy coastline of Cornwall, where the fragrant flower would be blooming right now alongside the bright splashes of primroses and pansies.

She bit back her tears in surprise, for she never, ever cried, not even at her mother's funeral. Her younger brother had told her she was the oddest being alive that day. And if that had been the worst day of her life, today was surely the second worst.

A faint plume of smoke curling from the chimney signaled her aunt's presence within. Jane knocked on the door. It soon opened to reveal a thin, plain woman with a careworn face, wholly unremarkable save for her pale cornflower-blue eyes and sincere, warm smile. Her thick nut-brown hair, threaded with gray, matched the color of her homespun day gown.

Faint wrinkles disappeared as sheer joy suffused Clarissa Fairchild's face. "Jane, oh, how I've longed to see you. And here you are!" she cried as she folded her niece into her arms. "With whom did you travel?" She looked outside, as though expecting an entourage. "Where is your maid?"

Jane moved away from her embrace. "I came alone, Aunt."

"Alone! Whatever could have possessed you?" she quizzed, darting a worried glance before hurriedly closing the door.

"It appears my arrival has gone by unremarked."

"Come, dearest. I've just put on water to boil. I want to hear everything." They bustled through the short hallway, Jane following her aunt blindly forward. Arriving in the kitchen, Clarissa walked to the cupboard and, without speaking, lowered a second cup and saucer. Jane sat stiffly at the table and watched as Clarissa added two heaping spoonfuls of Bohea tea to the teapot from her small cache. Jane let the silence stretch, taking an uncommonly long time to remove her gloves, pulling at each fingertip before meeting her aunt's gaze.

"Jane, I would not for the world distress you further, but please tell me you have not traveled alone all the way from the streets of Mayfair? And knowing you, you rode! Why, it must have taken you eight hours at least."

The worry on Clarissa's brow was distressing, so Jane forced a light tone as she replied, "Yes, but it was not so terrible a journey. I only worry that I had to 'steal' my own horse to get here."

Clarissa paused in the midst of pouring boiling water over the tea leaves and stared at her niece. "What do you mean, you had to steal your own horse?" Her voice was sharp, as she set a plate of small raisin cakes before her niece.

"Well, to make a long story short, Father has disowned me." During the shocked silence that followed, Jane removed her netted riding hat and smoothed her hair into place. "I must ask, I am afraid, if you will allow me to stay with you. I daresay Father will not look kindly upon you for harboring me, but then, he so rarely looks kindly upon anyone not offering him money for one of his children. Truly, though"—and here her voice broke slightly—"I have nowhere else to stay or I would not ask this of you."

"Of course you may stay here." Clarissa frowned, her puzzlement clear. "But what happened? Whyever would my brother disown you? Though you are welcome here for as long as you would wish, why not go to the house Mr. Lovering left you?"

Jane looked out the kitchen window as night descended upon the woodland. Lowering her head, she breathed in the delicate, moist scent of the tea before taking a sip. It smelled heavenly after the cold and dirty ride from London. "I sold the townhouse and everything along with it several months ago when Father sent the family solicitors to explain the once again dire circumstances of the family's estate." She made her voice as unemotional as possible. "It was that or the untenable option of selling breeding stock at Pembroke. Father knew I couldn't bear the idea of selling those horses. They are the last of the ones Mother and I bred, you know." Her composure was finally threatening to break. Wordlessly, Clarissa handed her a handkerchief. "I, once again, find myself residing with Father, reduced to an obedient dependent . . . for the most part."

"Which part?" Clarissa asked, refilling Jane's cup. "Obedient? Or dependent?"

Jane smiled sadly. "You know me too well, Aunt."

"But why after such a kind gesture would he disown you?"

"It is simple, really. This morning I refused to marry his choice of a husband. The moneylenders are calling, again, and so he signed a betrothal agreement without consulting me.

Knowing he was unlikely to gain my compliance, he posted engagement announcements in the morning papers. By doing so, he ensured I would be practically ruined in the eyes of the *ton* should I cry off. Not that I care so much. But it was tiring to always hear my name bandied about."

Noticing Clarissa looking with concern at her untouched plate, Jane forced herself to pick up a raisin cake and take a bite. "I learned the news," she continued lightly, "during my morning ride when a Mr. Kellery stopped after a good gallop on Rotten Row to offer his best wishes on my impending marriage. I laughed and said I would as soon marry again as he would. Mr. Kellery is a well-known older gentleman with a much-avowed dislike of matrimony."

"Yes, I rather think I recall him from my come-out days," her aunt said. "And I do believe he was avowing even then."

"Well, he looked at me with a strange expression and rode away shaking his head. Of course I wondered what sort of prank Mr. Kellery had played. He is a serious gentleman, not the sort to play word games."

Jane leaned back and closed her eyes, remembering the contentious meeting with her father that had followed. In the privacy of the breakfast parlor, her father had handed her the three morning papers and watched her. He had worn his usual expression of casual disdain.

A few minutes later, she had turned to the butler and addressed him. "I would have a private word with his lordship, please, George." The silence was oppressive as the butler left the room. Finally she looked up. "I see," she said very quietly, and then continued, "Father, this is impossible. I will not marry him."

"You will marry him, Jane," he said equally quietly. "You will obey me, as every good daughter would a father. I have given you a season in town with every chance to choose a husband. But you have failed, and now you must abide by my choice. I have found a man of good family and good fortune."

"Hmmm. Billingsley," she said. "Good family and good fortune. We shall forget for the moment his revolting personality, puffed-up consequence, and hideous person, shall we? For what can they signify in the face of ten—or is it fifteen—thousand a year?" A hot flush moved down her body, leaving her trembling with suppressed emotion.

"Do not overstep yourself, Daughter."

"By having the audacity to comment on the man to whom I have been sold?" She lifted the teacup from the saucer, but put it back when she could not control her shaking hand. "Really, you have treated me like nothing better than cattle, selling me off to the highest bidder. *Again*." Now that her anger had risen, she couldn't stop. "It is too bad you didn't have more daughters. Just imagine the profits had there been two of us!"

Jane could see the telltale sign of anger on her father's face. A large vein near the center of his pale forehead stood out, like a streak of lightning foretelling doom. His dark, watery eyes bulged. But still his calm tone remained.

"You will marry again, or you will leave this house," he said. "If it is the latter, I will not know you anymore. Nor will your brother, or your friends. However, I concede you do have a choice. What is it to be?"

Jane felt the cold tendrils of angry pride stiffen her spine. Rising from the table, she dropped her napkin over her untouched breakfast. "How much time am I to be granted before I take my leave?"

Her father narrowed his murky eyes. "None," he said as he left the room.

The kind old butler kept his gaze on the tips of his boots when he reentered the dining room. His heightened color proved eavesdropping was his forte. "Shall I go after your maid? She has just stepped out to run your errands this morning."

"No, thank you, George," she said, recovering herself. "I would only ask your help in sending a note to Mrs. Dougherty to beg off her invitation for tomorrow evening. It appears I will not be staying in London after all."

"Yes, miss," he responded.

"No, George, it is ma'am. You must remember I have been married."

"Yes, miss," he responded with a slow smile. Despite her unfortunate situation, she could not resist smiling back at the family butler who had always been so kind to her, especially during the five years since her mother had died. He had spent hours talking to her, walking with her in the pastures of Pembroke, and offering comfort when no one else had, all at a respectful distance, of course. She rose from the table and shook his hand before she reached up and kissed his wrinkled old face good-bye. She looked at the tears in his eyes, and brushed at them with her fingertips.

"George, this is for the best. I knew I should never have returned here after Mr. Lovering died. You were the only enticement." She smiled at his long face. "But how can I stay here when you refuse to maintain the family's appearances?" She laughed before adding to the bald and well-attired man, "Your hair needs cutting again, and those shabby clothes . . ." It was their favorite joke, and it would be their last.

"Yes, miss. As you say, miss."

"Now, George . . ."

Jane was awakened from her reverie by the soothing touch of her aunt. Clarissa pressed a cool, damp compress on Jane's forehead, easing the aching pain she felt. "And now, here I am, my dearest aunt, an uninvited houseguest, sitting in your kitchen." Jane grasped her aunt's hand in her own. "But for you, I will try to be obedient."

Clarissa laughed and shook her head.

Chapter Two

The bright morning sunlight hurt Jane's sleepless eyes as it filtered through the budding trees of Littlefield's landscape three mornings later. She descended a steep bank, slippery with dew, then guided her horse through a muddy stream. Salty breezes wafted through fields of verdant young grasses and wildflowers in the semidarkness before the rays of the sun penetrated the early morning sky and stilled the air.

She had known she would not sleep again when the bedcovers had twisted into an uncomfortable mass. Torturous thoughts had swirled through her brain all night. Only the wind rushing by her face during a good gallop could promise to banish her worries, at least for a little while.

Pax stumbled while scrambling up the steep bank of the stream. Jane leaned her weight forward and gave the animal more freedom with the reins. At the top of the bank, her horse stopped and snorted. Jane wondered what Pax saw, and squinted over her mare's alert ears.

A streak of black was in the distance. It was a horse and rider. Going far, far too fast. At breakneck speed, in fact. In an instant she urged her mount into a gallop. She thought that if she could not stop the runaway, at least she could be there to pick up the pieces when the rider fell off.

Her horse could not overtake the other. Jane changed tactics and circled around the opposite direction of the field to try to cut off the pair. As they drew closer, she could hear the man curse.

"Get the . . . devil out of here . . . private property," was all she could make out.

Then the horse, despite its lathered sides, lowered its head and ran faster than before. Jane stopped and watched the pair gallop out of control around the perimeter of the field. Finally, the huge horse headed toward her in full gallop and reared within a few feet of her horse. Jane's mount crow-hopped and whinnied as the man half slid, half fell off the tail end of the stallion. It took all of Jane's resources to stay in her sidesaddle. The man's brutally strong back was turned to her as he dusted himself off and watched the black horse jump the high fence that enclosed the field and take off.

"Are you hurt?" asked Jane.

Breathing hard, he turned to face her. The man's overly long black hair was touched with a few brushstrokes of gray on the sides. He was dressed almost indecently, a plain white shirt with buttons undone halfway and sleeves rolled up, no neck-cloth, not even a coat. She tried not to notice the torn green-stained breeches that left nothing to the imagination. If she was not mistaken, she could even discern the edges of a pair of men's smalls under a tear near the thigh. She felt a blush suffuse her face as she finalized her perusal by noting that his scratched boots were caked in mud and had probably never seen a boot brush. As her gaze moved back up to his face, his cold expression hardened even further. His angular face promised to brook little argument. She backed her horse up a few paces.

He looked furious as he wiped the grime from his brow. "This is private property, Madam. Were you unable to read the notices posted?" he asked, his gray eyes turbulent with anger.

She was not sure why she should be defensive for trying to help. "Pray forgive me," she said. "I thought you might have been in need of help."

"I see." He looked at her for an uncomfortably long moment. She resisted the urge to squirm as he stepped forward the paces she had given up. "And you thought you could stop that two-ton miserable sack of horseflesh?" he asked.

"I am most sorry to have invaded your master's property. Do be so kind as to overlook it. It shall not happen again," she replied, lifting her chin.

An uncomfortable silence ensued as the tall, muscular man turned to retrieve his hat. He returned with a glint in his eye, which Jane could not fathom. "Yes," he said, "his lordship will be most displeased."

He didn't speak or act like a servant, and yet his behavior and clothing were not gentlemanlike. He must be a gentleman in name only, reduced to earning a wage. His arrogant countenance showed he had refused to become accustomed to his low station in life.

His eyes roamed her entire person from the tip of her boots to her eyes. It was a completely improper action, and Jane felt anew the awkwardness of the situation. She wondered for just an instant whether anyone would be able to hear her if she needed to cry for help. She pushed this thought away and began to back up her horse. "I will ride on to enlist the aid of another stable hand and a new mount for you." She was pleased to note that despite her discomfort, her tones were cool.

"Oh, no, miss. I was thinking you might be able to convey me to the area yourself, as you were the cause of this trouble."

"Me? How dare you presume to blame me!"

"Well, you startled him just as I had got him almost under control."

"Nonsense. You had absolutely no control over him to start with."

"All the same, the least you could do is give *a poor bloke* a ride pillion back to the stables."

She stared at him in horror. Could he really mean to suggest she allow him up on her horse with her? It was too much. As he started to lead her animal to a felled tree to mount up, she pulled Pax up short. "Unhand my horse. I will ride on in search of help." She moved her riding crop from her saddle to her hand.

But he reached up and easily took it away from her. "You shall do no such thing. Stay still. It never pays to fight the inevitable." And with that, he grabbed the pommel and cantle of the saddle and swung up behind her. His bronzed forearm grazed her hips as he settled behind her.

"This is entirely improper," she began before he cut her off by putting both hands around her waist.

"Move on, old girl, before I use this whip."

Jane was appalled, unsure if his command was directed to-ward her or her steed. She dug her heels into the animal and urged her forward.

The heat from his large hands was unsettling. They almost encircled her entire waist. Flustered and angry that this arrogant groom had the impertinence to insist and force himself up onto her horse, she urged Pax into a fast trot, but to her dismay, this only made the man tighten his grip on her waist and move closer to her body. She could even smell the male essence of him. Jane immediately brought her horse back to a fast walk.

She thought she heard him laugh, but his voice was bland as he inquired, "Is your horse winded already, Miss, ah . . . Per-haps I should know your name, considering our circum-stances." He removed one of his hands to rearrange the saddle pad as he wrapped his other entire forearm around her waist. The strength in his arm unnerved her, as did his warm breath on her neck.

Jane hesitated. It was very improper of this man to insist on an introduction. It was the outside of enough. She decided to re-fuse an answer. It was difficult to cut someone when he was holding a part of one's body, but she persevered.

"So I am not to learn the trespasser's name, then? I am not surprised," the man continued.

Jane responded with a sniff. When they were finally past the stream, he directed her through a small grove of apple trees. She stopped at the foot of a manicured drive and allowed her gaze to drift over the estate. The structure was immense. Pale limestone cut into rectangles formed a symmetrical castle boasting at least two hundred windows. Jane almost forgot her passenger for a few moments while she admired the classic lines of the edifice. Conical evergreens framed the tall archway of the entrance as well as the entire outside of the castle and pathways.

"Do you like what you see?"

Her unwanted companion's warm breath on her neck reminded her of the discomforting state of affairs. "Who would not?"

"Indeed," he said as he leaned closer. "Shall we press on, then? I could arrange a tour of the Hall should you so desire. In fact, I could escort you myself, considering your unexampled kindness in condescending to share your horse with me."

She could feel his whiskers tease her ear. "You may dismount here," Jane commanded in a clipped fashion. "And I will depend on you not to discuss this incident with anyone."

"I daresay this means you will not offer to escort me to the main stables?" he responded. When this met with no response, he swung off the horse and slid down. Jane noticed a long tear on the right side of his shirt, which revealed a muscled shoulder with a jagged scar. She pulled her gaze away from him and leaned over to take the riding crop he still held.

"Have no fear, ma'am. For"—his eyes narrowed in amusement—"who would believe I was offered escort by a nameless trespasser in the neighborhood?" The man smiled for the first time, revealing straight white teeth. The sun appeared from behind a scudding cloud, and his eyes turned to burnished silver before he bowed and strode with purpose toward the drive.

Jane summoned as much dignity as possible as she urged her mare to trot back down the small lane while she wondered what on earth she had done to merit such a series of unfortunate events. Now, in addition to her long list of worries in London, it seemed she must add yet another here in Littlefield. She sighed. While her life had been far from perfect a day ago, it had been at least secure and proper.

For the first twenty-three years of her life, the most improper thing she had ever done was infuriate her music teacher. This entailed running away from home when she was twelve, following the severe scolding she had received from her father regarding a certain toad in the pianoforte. Her mother had found her down by the cliffs, huddled in the wild grasses of the shallows with her knees drawn up and her chin tucked down. She remembered the sensation of her mother's hands stroking her hair and whispering that she must return home. She had picked up her butterfly box and scribbling book and trudged homeward.

After stabling her mare, Jane walked toward her aunt's cottage. The thought of the scribbling book made her smile. Yes, that was it. Finishing the story she had begun to write two months ago would take her mind off of her current worries. It was a better idea than trespassing in search of the sea and good scenery.

Clarissa rose from her cramped position in the garden to welcome Jane at the gate. She removed her muddied gardening gloves and apron. "Jane," she said with obvious pleasure, "I have been waiting for you, dearest. I have something to show you which I think you will like!" The two women entered the cottage and made their way through the narrow hall into the kitchen. Jane's curiosity could not budge Clarissa's desire to surprise her.

Clarissa moved to the table and untied two old-looking packets. Jane watched her aunt unfold lengths of beautiful crepe and Alamode black silk.

"Aunt Clarissa! Wherever did you find this?"

"I remembered this morning that I had had the foresight to purchase several lengths of fabric before leaving my brother's residence in London. I knew it would be more difficult to find good cloth in the country." Clarissa folded the fabrics and placed them in Jane's arms. "Your father never should have forced you out of mourning. Your riding habit will have to do until this can be made up."

"It only mattered to the outside world. In the privacy of my heart, I could still mourn him," Jane said wistfully while examining the silks. "I can't thank you enough. It is too much."

Clarissa moved to place tea items on the table. "Your thanks are unnecessary. I will write a note to my brother, insisting he send your clothes for the end of the period."

"He won't relent. My father was very clear that I not take anything. It will be a point of pride. He will be furious enough when he realizes I took my mare." She kept her eyes on her hands, which held the riding crop she had just picked up.

"Aunt, I must warn you of a particularly vexing event during my ride this morning." She went on to relate the particulars of the meeting with the stable hand.

Clarissa was confused. "You say the man was very tall with black hair? It cannot be the man who oversees the stables, as that is Matthews and he is balding. I know all the inhabitants of the village, and most of the servants at Hesperides Hall are at least familiar by face. Are you sure it was not the earl himself? He fits the description," the aunt said as she poured the boiling water into a pot.

"But this man was wearing a torn shirt without a neckcloth and breeches that were beyond description. He threatened that the earl would be furious for my trespassing."

"Well, then it couldn't be Lord Graystock." Clarissa set a loaf of bread and some preserves onto the small wooden table. "Ah, but I remember . . . The rector was mentioning the earl was expecting a guest or two at Hesperides. He must be one of the gentlemen or a manservant of one of the guests."

"You know the earl? Lord Graystock, you said?"

"I have not been presented to him, as he has only lately returned. However, I have seen him in church and he is an austere gentleman, as befitting his station." Clarissa paused to pass Jane a small plate. "Before he assumed the mantle of the title from his father, he was married to a young lady. But it was for just a short while, well before I came here."

Jane stood up and moved to look out of the window. "What happened?"

"She died when she lost the child she was carrying. Apparently, it was a dreadful time. The neighborhood had waited more than two decades for a new mistress of Hesperides, and she was there for only seven months. She was young, only eighteen." She paused before rushing through the last of the explanation. "There was much talk about the circumstances of her miscarriage and death."

It had begun to rain, and from the window Jane sensed the reflection of raindrops on her face. "What kind of talk?"

"The kind that breeds from idleness in a small village."

"So, he became lord of the realm of Littlefield and reigns supreme over the area's society, who bow and scrape to him while gossiping behind his back?"

"No, Jane. You are mistaken somewhat," her aunt answered, taken aback by her tone. "The young gentleman purchased a pair of colors in the cavalry in the spring of aught nine, soon after his wife died. He vowed not to return. Reverend Gurcher said it was to escape the nightmares that haunted him. Although the rector should have never confided this to me," Clarissa added. "It is said he sold out when his commanding officer insisted, after he had very nearly lost an arm to a saber at Waterloo."

Jane squeezed her eyes shut. "I should not have surmised what I did."

"It is worse still," continued Clarissa. "His father, the old earl, died two years ago, convinced that his elder son would never return." Clarissa added that he also had one other sibling, a brother.

"And the other son?"

"I have never met him, as I have lived here for just the last seven years. No one seems to know much about him other than the fact that he does not reside here."

A long pause followed Clarissa's words. Jane turned from the window to face her aunt. Clarissa's pale blue eyes stared up at her from a drawn and tired face. Jane felt most unsettled and had to fight the urge to ask more questions. So, instead, she turned the conversation to arranging for suitable accommodations for her horse, still at the smithy's small stall.

The Earl of Graystock was pensive as he retired to the old, cracked leather chair near the fireplace in his library. The book he had left draped over the arm failed to engross him after a dutiful ten-minute read. He turned to look at the flames in the fireplace and allowed his mind to drift to the woman he had left on the drive.

He remembered her fragile, proud profile as she had moved toward the lane. She had brushed fine wisps of pale gold hair from her porcelain cheeks as she urged her mare into a trot. In a hurry to get herself as far from him as possible, no doubt. And for that he could hardly blame her. What had come over him? He had never treated a lady in such a fashion before.

But she knew how to fight back. A slow smile spread across

his face as he remembered her calculating perusal of his person back in the field. Those slanting eyes of hers were devilish. He had never seen eyes so mesmerizing—rims of blue with yellow in the centers. The colors played tricks on the senses. It had been next to impossible to drag his eyes off of her. It had been almost as hard to take his hands off her soft, tiny waist. And he would not soon forget her intoxicating feminine scent, which seemed to have been nothing more than lavender soap and sunshine. Lavender soap and sunshine, indeed! He shook his head. This was not like him.

He sighed and knew he would go out of his way to never learn her name. Young women, especially ones of her stamp, always led to trouble . . . of the never-ending variety. Just the thought made him weary. He picked up his book to have another go at it.

Just as he deemed the book hopelessly dull, Gooding arrived on the heels of the butler, who entered carrying a tray of brandy. "Ah, Gooding, you have arrived at last," Rolfe exclaimed as he looked over the compact medium frame of the slightly older gentleman.

"So you have been pining for me these many days since last we met, dear chap?" replied Gooding, in good humor as always.

It *was* good to see his subordinate officer so soon again after quitting London. He had spent much time with Gooding during the war. But now that the war was over, it was difficult to change the nature of their acquaintance.

For almost six years, Lieutenant Colonel Lord Hesperides, now the Earl of Graystock, had been Gooding's superior. For six years, Gooding had obeyed his every command without question. And now, Rolfe was coming to realize it was up to him to change the nature of their relationship to make it on more equal terms. All in all, Rolfe had no true friends, as he was a self-sufficient character, preferring his own company to the tedium of entertaining others. He sometimes wondered if he was this way by choice or by circumstance. Gooding was one of the very few acquaintances he preferred to keep.

"How go the roads?" he inquired, stepping away from his usual introspection.

"An awful quagmire. The spring rains left me hock high in mud from London to Arundel. The last few miles from there reminded me of the deluge in northern Spain. Your area is in luck, as the coastal winds are blowing off the worst of it." Gooding mentioned he had stopped at Littlefield's inn to repair a snapped rein and wipe the worst of the offending mud from his attire before continuing on to Hesperides.

"I'm afraid you might have to bear with my presence longer than overnight, as your town's smithy is absent and I have a ruined bridle to repair."

Waving away the butler, Rolfe moved toward the sideboard to pour two glasses of brandy. The ancient servant in turn cleared his throat to gain the earl's attention.

"Yes, Hastings?" came the reply to that standard attention-getting device.

"Your lordship, may I presume to suggest the services of Matthews to aid Sir Thomas?"

"Of course. Have Matthews attend to the tack."

"Hmm, a Mr. Matthews? Indeed, I have a letter for him in my possession. It was put in my care at the inn when I indicated my final destination." Gooding placed in Hastings' tray a rather soggy envelope that bore the stable master's name. Hastings closed the brass-handled doors as he exited the formal room. "Recapturing your earliest role of messenger, are you? Upon my word, were you able to refrain from a bit of spying?"

Gooding laughed and held up both hands. "I admit to the first, but before we continue, may I help myself to a bit more of your brandy? Purely for medicinal purposes, you understand."

Rolfe nodded and in a matter of moments extracted a promise from Gooding to remain at least a fortnight at Hesperides.

"An invitation to stay at Hesperides is an honor not to be refused. I would be delighted to forestall my journey southward. My housekeeper will also be delighted to learn of the additional fortnight before my arrival," said Gooding with a grin.

"A house party will also be forming in the autumn. You would be a much-welcomed addition then, as well."

"I would be honored," Gooding said with a merry smile, his

brown eyes twinkling. "It is a long time since Hesperides has seen a party, is it not, sir?"

Rolfe paused. "You must call me Graystock now, you know." Gooding's face brightened as he nodded in agreement. Rolfe continued. "It was my grandmother's idea. While she is not a formidable relation, she has a way of forming ideas and plans in an altogether vexing fashion." Rolfe did not add that the tough old bird had had the audacity to remove from the Dowager House to the Hall without his leave. At the age of ninety, Grandmamma was not to be questioned, for fear of killing the old girl. He was certain her mental faculties were eroding, so he viewed her move to Hesperides not with trepidation but with relief, feeling he could keep a better eye on her. Rolfe had decided she had become quite unbalanced the day he had received letters from two families indicating their delight in accepting invitations to a house party in October. As it stood, the Kellerys, the Smiths, and now Gooding would be filling the Hall's apartments when the leaves turned.

When he had confronted his paternal grandmother about the letters, she had insisted she had already discussed the plan with him, much to his surprise and her annoyance. With a cynical mind and a knowing eye, he asked for an explanation.

She harrumphed. "I'm fatigued with the boredom of life in the country. If I'm to be locked up here, and deprived of my friends in town, then at least let us have some amusements."

"But, Grandmamma, you're not locked up, and well you know it. And your friends are all . . . well, dash it, well . . . dead!"

"Dear boy, I'm not senile," she laughed. "It's time to make new friends. The others are six feet undergound and therefore, well, just not as much fun as they used to be. And don't start telling me what good friends I have at the rectory and in the village."

Rolfe looked at her. "But you don't even know the Kellerys or the Smiths."

"I knew their grandparents, and a merry lot they were."

Rolfe knew that when she reverted to this sort of common language there was no use continuing. And possessing the intuitive qualities of an officer, he knew when to retreat. "All right,

Grandmamma, you shall have your house party. But I cannot promise I will be here."

Having gained the advantage, she folded her hands in her lap, smiled her most endearing smile, and continued to press her point. "But, my dear Rolfe, you cannot mean you won't be here for the harvest festival and Michaelmas celebration?"

He sighed and looked at the ceiling.

Rolfe and Gooding were on the point of quitting the room when Matthews entered. The stable master wore the same uncomfortable expression that almost all of the servants of Hesperides attempted to conceal. "My lord, may I be so humble as to ask how you would like me to answer this letter?"

It was the same letter Gooding had handed to Hastings not one half hour before. Rolfe opened it and perused the contents.

April 27th
Dear Sir,
I must beg your pardon in advance for forwarding this application. A near relation has lately arrived and is in dire need of stabling her mare for an indeterminate length of time. The small size of Littlefield leaves us without a place for the horse. If I knew where else to look, we would of course not dare to apply to you for guidance. While we understand it to be out of the question to request shelter in the earl's stables, we hope you might be able to provide us with suggestions for alternate venues by day's end if at all possible.

I remain, kind sir,
Clarissa Fairchild

Rolfe lowered the letter. "It seems the St. James stables are to become open to the public," he commented. He stared at Matthews. "Really, is there no other possibility? Who is this Clarissa Fairchild?"

Rolfe was surprised to see Gooding's ruddy face turn white. That gentleman snatched the letter from his hands to examine it.

Keeping his eyes trained on the floor, Matthews responded, "My lord, the inn's stables have yet to be rebuilt since the fire."

He paused before adding with an uncontrollable stammer. "Miss Fairchild is a-a, sp-sp-spinster in the neighborhood."

"Well, go to it, man," Rolfe commanded. "Inform the lady that accommodations shall be provided for the animal in question. And have my steward inform the innkeepers I would request a word with them."

Rolfe noticed Gooding had regained his composure after the stable master departed. "I take it you might have a comment or two regarding the letter? Or is it the letter writer?"

Gooding had regrouped and was able to answer with a semblance of calm. "Actually, I was thinking perhaps the mare could teach your stallion a few manners."

Rolfe scrutinized Gooding's face for a long moment. Then he smiled and guided his friend into the formal dining hall. Despite the urge to goad him further, Rolfe had the kindness not to pursue the topic.

It had required all of Sir Thomas Gooding's fortitude to entertain his host and his grandmother that evening. Now, in his bedchamber, away from his former commander's knowing eyes, he could contemplate the lady in question.

He remembered his good fortune in encountering Clarissa Fairchild almost a decade ago in London. No one else had seemed to admire her serene, intelligent expression. It had been said she was past the first bloom of youth at seven and twenty, but perhaps the *ton* had been brutal in its appraisal of the young lady. He had heard that for eight long seasons, Miss Fairchild attended soirees, balls, and entertainments of every kind, with little success. Of course, she had been greatly admired by all of the other young misses on the marriage mart. Although Thomas had sometimes wondered in his most cynical rare moments if these young ladies' friendships were not due to the fact that she could make some of the less than beautiful young ladies look to advantage in comparison.

Thomas had noticed that she suffered from the most acute sort of self-doubt. Miss Fairchild was indeed not pretty. She had a gangly frame, and pale eyes in an unremarkable face framed by ordinary brown hair with little curl.

However, Thomas, then untitled, had gotten a peek beneath

the controlled façade of Miss Fairchild. He had chanced to be seated next to the làdy in question after the supper dance at a ball. After ten minutes of conversation with the beautiful but decidedly giggly chit with whom he had just danced, Thomas hoped that the plain lady seated on his other side would be capable of better conversation. And indeed she was. No nerve-jangling fits of giggles, only rational, intelligent conversation with an occasional warm laugh and beautiful smile. And while he might not have been a fair way in love with her by the end of the second course, he had been enough caught by the clarity of her eyes to ask for the honor of her hand for the next set.

This grand gesture led to a small posy of flowers that was received by the lady with much gratitude the next morning. And so began his short courtship of Clarissa Fairchild. For within two months' time, Thomas found himself upon one knee. He was won over and much flattered by Clarissa's immediate acceptance. They planned their wedding, very sure of themselves and their love.

When he approached Clarissa's brother, Edward Fairchild, however, Fairchild had looked at him with disdain. His sister, Fairchild had said, would not be marrying him, nor did she ever want to see him again. Thomas' feelings upon receiving the startling news of her rejection of his suit cannot be overstated. He had insisted on an audience with Clarissa. He had pleaded his case with the brother, all in vain. He pursued the matter in Cornwall for several weeks, again all in vain, as no one there knew where Miss Fairchild could be found. Desolate, he had joined the war effort against Napoleon. His father's patron, in a great act of charity, had purchased a small commission for the good son. In due time, and with duly heroic diligence and acts, he was knighted, two months after Wellington's victory at Salamanca. That same month saw the title of Lord Wellington conferred upon Arthur Wellesley and Thomas' marriage to Miss Lucinda Vandermay, an ugly Dutch heiress.

After a seven-year absence from Clarissa Fairchild, Thomas had not expected the light-headed, buzzing sensation he felt upon hearing her name. He paced the floor of his bedchamber in an agony of angry indecision. He could make known to her he was at Hesperides, thereby showing her that his interest in her had dissipated, or he could steal away into the night to find her and drag the truth from her. Contemplation of the second course of action brought a sort of warm glow to his being, but ultimately his pride got the best of him and forbade a mad dash into the night.

Chapter Three

Jane lowered her eyes. Her only consolation was that as she was in the back of the church and he was in the front, she might have a chance of avoiding his notice. She whispered to her aunt the necessity of departing as soon as the last notes of the recessional were sung.

Jane's plan to escape unnoticed was thwarted when the rector, in sycophantic tones, invited the earl to perform a reading. All hope was lost when she could not make herself small enough to escape detection. Each time his cool, dark gaze swept the small congregation as he read the familiar words, she longed to cringe and avert her face. But she forced herself not to. On the final two sentences, his attention rested on her alone, and she gave up her pretense and stared back at him. She noticed he had replaced his poor man's costume with an immaculate, form-fitting bottle-green coat with gilt buttons, and cream-colored breeches met black boots polished to perfection—a gentleman's attire in every respect. His unfashionably long hair and arrogant, hooded expression were the only evidence remaining of the man she had met a few days before.

The reading done, he returned to his seat beside the rector's wife and whispered in her ear all of one minute. The tightly coiled curls on that lady's head bounced as she gave a backward glance toward Jane and her aunt. Jane felt the weight of the entire congregation's eyes upon her as they filed out. Clarissa's arm linked with her own as they nudged through the church doors into the bright sunlight. Without a word, they walked swiftly toward the cottage. But the high-pitched voice of the rector's wife calling their names pierced the crisp air and shattered their purpose.

"Oh, Miss Fairchild, oh, dear me, Miss Clarissa and Mrs. Lovering . . ." trilled Mrs. Gurcher, out of breath. Her voluptuous frame trundled up to them. "My dears, would you be so kind as to attend our little gathering at the parsonage? The earl and his grandmother and friend have condescended to take tea with us."

This was worse than Jane had anticipated. Much worse.

With as much hauteur as the two quaking plumes in her purple bonnet would allow, Mrs. Gurcher continued, "My dears, you have the singular honor of having had the earl ask particularly for your company. Upon my word, he has never asked such a thing before."

"We would be delighted. However, we planned a picnic by the sea this very day, so I am inclined to refuse your very kind offer," Clarissa responded.

"But I am not to let you get away! The gentleman with the earl insisted. See how they await your joining our small party?" Mrs. Gurcher motioned toward the group behind them. It was impossible to continue to refuse. With clutched hands and leaden footsteps, Jane and her aunt turned and walked to their fate of weak tea and uncomfortable conversation. Jane glanced at her aunt when Clarissa stumbled, only to read confused hesitation on her face, which was now devoid of color. She did not know what had caused the change in her aunt's demeanor, but she did know it was up to her to do the proper. She looked toward the earl and the other gentleman and refused to be bullied. Jane straightened her spine, changed tactics, and faced the enemy with fortitude.

Upon the rector's presentation of Lord Graystock to Jane, the earl bowed over her hand. "Mrs. Lovering, it is a distinct honor to meet you." He raised his heavy-lidded eyes to her face.

"My lord, I must thank you for your kind offer to stable my

horse while the inn's stables are being repaired," Jane said and lowered her gaze to the hem of her new mourning dress.

Tilting his head to examine her face, he replied, "Come, Mrs. Lovering, is it not a gentle-born person's duty to aid another in distress?"

"Quite so, my lord." She paused and looked up at him before adding under her breath, "Especially when the person in distress identifies himself."

"Touché, Mrs. Lovering."

His smile actually touched his silver eyes, but Jane was too distracted by Clarissa's obvious discomfort to examine the phenomenon further. She noted that when introduced to the other gentleman, a Sir Thomas Gooding, Clarissa would not look at him. And he, in turn, barely seemed able to utter the required niceties. Neither claimed a prior acquaintance, but Jane thought he looked vaguely familiar. Perhaps they had met in town.

As they walked toward the parsonage, the earl's grandmother addressed the two younger ladies. "I understand this little tea has interrupted a seaside picnic you planned for today. How I long to see the sea. But these old bones of mine make it difficult to go very often."

"We would be delighted to have you join us on an outing to the shore, if your health allows it, any one of these days," responded Clarissa, who seemed to have pulled herself together.

Mrs. Gurcher proudly herded the distinguished group into the front drawing room of the parsonage. At each moment her voice seemed to trill a bit higher and at times took on a warbling sound, especially when she learned that Cook's little cakes were not quite ready. Clarissa and Jane, distressed to learn the requisite twenty-minute tea might stretch into forty minutes, hid their emotions. Strong constitutions and a thorough education in the fine art of stretching the topic of the weather fortified them.

The two gentlemen refrained from contributing to this portion of the conversation. Rolfe meditated on the delectable Mrs. Lovering. The severity of her black gown emphasized her delicate neck and the slenderness of her frame. His hands gripped the arms of the chair as he remembered the feel of her small waist. When she looked up at him, her creamy complexion showed the hint of a blush on her high cheekbones. Ah, and those divine aquamarine eyes of hers—so remote when she was ill at ease.

It soon became apparent that his grandmother had quite taken to heart the fine weather and proposed taking advantage of the folly of a picnic on the bluffs overlooking the sea that same day. Rolfe arranged the plan with alacrity, and now the two younger ladies were the ones found lacking a topic of conversation. A plan was therefore fixed with several modifications. Lady Graystock was to be attended in her carriage by Miss Fairchild and the good Reverend and Mrs. Gurcher. The two gentlemen and Mrs. Lovering were to ride. The dowager countess suggested the servants at Hesperides would prepare a large picnic. Finally, with varying degrees of reluctance, all parties agreed to meet at the Hall. The much-anticipated cakes were consumed and the party, blessedly, was at an end.

"Quite uncommonly good-looking chits, I say," stated the grandmother during the return carriage ride to Hesperides.

Rolfe sighed. "Grandmamma, Miss Fairchild cannot be called a chit by any means. She cannot be younger than one and thirty."

"Actually, she is four and thirty, to be exact. Her niece must be at least a decade younger," said Gooding before pausing to look at Rolfe. "I'm surprised you did not recognize Jane Lovering. She was engaged to dear Mr. Billingsley less than a fortnight ago." Gooding paused and then continued, "She was at some of the *ton*'s squeezes this spring."

Grandmamma laughed. "How could he see the girl or anyone else, for that matter, if he don't go to the squeezes?"

"She was married to Cuthguard Lovering for two years before he died," offered Gooding as an afterthought.

Grandmamma sat upright. "Cutty Lovering? For goodness' sake, he was quite ancient. He had a son from his first marriage whose age must match Mrs. Lovering's. He was sixty if he was a day when I last heard of him."

Rolfe was too much of a gentleman to conclude aloud that the girl might have been after Cutty's moneybags.

"It was considered an odd match at the time, as her family is

quite well-to-do," Gooding said. "Lord Fairchild never should
have allowed it. But she always sat silently beside her husband
at several small dinner parties I went to, attending his every
need."

Rolfe tapped the tips of his fingers on the carriage door as
Gooding continued, "In fact, I was a bit surprised to hear she
had accepted an offer before her year of mourning was properly
up."

Silence descended within the carriage, except for the clopping of the horses. Grandmamma gave up the fight to keep
awake and drooped into her grandson's shoulder. He sighed and
pushed a pillow under her head.

"What is she doing here instead of gazing adoringly at
Billingsley's puppy face in town?" Rolfe asked a few minutes
later.

"Which of us has the nerve to ask her directly?"

Rolfe looked at his friend. "I'll ask her if you will tell me
what precisely is the nature of your acquaintance with Miss
Fairchild." He paused when he received no answer. "You know,
Gooding, you might try at a bit of conversation the next time
you encounter her. Otherwise your feelings will be too obvious." Gooding's face grew darker by the second. Rolfe had
never seen him except with an open expression. "Good God,
man, you're in love with her, aren't you?"

Gooding opened his mouth to speak, but no sound came out.

"Mrs. Lovering, may I be so bold as to inquire as to what
brings you here to our small neighborhood this time of year?"
asked Rolfe as he brought his chestnut gelding close to her
mare. The two were riding ahead of the group on the lane leading to the bluffs.

"Why do you ask, my lord?" Jane responded.

"Well, you are newly engaged."

Her heart sank. So word of her engagement had already
made its way south. Arrived, no doubt, with Sir Thomas.

"And your fiancé is in London," Rolfe continued. "So, one
wonders what could possibly entice you to spend a few weeks
during the season in our charming but smallish neighborhood."

"Why, my aunt, of course."

"Of course." He lifted a brow.

His words were polite enough, but Jane, feeling needled, continued, "And may I ask you, then, my lord, what enticements have driven *you* from town during the height of the season?"

"Why, my grandmamma, of course."

"Of course." She echoed his words right down to the arrogantly lifted brow.

"Come now, Mrs. Lovering, surely we know each other well enough for you to confide in me."

Jane refused to meet his gaze.

"I see I am not to have the pleasure of an answer from you. But then, that is a favored style of yours."

"If you insist on playing the inquisitor, I will admit that I am not engaged, nor was I ever engaged, to Mr. Billingsley. There was an error, you see, in the newspapers," she added with what she hoped was a carefree smile.

Graystock forced himself to listen to her words without interruption. The smallest dimple marred the smoothness of her cheek. It almost made him lose his train of thought.

"And I can never resist an invitation from my aunt for a visit. She is the dearest person in the world to me."

"Ah, an error in the papers, you say? That is a fine mess. Your father, I would assume, has sent his solicitors to contend with this? A lady's reputation would be beyond repair if the matter was not attended to immediately."

"I thank you kindly, sir, for your concern," she said, chewing on her lower lip. "The situation has been taken in hand. But now I feel we are neglecting your friend. Let us drop back."

Her lips were quite kissable, and it was a shame the damage she was doing to them. He sought her gaze without success. "You have perfected the fine art of evading questions, I see."

She pulled up her horse. "And you, sir, have perfected the fine art of interrogation."

He stopped too and realized he would have to try a different tack, lest he win the proverbial battle but lose her company. "I do hope our stables have provided adequate care of your mare. She is a fine horse."

Mrs. Lovering leaned down, patted the horse on the shoulder, and urged her forward again. "Yes, and again, I must thank you for offering to provide shelter for her." She paused before adding, "I suppose I must also apologize for trespassing last week, and for any embarrassing comments I might have made." Her brow furrowed in agitation. "If you had but told me who you were—"

He interrupted her. "Mrs. Lovering, most sincere apologies are not given with an excuse. However, I accept your apology and now that we have been introduced, I invite you to explore the grounds of Hesperides at your leisure. I simply ask you to refrain from passing through the unfortunate field where we met. I am in the process of training my new mount, and distractions do not bode well, as you saw for yourself." He could see from the blush creeping up her neck that she was mortified by his rebuke in the middle of her apology.

"My lord, I do apologize most profusely. Please allow me to show how sincere I am."

He was intrigued and wondered what trick she had up her sleeve now, the minx. "Yes, do continue."

"May I offer my assistance with your stallion? Before you decline, please know that I have had no small experience in the training of horses. My family owns and breeds horses in Cornwall."

He stared at her. No lady would offer such a thing, let alone discuss horse breeding. It was a blatant slap in the face to his ability as a horseman. He looked into her slanting eyes and perceived the smallest trace of a smile on her face. "You are too kind, but I'm afraid I must decline your offer."

"Just as I thought. You can't bear the thought that a female could possibly be of help to you." She turned to go back toward Sir Thomas Gooding and the carriage.

He was outraged. No one dared speak to him in such a manner. He bent down and caught her reins as she finished the turn. "Mrs. Lovering, I must revise my answer if you will allow. Meet me in the aforementioned field at a bit past dawn tomorrow—if that is not too early for you?"

Her smile was her answer. He dropped her reins and watched her trot toward the carriage in the distance. He wondered later if he had accepted her challenge in anger or from an extreme desire to see the stallion deposit her misplaced arrogance on the ground alongside her intriguing little derriere.

The sky was a deep azure blue, the heat quite uncommon this time of year. As the scattered group proceeded toward their goal, the wooded area gave way to sandy soil and a few stunted pine trees. The only other vegetation daring to survive winter's high winds was crabgrass and longer sea oats. The carriage stopped well before the final berm fronting the sea. Throughout the journey, Mrs. Gurcher had made the most of a captive audience. She tittered and gossiped and commented on each new piece of scenery as if no one in the carriage had ever remarked on any of the views of the neighborhood before.

The rector, who had learned better than anyone how to ignore his wife, kept his nose buried in a tome of sermons. Lady Graystock alternately used her fan in the hot carriage and dozed. And Clarissa was reduced to near silence, attributable in equal parts to a growing headache and an acute attack of nerves—something she rarely experienced in her life. Each of the two times she dared to peek out of the small window, he was of course looking back over his shoulder, and caught her glance.

His glances had been filled with . . . nothing. Well, no, not exactly nothing. It was more like a stranger's glance, as if he didn't recognize her—except that he kept staring at her, throughout tea and now during the ride. She felt like a spider had caught her in its sticky threads and was keeping a disinterested yet bloodthirsty eye on her to make sure she didn't extricate herself.

She shut her eyes and leaned back into the cushions as Mrs. Gurcher exclaimed for the fourth time how hot the weather had become. With a heavy heart, she realized she should emulate her niece's example and face the music. She resolved to have a private word with the gentleman if she could arrange it with discretion.

The picnic by the sea was a grand adventure, according to Mrs. Gurcher. The aging countess looked almost happy except that it was clear she did not possess enough energy to wrest the conversation away from the high-pitched nonsense of the rector's wife. As the afternoon continued, Clarissa realized it would be well nigh impossible to speak privately with Thomas. That gentleman ate and just stared at each person in the group as they spoke. At length, Clarissa was roused from her reverie by Lady Graystock.

The countess called out to Jane to ask if she would be willing to read a bit to her. "With my eyesight growing dimmer by the year, I delight in having people read to me," the dowager countess said as she opened her book and handed it to Jane.

"It would be my pleasure. I take great joy in all of Burney's work, ma'am."

Rolfe watched as Mrs. Lovering settled beside his grandmother to accommodate her wishes. He would have liked to get her alone again, but knew the merits of another tête-à-tête would not outweigh the disadvantages. He was thoroughly annoyed with her. Furthermore, he was even more disgusted with himself for not ignoring her verbal sparring. He very much regretted allowing her to try his horse on the morrow. He even wondered how he had ever become a lieutenant colonel, overseeing the movements of a four-hundred-man battalion, when he was incapable of making a mere widow cower in his presence, or at least show the respect due his title.

She continued reading aloud and seemed absorbed, but he doubted she was as oblivious to his gaze as she would have him believe, due to a slight flush on her part. Miss Fairchild and Gooding looked miserable. In fact, the only person present who seemed at all at ease was the rector, who sat with a book of sermons, unaware of the scene before him.

The entire outing was becoming tedious and had not held the amusements he had expected. He had not obtained his object of further discomposing the winsome Mrs. Lovering. If any comedy could be found at this event, he must at least contrive for his friend to endure a clandestine meeting with the staid Miss Fairchild. Swinging to his feet, he announced his intention to take a walk. He offered an arm to his grandmother and suggested Mrs. Lovering might enjoy walking with Mr. and Mrs. Gurcher, as the rector could also trace his roots to Cornwall.

That left Gooding with the spinster. A quarter of a mile later found the last couple trailing the other parties.

The major's thoughts battered his brain for a good ten minutes before he finally broke the silence. "You avoided me, Clarissa—for eight years. I deserve to know the reason." Before she could reply, he continued, "I was convinced you had a change of heart and did not possess enough courage to face me. Or perhaps there was someone else. Whatever it was, you owed me the courtesy of a private interview."

"Sir, I beg you not to be angry. What happened was so very long ago and could not possibly be of much importance. I am very sorry if I ever caused you any pain."

Years of worry, which had evolved into years of anger, itched his brain. "Pain? Is that what you call a six-month search throughout every last borough of Cornwall? Or several ugly meetings with your brother? Or the concern I had for your well-being? Clarissa, this will not do." He placed one palm against her cheek and turned her toward his gaze.

She looked at her shoes. "Again, I am sorry for any discomfort you might have endured on my behalf. However, I cannot find that you were concerned overmuch, as you did marry after all. You can at least rest assured that I have led a productive, comfortable life since last we met. And there was not someone else, as you suggested."

"Well, then, why did you leave? Why do you not give me the courtesy of an explanation? Surely you can tell me now."

"Can I, sir? Can you possibly imagine the position of a plain younger sister on the shelf, so to speak? Who is under the care of a demanding brother?"

Gooding stared into her large blue eyes and took a step back. "Is that it, then? You dared not defy your brother and place your future well-being in my hands? Or was it that the lower end of the social register did not appeal to you?" He tried and failed to keep his anger in check.

Clarissa interrupted him with dismay. "No, no, you misunderstand."

He in turn interrupted her. "You are right, Madam. I do not understand you." He strode off toward the picnic area to retrieve his mount, leaving Clarissa to explain to the others the reason for his departure.

As Jane rode through the dawn's mist, she shivered and wished she had a warmer cloak. She had dared not borrow her aunt's, as Clarissa would need it herself if she went outside this morning. She let her horse, Pax, have her head, and pondered Clarissa's reaction to Sir Thomas yesterday. The most she had been able to learn from her aunt was that Sir Thomas had been a former suitor years ago, which was news indeed. Jane's father had often complained that Clarissa had never gained the notice of any gentlemen of the *ton*, and she was another of the many monetary concerns with which he must contend.

Jane reflected on the fact that her father was again in debt. More than just a little. So far, no one outside the family knew. But soon the creditors' demands for payment would lead to refusals to supply goods or services. Surly behavior by unpaid servants would follow. Jane knew this only too well, as they had endured three months of such before she had acceded to the plan for her to marry Cutty Lovering.

Despite all her past help for her family, she felt a bit guilty now when she thought too long about her recent defection. But then she reminded herself it would not have been enough even if she had agreed to marry the foppish Mr. Billingsley with his extraordinary shirt points that seemed at times higher than the tilt of his roman nose. It had not been enough when she had married Cutty, and he had given a great deal. It had not been enough when she sold the small townhouse bequeathed to her upon his death. It seemed nothing would ever be enough.

She just could not understand it. The family's estate and the breeding farm were prospering. Yet her father had insisted on investing in risky speculations that proved ruinous time and time again. She had pleaded with her brother to speak to their father. But Theodore refused to do so and spent most of his time away from home at house parties with his friends.

She reasoned with herself that she must let her father make his own way without her again marrying to fill the family coffers. But she couldn't help worrying about all of their futures as she wondered what they would live on. If only her father had agreed to her wish to return to Pembroke, after Cutty died, to oversee the family's horse-breeding operations. But he had refused, saying that she was a grown woman and had to give up her infatuation with horses. What she really wanted was to find Harry and marry him before she waffled again and allowed herself to be persuaded to marry a rich man. She and Clarissa could become governesses if Harry would not have her, perish the thought. It all seemed so dreary. She remembered all the agonizing hours she had spent with her own governesses and wondered if fate was going to repay her for all the pranks she and her brother had played on the poor women.

She resolved to write to Harry, and also to finish her latest scribbling effort. Clarissa had read some of her prose and encouraged her to send her work to a publisher. Her father had insisted that only bluestockings became published authoresses. He had forbidden her to write, as he thought it would scare off any potential husband.

Lost in thought, Jane almost failed to notice she had arrived at the field. It was eerie in the mist with the dark tree trunks and branches covered with a hint of new leaves.

"Mrs. Lovering, it is almost time for breakfast. I assumed you had forgotten our engagement." The earl was attempting to bridle the stallion, who kept pawing the ground. He was wearing the same deplorable outfit in which she had first seen him. Almost against her will, she verified that one could positively see the man's smalls through the tear on the hip of his breeches. If anything, it had grown larger!

"Fear not. I would not dream of depriving you my help in taming your beast, sir." Jane averted her eyes, jumped down from her sidesaddle, and secured the reins to a tree. She had a difficult time maintaining a composed expression, as his arrogance seemed misplaced given that he had new mud stains on his shoulder and cheek. "And how lovely that you dressed on my account!" she continued.

She detached the riding-habit skirt, revealing form-fitting, dove-colored riding breeches. She had had her seamstress make the skirt of the habit and breeches to her specifications years ago, much to the shock of her father.

"As did you, I see, Madam," the earl said with one eyebrow raised.

"If I am to get on, and more importantly stay on, your animal, it will have to be astride. I would only ask that you not discuss my attire with anyone."

Lord Graystock rolled his eyes and smiled. "Heaven forbid, Mrs. Lovering. I fear your reputation could not bear another mark."

"And yours, sir? Is it superior to mine?"

"I daresay it could withstand word of my riding astride wearing breeches." His eyes roamed slowly down over the offending article of clothing. "Not that I am complaining, you understand."

Jane refused to allow him to make her blush. "Yes, well, at least my smalls are covered."

"More's the pity," he said, from much nearer than Jane recalled him being.

She disregarded the comment and walked toward the animal in the middle of the field. "Now, sir," she said, taking possession of the bridle from the earl along the way, "let us see what is to be done about this recalcitrant stallion of yours. And by that—lest you find yourself confused—I do mean your horse." She was rewarded by his laugh, which caused a sensation in her midriff that she would just as soon not examine.

When she was within reach of the warm, moist breath of the stallion, he snorted, wheeled around, and galloped away.

Lord Graystock chuckled. "You must have better methods in your repertoire. I daresay your entire arsenal won't do the trick."

"We shall see," Jane retorted as she watched the horse. She felt little of the self-confidence she tried to show. The stallion exhibited a sort of wildness in the eye that she had rarely seen before.

"Care to wager on it?" he asked.

"Wager on what?"

"On your ability to ride the beast, of course. Or perhaps"—his eyebrows quirked insolently—"we should better your odds by making it on your ability to capture him?"

"I have never wagered in my life."

"Are you unsure, Mrs. Lovering, of your abilities?"

She looked at him for a long moment. "What would I win?"

He smiled. "More importantly, what would you lose?"

They paused for a moment, each thinking as quickly as possible. The earl closed the gap between them.

"A kiss. If you lose, that is," he said.

"No," she said.

"A kiss if you win, then, if you prefer."

"No," she said again.

"Then we are back to if you lose."

She knew he expected her to refuse again, stomp off and refer to her reputation and the like. What could she counter it with to wipe the smug expression off his face and end this entire wagering business?

"All right," she said slowly. "But if I stay on the brute, you'll marry me." Really, she only wanted to see him unsettled, just a little. Titled gentlemen were so sure of themselves, this one in the extreme. He antagonized her beyond measure. And she knew she could unseat herself if she did manage to ride the beast. She could tell by the strained expression on his face that she had outmaneuvered him.

"Mrs. Lovering, ah, your wager is so very tempting, but . . ." She smiled as she realized he was not going to accept the challenge. "But not very equal in terms. What say you to upping my end to a bit more than a kiss?"

She felt flustered and annoyed. "I think not," she responded as she jutted out her chin.

He looked delighted. "Ah, well, then, let's shake on the original wager," he concluded as he reached for her hand. "And by the by, he seems to favor trees. Best be careful."

She was too embarrassed to ask for clarification of the original wager or the comment regarding the trees. The truth was, the infuriating man had her doubting her own abilities. Jane had ridden many young, difficult horses but never a difficult stallion in his prime. And she was distracted by Graystock, who sat on a log in the shade of a young sapling, watching her with a hooded expression in his gray eyes.

After a full hour, the stallion was caught, bridled, and shaking. She had got within a few feet of the horse and then turned her shoulder to him while pretending to be working on the bridle. The horse's curiosity had gotten the best of him in the end, as she had known it would. He had walked up to her and put his head over her shoulder. She had shown him the bit, and he had allowed her to slip on the piece of tack with only one whinny and a head toss.

Jane checked the tightness of the girth and swung up into the saddle with well-practiced ease. Before she was seated, the horse began backing up at full speed and then reared. She leaned forward and pulled down hard on the reins. With a half turn, the stallion came down on all fours at breakneck speed. Instead of hauling back on the reins, Jane let the animal have his head. After circling the field four times, he changed tactics.

She was going to get hurt. She could feel her tenuous control over the animal slipping from her grasp. Desperate to unseat her, the stallion began bucking and twisting in midair. An abrupt stop after a near-fatal sideswipe of a tree found Jane somersaulting off the horse's back. She fought for control of her lungs when she realized the wind had been knocked out of her. The earl's shadow fell across her face as she tried to sit up.

"Are you hurt?" he asked. When she did not respond, he began feeling her legs and arms. She pushed away his hands and tried to get enough air to speak. Really, she just wished he would give her space and time to regain her senses. When she opened her eyes and sat up, she noticed a gash on her thigh. The earl examined the wound as she tried to compose herself.

"You are in luck," he said grimly. "Looks like you'll not need stitches." He pulled a flask out of the leather saddlebag lying in the grass and began sprinkling the contents on the slash. She bit her tongue as the liquid burned the raw edges of her skin. He untied his loose neckcloth to bind the wound.

"I'll send a doctor to see to this, once you return to your aunt's house. It should be fine as long as it doesn't become putrid," the earl added, rocking back on his knees.

"I'm fine, really, just fine," insisted Jane, embarrassed. She paused before continuing, "I now see how your breeches came to be in their current state of disrepair."

He smiled. A heavy silence descended on them as the earl looked at the widow's person for any other signs of misfortune.

"Well, then."

"Well, then, what?" asked Jane, trying on her most innocent voice but feeling all the nervousness of a never-been-kissed girl of six and ten.

The corners of his lips curled when he looked at her and pushed a strand of hair from her eyes. "I fear you have a bit of dirt on your face." His large hand felt warm as he brushed the earth from her face. She could read desire in his gaze.

"As do you, my lord." His hand touched her cheek again and she held her breath with anticipation and a bit of fear. "Are you going to kiss me now?"

"Was that not the wager?" he asked with a lazy drawl.

She looked up at his heavy-lidded eyes and whispered, "Yes." Jane felt as if it were inevitable, yet she was so uncertain. She had always been in control of every situation. This was uncharted territory. Forbidden territory, really.

As he pulled her to her feet, he took her hands. "Come, come, Mrs. Lovering. I am a gentleman. I would not take advantage of you without your permission, especially when you have already suffered battle wounds."

She looked at him.

"I'll take that as permission to continue." He cupped one side of her face with his palm and lightly kissed her. She could feel the hot creep of a blush forming and dared not look up at him. "You are embarrassed now," he said.

She raised her eyes to his with anger. "I am not." She deliberately reached up and placed her arms around his neck. She tugged his head down to her and placed her passive lips on his.

She felt him laugh against her lips. "Oh, no, Mrs. Lovering," he said. "That's not the way of it at all." He leaned one of his hands against the apple tree behind her and pulled her waist close to his body with the other arm, forcing her to arch into his broad chest. "This is the way," he whispered as he lightly bit at her lower lip and then used the tip of his tongue to gain entrance beyond her lips. She felt awash with heretofore-unknown longing and excitement. No one had ever kissed her like this. His tongue urged her to respond in kind, as she yielded fully to his embrace. She shivered with desire, and a small moan escaped her lips.

His fingers moved to her buttocks and pressed her to his

arousal. Jane almost recoiled in shock. She had been around horses all her life and knew exactly what was pressing into the juncture of her thighs. Never had she been so out of breath or so embarrassed. She let him continue out of a mixture of unknown desire and curiosity and the fact that she could not seem to call forth any words to her mouth. She breathed deeply. The scent of male and cologne made her throat ache. She could hear his ragged breaths as his mouth moved down her neck, feathering kisses to her breast. She stopped breathing when she felt his warm palm massage her breast through the thin fabric. He gathered her hand in his other and raised it to his lips.

"Really, my dear, we should continue this in the cottage nearby," the earl whispered.

His words jolted Jane into action. She shook off the mesmerizing trance and confronted the earl. "I think not."

"Mrs. Lovering, you are a widow. I am a widower. What more need be said? Do you not long for a liaison? I am here for you now, for the asking," he whispered as he nipped the lobe of her ear. She placed her hands on his chest and pushed gently.

"You are very kind to offer. However, I am not inclined." Her words hid the truth. She was terrified by his suggestion. As Jane did not want to show her fear and naiveté, she continued, "Perhaps another time—if I am ever inclined, that is."

Lord Graystock gazed at her. "If I did not know you to have been married, I would take your reaction to be that of a very green girl. Or are you just a coquette?" he said.

He could see through her. Jane reached down to retrieve the wrap skirt and secured it. She dared not say another word, lest she say the wrong thing. Distance was the answer. She walked to her horse and mounted without looking back.

"I hope I have not scared you. It wasn't my intention."

"You did not scare me, my lord. I am expected by my aunt. She was unhappy with the idea of my riding your horse. It seems a groom's sister alarmed her with a description of your brute. It is long past the time that I should be on my way."

"There will be no further training sessions, then?"

Jane refused to take the bait. "Good day to you, sir."

"And good morning to you, Mrs. Lovering," he said, and stood looking after her long after she had gone from sight.

Chapter Four

Jane felt ridiculous as she rode back to the cottage. She hated speaking falsehoods. And yes, it had been a falsehood, if only one by omission. As she trotted past the hedgerows with jonquils just raising their thin necks toward the sun, she cursed her inexperience with men. It left her feeling embarrassed and unsure of herself.

Since Cutty's death, several young gentlemen throughout the season had paid court to her with her father's urging, despite her state of mourning. Some—Mr. Billingsley was the prime example—were more determined than others. At each encounter, she felt no desire for any type of intimacy, physical or emotional. She did not want to be anyone's possession. She had learned to avoid intimate settings such as Vauxhall at night and walks in gardens during evening entertainments. She had even fended off Mr. Billingsley's amorous advances in an open carriage in Hyde Park when they found themselves in a secluded area. He had become so annoyed by her repeated refusal to accept his ungainly embraces that he had proposed marriage on the spot. She had had no idea that he was serious and would arrange an audience with her father. If only Cutty had not died, she wouldn't have had to endure these sorts of situations.

Cutty had been a kind, generous man who had loved her. He was old school. Jane had slept each night of her married life with her husband. He had respected and cared for her in every way imaginable. Each night he had kissed her cheeks, held her, and even brushed her hair as she sat at her escritoire in her cozy bedchamber. But, he had explained, he was unable to . . . well, to complete the act that could conceive a child. In truth, it was the reason she had agreed to marry him.

She remembered how shocked she had been by Cutty's proposal several years ago. Before she could refuse, he had explained his offer and her options. Cutty had said her father, in a drunken stupor, told him he was going to give her hand to Lord Wythe in return for restoration of the family's finances. Cutty had endeavored to dissuade him from the appalling idea, as Lord Wythe was of questionable character. With much mopping of his brow, Cutty had even relayed to Jane in whispering tones that he understood Wythe was barred from visiting certain establishments of willing females due to the nature of his perverse sexual proclivities.

Cutty had been relentless in his efforts to change Lord Fairchild's mind, all to no avail. In desperation, he had finally offered to wed Jane himself. He had explained to her that he had initially pondered the thought of lending money to her father. However, he had been almost sure that if the Fairchild finances were ever in doubt again, Jane's fate might become entangled with Lord Wythe once more.

Cutty had always been kind to Jane when she was growing up. She had first met him the summer following his wife's death. He and his young son had ridden neck or nothing over the downs of Cornwall, always inviting Jane to help chase away their grief.

So Jane had given up her dreams of marrying Harry. She had felt too much gratitude toward Cutty to even mention her desire and too much fear for her family to discuss it with her father. Cutty had in return promised to protect her, love her, and care for her in all ways save the marriage bed. He apologized to her for not being able to give her a child, but told her that at least he would never hurt her or force her to do her duty, as so many women deplored. And she in turn, free from the recent unhappiness in her familial home, blossomed. It was a pleasant, idyllic time, and only occasionally, very occasionally, did she feel something was missing. It was then that she would wonder about Harry, her first true childhood friend and love. Her intense loyalty to Cutty, however, forced many daydreams to be cut short.

She wondered if Harry was back in Cornwall after all the years at university. His sister, Fanny, had written to her that he was expected. And had he had the chance to brave the wilds of foreign soil in quest of elusive winged species? Mostly, she wondered if she still held a special place in his heart. He was the only man with whom she felt she could trust her secret if they ever married. For no one knew she was still a virgin. It was a fact that embarrassed her and could cause additional problems if ever revealed. For Cutty had explained that ancient marriage laws could render their marriage void, since it was never consummated. Because of this, he had arranged an independence for her upon his death.

What Cutty had forgotten was Jane's love of her family's stables in Cornwall, a fact her father had used to his advantage. On darker days, she worried that Cutty's heir by his first marriage, his son, Richard, might try to retrieve the money if it was learned that her marriage was never consummated.

Her greatest wish was to go to Cornwall, find Harry, and wed him. Material wealth was nothing to her. Her years with Cutty had proved beyond any doubt that wealth did not constitute joy. In fact, happiness died a quiet, slow death when the soul was not nurtured by a great love, or at least some hope for romantic love.

But if Harry wed her, what would become of Clarissa? By Jane's refusal to marry Billingsley, her family now faced financial ruin. Jane worried that her aunt's quarterly allowance might end. She could not bear the idea of Clarissa working for her living. And it was doubtful that Harry could be persuaded to include Clarissa in their wedded bliss, for Clarissa and Harry had always agreed to disagree on every topic. And so the arguments and answers swirled in her mind and terminated in another wracking headache.

"Jane, dear, you must stop writing and prepare for tea at Hesperides," Clarissa called from the hall.

Jane obeyed her aunt by arranging the stack of writing papers, wiping her quill, and closing the drawers of the small escritoire. She looked at her ink-stained hands and sighed.

Clarissa bustled into the guest chamber holding up the pressed black silk gown. A quarter of an hour later found Jane dressed and unsmiling as her aunt brushed her hair and swept it back into a knot high above her neck. Jane took her aunt's place and smoothed back Clarissa's brown tresses tinged with gray.

"A fine pair of guests we will be. Without conversation, and schooling our features, if my guess is correct," Jane said.

"But I do like the grandmother. She seemed taken with you at the picnic," said Clarissa as she hid her long hair in the confines of a lace cap. Jane picked a piece of lint from the dull brown-colored gown Clarissa almost always wore.

"When one's only competition is Mrs. Gurcher for friendship, I am not sure it is a fair game," retorted Jane.

"Yes, well, I have never been invited to tea at Hesperides until now. I am sure you are the reason," Clarissa said as she moved through the passageway toward the door of the cottage.

Jane changed the conversation as she adjusted the tilt of her black silk bonnet. "It is only a tea. They cannot hold us longer than the appointed hour."

Thomas was at war within his own mind. Propriety and good sense told him he must attend his host's modest entertainment of tea this afternoon. Anger and pride insisted that he be anywhere but in the conservatory overlooking the tiered gardens of Hesperides at four o'clock. The meager hunting party consisting of the earl, the gamekeeper, and himself had proved unfruitful. And he was not in a mood to attempt to lighten the earl's typical brooding frame of mind. He gave thanks for the hundredth time that hunting was a silent venture by necessity.

As they walked up to the large oak doors of the Hall, Thomas reviewed all his proposed excuses for not attending the ladies at tea. A glance at the earl's harsh, squinting profile above the deep gray collar of his long hunting coat resolved him to his purpose. As he opened his mouth to make his excuses, Graystock interrupted him.

"You're not considering retreat, are you?" The earl accepted the bows of the footmen and continued, "You are my friend and guest. And as such, you must endeavor to entertain me."

"That's what the chits will do, Graystock."

The earl preceded Thomas into the conservatory and added under his breath, "Ah. But you will outdo them if recent history is any indication." The ladies all rose upon the gentlemen's entrance, save the dowager countess. The earl moved to his grandmother, whose large frame was ensconced in a deceptively delicate love seat. He raised her hand to his lips. Rolfe bowed to the other two ladies as Thomas moved forward to pay his respects to at least two of the ladies.

The party of five somehow managed to offer a contorted view of refined society for the first half of the visit. The usual topics of weather and the small upcoming and past country entertainments were discussed at length, with nary a blush or a frown. If one looked closely, thought Thomas, one might have noticed he and Miss Fairchild did not direct questions to one another. Graystock did not follow suit with Mrs. Lovering. It was clear the earl enjoyed provoking her in a very mild way.

Lady Graystock sighed loudly, drawing everyone's attention.

"Whatever is it, Grandmamma?" asked the earl.

"I daresay I have overexerted myself today. I think I must be escorted to my chamber. But I would dearly like to continue the pleasure of our guests' company." She paused to look at Jane. "My dear, would you be so kind as to do me the honor of reading to me again? Your voice is exquisite, and I long to hear the next chapter of the novel we started during our last outing." The dowager countess lowered her eyes in a pitiful expression.

Graystock appeared exasperated. "Really, Grandmamma, you cannot impose upon Mrs. Lovering again."

The lady insisted, "No, it is not an inconvenience. I should be delighted above all things to give you this small pleasure. And I, too, delight in the works of Burney." She rose to her feet and set her cup and saucer on the tea tray.

The earl looked at Thomas and indicated to him with a nod toward Clarissa that decorum necessitated someone escorting her to her cottage. Thomas ignored the suggestion and turned to offer his arm to the dowager countess.

"Miss Fairchild, please allow me to escort you to your door," offered the earl.

"Oh, goodness, my lord, no, thank you. It is entirely unnecessary," responded Clarissa with a slight blush. As she placed her hand on the earl's sleeve to be led to the main hallway, Thomas watched her but refused to bid her good day.

The dowager countess' old, faded eyes fluttered open as Jane closed the volume.

"That was lovely, my dear. Thank you so much for reading to me. Your voice is excellent, and you read with such animation."

"You are too kind," Jane responded.

"It has been many years—too many years—since I have had female company in residence with me." With a sigh, she continued, "But it is a fate I am resigned to."

Jane wondered if the dowager countess was trying to draw her into a conversation or if she should refrain from making a comment. After an uncomfortable silence of a few moments, Jane asked, "But the young countess provided you with companionship for at least a short while during the last decade, did she not?"

"Good heavens, no, my dear. She was a mere child, all giggles and bounces, and altogether afraid of me. Her greatest pleasure was evening soirees and balls before she married."

"But who can blame her? I assure you I was the same at her age," Jane said with a smile.

"Yes, well, she was very young," she agreed. Then the dowager countess looked out toward the darkening light of the window. Jane thought she heard the older woman mutter, "But she was never capable of bringing happiness to Hesperides." Then louder, "But I shall not speak ill of the dead, as I must face Mr. Gurcher on Sunday. Surely God will punish me by forcing me to endure tea with Mrs. Gurcher again." With a twinkle in her eye, she looked at Jane. "But then, you will save me by proposing a walk to your aunt's cottage to admire the garden, will you not?"

Jane smiled. "If it would please you. We would be delighted by a visit."

"Yes, and it will infuriate Mrs. Gurcher," noted the dowager countess without any remorse. "Help me arrange these pillows, my dear, will you? I will take my afternoon lie-down now, I think."

Jane hastened to her side and helped the elderly lady retire before moving to the adjacent sitting room. She walked to the window before departing. A light spring rain tapped against the windowpane as she closed her eyes and rested her forehead against the cool glass.

She still did not know what to make of the conversation. It seemed to be in conflict with what her aunt had intimated about the earl's marriage. Jane wondered why the young countess had not brought happiness to the Hall while she was alive, but then decided it was likely the grandmother had not known the true feelings between the young couple. She shook her head. Jane had enough worries of her own to sort out. The trials of the earl-dom were not her affair.

She closed the outer door to the dowager countess' sitting room and bedchamber. With the approaching dusk, long shadows filled the carpeted hallway. Leaning against the paneled wall opposite her, a tall, broad-backed figure stood with crossed ankles. His silver eyes stared at her from a brooding face before he said something incomprehensible to her. With two long strides, he was in front of her. He grasped her shoulders in a firm if not painful grip. Jane, in her embarrassment, felt rooted to the spot and was unable to think of anything to say.

And then he said it again—"Come with me," in a commanding, harsh whisper. He led her farther down the hall into a sitting room and adjoining chamber, then closed the door. She noticed the beautiful blue toile curtains and tapestries lining the windows and walls of the spacious room. Beyond a short corridor, she could see a massive carved wooden bed with the same toile curtains. With shock, she realized she was in an inappropriate position. A position she had avoided her entire life.

The earl fingered the soft silk of her sleeves. His large, warm hands slowly slid down her arms. Jane felt the callused palms and inched away. "Are you afraid?" he asked.

She tilted up her chin and lied. "No. Should I be?"

"I would reconsider your answer," he whispered. His forefinger traced a line from her lips to her breast. Her nipple hardened as she gasped in surprise. She knew she was blushing.

"What on earth do you think you are doing, my lord?"

"Trying to get my faced slapped, Madam."

"Well, I should think . . ." she started.

"No, don't think," he interrupted. The earl's shadow fell across her face as his warm breath reached her cheek, giving her ample time to draw back. When she did not, his full lips met hers as he drew her into the circle of his arms. Her mind raced with shock as the reality of the scene unfolded. She must take hold of herself. But she could not. The effort to say no was too far away. She felt drugged by the raw, male, familiar smell of him. In embarrassment, she felt his tongue curl against her own and tasted brandy. Harry had never kissed her like that. His kisses had always been chaste and brief. This was intoxicating and knee-weakening. His hands were loosening her gown while he looked into her eyes. She felt paralyzed by the excess of emotions coursing through her.

"Are you more inclined now, Jane?" he asked, whispering into her ear as he placed one of her hands on his shoulder. The intimacy of hearing her given name on his lips was almost more provocative than what he asked.

She was too embarrassed to answer. All she knew, for some unfathomable reason, was that she would not back down now.

He lowered the edges of her dress and shift and sucked in his breath. He seemed almost dazed, Jane saw, when he leaned down to taste the tip of her breast. His hand rose to trace the contours of the other. The twin sensations of overwhelming shyness and an unfurling desire made her stand perfectly still. He suckled her and gently touched the sensitive tips with the palm of his hand. Jane felt a rush of heat and a painful longing run through the core of her body as his rough face etched itself on her breasts. She stopped breathing as she combed her fingers through his thick black silky hair and arched her back.

Rolfe paused and looked up at her with half-closed eyes. "You must tell me to stop if you so desire." She stared back at him.

"I insist, my lord . . ." she whispered.

"You must say it with more force, Mrs. Lovering," he said dryly.

"Are you intoxicated, my lord?" she retorted with as much dignity as she could muster, considering her state of undress.

He smiled and picked her up like a child then made his way through the passage to lay her on the bed in the darkened room. He pushed off his coat and undid his white neckcloth. As he pulled the linen shirt over his head, she noticed the large bulge in his buff-colored breeches. She felt goose bumps on her arms as fear waged war with desire.

He leaned over the bed and peeled back the layer upon layer of dress clothes, petticoats, underclothes, and her shift until she lay naked upon the bedcovers. She watched his gray eyes dilate with passion as he drew the pins from her hair. Waves of her hair fell past her shoulders onto the pillow.

He sighed. "I want you. I want all of you right now."

She lay still on the silk comforter, her mind and body torn between an unknown, intense need and complete embarrassment.

In a haze, she remembered spying on a stallion and her mare in heat in the middle of the hot summer stable when she was fourteen years old. She had stared in shock and wonder as the stallion nipped the mare on the shoulder, forcing her to submit to the mounting. Then, the earsplitting squeals from the animals as the male entered and pumped his seed into the female. She had stayed hidden long after the men overseeing the breeding session had separated the animals and departed. She loved her horse and had wanted to know everything about her. But it had been more than she could have imagined. And now she wondered how she would endure this interlude, which was sure to embody pain.

Rolfe looked into her half-closed aquamarine eyes as he edged onto the bed and pulled her body close to his. He wondered how much of his intense attraction to her was due to his five years of self-imposed celibacy. His mouth followed the trail left by his hands as he discovered her body. As he kissed her soft, small waist, his hands caressed her slim, firm thighs. Her legs trembled as his fingers moved up along her inner thighs and pushed them apart. When he reached the downy, darker curls of her femininity, she gasped. He massaged the center of her womanhood and was gratified to feel wetness. He leaned forward to tease the tip of her high, full breast to tautness again with his lips and heard her indrawn breath. She lay silently as he tried to enter her with two fingers. He was stilled by the realization of untried tightness. His mind reeled, and for the first time in many years, he felt very unsure of himself.

But then, it could not be true, he reasoned. He knew it could not. She was a widow. As he probed further, he could feel her stiffen.

He withdrew his fingers and sat up. He leaned over her to pick up his fine lawn shirt off the floor and drew it over his head. "Mrs. Lovering, we must stop this nonsense, immediately." He paused before adding, "I do not take pleasure in deflowering virgins. And I am not on the marriage mart."

She lay on the bed and looked up at him. "I would not have you as a husband, my lord," she said low. "But you yourself brought me here, and proposed a rendezvous not long ago. Have you forgotten?"

"You are an innocent. I should have recognized the signs."

"You said I was a widow and you a widower. You suggested a liaison, and now you lack courage? Is that it?"

His eyes drifted to her beautiful breasts once more, and he felt drugged as he once again cupped the curls of her womanhood. A jolt of raw desire raged through his body when he felt a rush of dampness. He swore and raised himself from the bed to strip off his boots and breeches and to take off his shirt for the second time. In the dark, faraway recesses of his mind, he knew he would come to regret this inability to deny himself.

He spied apprehension in her eyes at his nakedness. As he moved onto the bed again and eased his body close to hers, she tensed.

"Please tell me what to expect," she said in a small voice.

"You will feel pain. That is certain," he murmured in her ear, giving her one last chance to stop. He wondered which would be worse, stopping now or finalizing the act. He accepted her silence as an invitation to continue.

He grasped her hand on the silk covers and slid between her

legs. The fingers of his other hand delved between the folds of her femininity. He dipped his head to suckle her breast again. She reached for his face as he closed his eyes and breathed deeply her faint lavender scent. He fought to control the hard edge of his desire as he pushed her hands back and kissed her. The pressure within him pulsated with need. A rosy blush overtook her porcelain face as his fingers explored the most intimate places on her person. He kissed her delicate neck as he stretched the barrier within her and massaged the firm bud of her desire.

Suddenly he heard her breath catch and she seemed to be on a precipice, hanging by a thread. He felt the unfulfillment of all the years gone by dissolve in that suspended moment in time. In that instant Rolfe pushed inside of her. She clung to him and held her breath as he began the necessary, painful stretching. Breathing hard, he strained to maintain control. He moved slowly in and out of just the mere edges of her for long moments. Then, closing his eyes, he firmly plunged inside her, past her barrier, past her innocence, filling her completely. In a fog, he could hear her calling him.

"Please, oh . . . wait, wait, please."

He stopped and looked down at her face. Her expression filled him with pain. With more control than he knew he possessed, he rested his forehead against hers and closed his eyes. "Jane, I shall stop if you insist. But, my dear, the damage is already done."

"Is it over?" she asked in a high, nervous voice.

"Not for me, no."

"Will it hurt if you continue?"

"Possibly, a little, I think," he said hoarsely. He felt that the slightest movement might cause him to explode. He continued, "Jane, hold me, and let me take you."

She wrapped her arms around his back, and he guessed she was keeping her panic at bay. Slowly, he withdrew and massaged just the outside edges of her again. He teased the opening until she could bear it no longer. She pulled his buttocks down toward her, and he began an excruciating, slow rhythm.

Now the aching pleasure he felt was almost painful in its intensity. As he broke rhythm, he pressed deep into her. She gripped his shoulders and twined her long legs around his. He strained to move the last fraction of an inch closer to her being.

Abruptly, he stopped, and pulled out of her. He savored the intense release of his seed onto her soft belly, and listened to her breathing.

Wiping away the evidence of his passion with the sheet, he moved to cover her again with his body as he buried his face in her golden hair, breathing in her feminine scent. She loosened her grip on his shoulders and caressed his back. He felt satiated and at peace—sensibilities that had eluded him for such a very long, long time.

He arranged her in the cradle of his arms as he withdrew her arms from around him. The strain of holding back had taken its toll. He had used the last drop of his innermost resources of strength in his care of this woman. The loss of her innocence had tasted bittersweet. An overwhelming feeling of protectiveness enveloped him as he held her in his arms and tucked the bedcovers over both of them. He pulled her body close to his. His hand found its way to her breast, and he could feel her erratic heartbeats.

She covered his hand with her own. In a low voice she whispered, "Thank you."

The cold stirrings of doubt battered his thoughts as he stared up at the bed hangings overhead. "Thank you? Is that really what you should be saying to me? Should it not be, 'Damn you'?"

"Perhaps. However, all I can feel at this moment is a sense of gratitude."

He continued as he sat up in bed. "What could you have been thinking to allow, nay, encourage, your own seduction when you were a virgin?"

He watched a deep blush suffuse her face as she sat up, holding the bedcovers to her breasts. She pulled her shift from the top of the heap on the floor and put it on. "I am sorry to have troubled you, my lord. But do not forget it was you who brought me here," she added with a tight smile. She trembled despite her attempt to portray a cool exterior. She rose from the bed and stepped into her gown.

Rolfe sighed and ran his hands through his hair. He looked up at her as she struggled to fasten the buttons at the back of her prim mourning dress. He stood up, shaking his head as he walked straight toward her. Jane blushed anew and lowered her eyes, but not before he saw her look down his frame. The entire scene seemed so incredible and unreal still.

"Stop looking at me that way, or I will force you into my bed again," he whispered. "And stop using my title in the bed-chamber. It is entirely inappropriate." He reached out and cupped her face with one hand. "I desire to hear my name on your lips."

In embarrassment she looked at the jagged scar just below his shoulder. She stared hard at it. "Is this the wound that almost cost you an arm at Waterloo . . . Rolfe?" Her gaze moved down the rest of his body, stopping at his torso.

"Do you see what you do to me?" Rolfe asked, ignoring her question. He pulled her into his arms and began to kiss her neck and shoulder. Something on the bedsheets behind her caught his attention. Several crimson stains marked the linen sheets. He stopped suddenly. "Are you all right? Are you in any sort of pain?"

As her gaze followed his to the bed, she responded with keen embarrassment. "Yes, I mean, no. I'm all right, really just fine. But I must go before any more time passes." She began pinning up her hair as she turned her back to him to present the many buttons that needed attending. His fingers completed that task instead of choosing the task he would have preferred, that of caressing the soft, fair curls at the base of her neck.

She turned as he looped the last button. He was amused to find that her severe black gown was formidable armor he was unlikely to easily pierce again. She insisted on returning to the cottage alone, despite the rainy, dark sky. But the earl refused to be put off, despite Jane's worries concerning appearances if they were seen walking alone in the evening.

"Come," he demanded. "We will go out by the doors leading from the ballroom. No one will see us. I insist."

With a firm grasp of her hand, he led her as one would lead a wayward child. Down the back staircase, through the ballroom, and out into the semidarkness, they made their escape unnoticed save by one oddly smiling old lady at her window clutching a volume by Burney.

Chapter Five

The cold day broke without a cloud in sight, a circumstance that proved to be at complete odds with the overcast tint of Rolfe's mind. He had awoken several times during the night, only to smell Jane's sweetness imprinted on his bedcovers. By dawn, he paced his room in deep thought. He was in a predicament he had sworn to never ever face again, that of marriage. The ways of a gentleman forbade him to consider any other solution. He only questioned whether he had consciously or unconsciously chosen to be in this state of affairs. No, he reasoned, he had had no way of knowing she was a virgin—except her behavior in the field when she had been by turns hot and cold. Rolfe rang for his valet and chose a black coat to match his mood. Forgoing breakfast, he stalked out of the Hall toward the stables.

Despite Jane's certainty that she would be unable to sleep at all that night, she slept within moments of dousing the candle on the bedside table. However, this blessed release was interrupted when she awoke in tears.

At first the dream had been so lovely. She and Harry were walking in a field together, searching for butterflies. But as she caught an elusive pale yellow winged insect, a pair of bronzed male hands covered her own. When she looked up, she saw the earl naked, with the saber wound oozing blood down his arm.

Halfway between sleep and consciousness, she awoke and felt frozen with unknown fear.

And then, she heard something—footsteps belowstairs. She slipped from under the covers as quietly as possible and moved to the door to listen. Harsh whispers seeped through the thin door. A man's and a woman's voices.

In a panic she thought it might be Lord Graystock, but it occurred to her that the earl's voice was lower-pitched than that of this gentleman. In her relief, she sagged against the door, which emitted a long squeak. Abruptly the voices stopped. For long moments Jane dared not move. She tiptoed to her escritoire, lit a candle, and pulled out her writing paper. With Sir Thomas in the parlor, Jane was sure there was not a chance she would fall into slumber again. And she had awoken with a firm resolve to put into motion her long-repressed desire.

As she stared at the blank page, Jane replayed her actions of the afternoon. She swallowed as she recalled the images. Her conscience wreaked havoc upon her person.

On one shoulder, her conscience whispered in her ear that what she had done was evil and she was going to the devil. She had had relations without marriage.

On the other shadowed shoulder, Cutty's voice reminded her he had always wanted her to be happy and find love. He had told her she would know it when she felt it. She did know it. Her heart belonged to Harry. What she had experienced with the earl was pure lust on his side, with a large dose of curiosity and shock on her part.

And, of course, pride. Her damn pride, she thought. It was the one fault she had tried to cure repeatedly, with no great success. If she had just had the courage to push the earl away, and to bear his barbed tongue, she would not have succumbed.

But her practical nature took over, and she was honest enough to admit she was relieved the problem of her virginity had been removed. Really, her situation had been absurd. During her entire youth, it had been instilled in her to protect her virtue and reputation. In the year since her husband's death, she had agonized over how she could keep the secret of an unconsummated marriage. It had been a ridiculous worry, as who would have known unless a physician had examined her? But she had been uneasy that her innocence on the subject might give her away. She knew she blushed upon the slightest mention of the marriage bed. She was sure married women had a certain knowing eye after succumbing to the other sex. She had felt "virgin" was imprinted on her forehead at times.

And now the problem was gone. The earl was a gentleman of unquestionable character. She had no doubt whatsoever he would guard her secret to his grave. It had been perfectly obvious he had been repulsed and horrified by her innocence. It was ironic, really. She had been so sure, after all the lectures of her numerous governesses, that men would be positively panting after her untouched innocence. And they had been, except for the earl.

With a shaking hand, she wrote a letter to Harry. It was the hundredth time in the last year she had done so. But each time before, it had been in her head, not on paper. Scratching her words with care, she tried to find the right phrases to convey her request to her oldest friend.

She wrote she would be there within a week, and still desired to be with him always, as they had spoken of during their youth. Would he still have her? She described her feelings, and her desire to make him happy, yet wrote too of the humiliation in baring her feelings. It had been ingrained since birth that a female must never reveal these types of thoughts before a proper declaration by the gentleman. In a way, it repulsed her. She begged forgiveness for her boldness and explained the situation regarding her father. Upon rereading, she wanted more than anything to toss the papers into the fire. But with a deep breath she sanded the letter, sealed it with wax, and wrote the directions with care.

With the slightest of sounds, the door to the cottage closed, and Jane moved to the window in time to see the gentleman walk into the night.

The cold wind cut through the fine cloth of Rolfe's somber spring coat, invading his very being as he rode away from the stables. The newly formed pale green leaves did not yet cover the naked branches of the oak trees on the front lawn. He struggled to still his swirling thoughts while he rode past the long regiment of poplars lining the grand entrée to Hesperides. He continued down the lane leading to the village for a mile or so. A movement up ahead caught his squinted eye.

"Of all the . . ." he cursed under his breath. A few more paces brought him to a halt several feet from her.

"My lord," Jane said with eyes downcast.

Not bothering to dismount, the earl nodded his head once, a fraction of an inch, and responded, "Mrs. Lovering."

When neither of the two parties continued after a moment or two, Jane cleared her throat. "I had no intention of disturbing you. I was just taking a bit of air."

Her face was very pale. He looked at the neat center part of her flaxen tresses, peeking out of her modest black bonnet. She appeared very proper, in mourning, from tip to toe. His body flooded with heat as he remembered he had seen and touched every part of her delicate person less than fifteen hours before.

"Please do not allow me to impede your way. Carry on," Rolfe stated in his usual brusque tone.

She appeared shocked by his words. Without an utterance or a backward glance, she continued past him. It was on the tip of his tongue to turn back and stop her to engage in further conversation, and he would have if his feelings had been less.

The farther she walked, the angrier she became. She could not decide why she was so angry and could not say what he had said to offend her, but he had done so. But, she reasoned with herself as she turned back toward the cottage, what had she wanted him to do? Acknowledge what had happened the day before? Suggest another rendezvous? Get down on bended knee and beg her to accept him in marriage? Certainly not any of those suggestions. It was better this way. And besides, he had less than no interest in wedding her. He had made that perfectly clear. He even thought that she had allowed her own seduction in hopes of forcing a betrothal. It was too humiliating to contemplate. Besides, she would as soon wed herself to this arrogant cock as to that mushroom, Billingsley. They would just pretend nothing had ever happened between them. She touched again the envelope in her pocket and resolved without further ado to post it this morning. She chuckled to herself as she tried to picture the earl down on his knee in the dirt, pleading for her hand. She stopped to pluck a few wildflowers and smiled as she dreamed of Harry with his sandy brown hair that matched his eyes. Yes, she would post the letter this very morning.

Thomas moved past the carpeted staircase onto the marble front hall. His steps echoed throughout as a footman opened the double doors leading into the breakfast room. He kissed the hand of Lady Graystock and wished her a good morning.

"Dear boy, please help yourself to the sideboard. You must be famished," the earl's grandmother said, her eyes twinkling.

"Yes, well, thank you, my lady," responded Thomas without looking into her merry old eyes. He did not want to ask her why she thought he might be hungry. He walked to the resplendent table and fished a few kidneys and sausages onto his plate.

"My dear grandson, Rolfe, has written a missive for you. It seems he has left us to fend for ourselves. But he insists that you stay here to entertain me and shoot some of our doves, and fill up the larders with fish," she continued.

Thomas reached for the letter and broke the seal. He scanned the note. "Oh, Lady Graystock, I would not presume to stay any longer if the earl has departed."

The old lady smiled and slathered a good deal of butter on a muffin as he read her grandson's letter.

Gooding,

Please do not presume that my departure necessitates your leaving. Most to the contrary, I do insist that you stay and endeavor to entertain one or two ladies in the neighborhood, that being Lady Graystock and another lady whose eyes refuse to meet yours. I shall be gone no longer than a sennight. Pressing business requires my immediate attention in town. Before you toss this into the fire, I do beseech you again to restrain your natural instinct to flee. In fact, I must beg you to consider that if you do not stay with my grandmother, she is likely to invite additional people to the Hall, with great embarrassment to me. Gooding, I am counting on you. With any luck, I will return shortly. I remain,

Graystock

As he folded the letter, Lady Graystock took Thomas' hands in her own. He glanced down to see the many wrinkles on her large, blue-veined hands. "My dear," Lady Graystock said, "please indulge an old heart and stay with me."

Thomas was most eager to use this excuse to put as much distance as possible between himself and Miss Fairchild. But it was impossible not to heed Lady Graystock's request. As he gave his accord, he contemplated how many days would have to pass before he could quietly but firmly leave. He had underestimated the united strength of the Graystock bloodlines.

"As you wish, Madam," responded Thomas.

Jane concentrated on the sheet of foolscap on the small kitchen table. It was covered with great splotches of black ink and smudges. She sighed as she reviewed her work. With much deliberation, she crumpled the paper. What was wrong with her? Her writing was bad, and she could not seem to lose herself in the story as in the past. Her main characters would not behave in a manner that pleased her. The protagonist was not moving the story along as forcefully as she wished. The descriptions were abysmal, the heroine witless, and the dialogue stilted. Jane was grateful when she heard the front door latch open, for it signaled a good excuse to end this torture.

"Jane, dear, I have such news!" her aunt exclaimed as she bustled in, carrying several small parcels. "I'm sorry to be so late, but Mrs. Gurcher and Cynthia Richardson would not let me escape from the butcher without filling my ear with the latest *on-dit*," continued Clarissa, a bit out of breath. Jane shuffled and tapped her sheath of papers on the well-worn table before tying the bundle with an old red ribbon and placing it in a box.

"Pray tell, what is the news?" asked Jane. She felt her chest tighten as she wondered if anyone could possibly know of her liaison with the earl.

"Mrs. Gurcher said the earl left for London this morning in great haste," she responded. "This is a shame for you, Jane."

"Please, don't say that. I have no interest in any dealings concerning that gentleman. He is arrogant, conceited, and abominable in every way," Jane stated firmly.

"Careful, my dear. He is a gentleman, and I have not witnessed any bad behavior on his part. Are you sure you are not still angry from the embarrassment of him hiding his identity from you the first time you met?"

Jane paused and then laughed as she began laying the small dining table with silverware. "It is vastly unfair of you to remind me of that. You know what a bore he is." With her eyes focused on the table, she rushed into forbidden territory. "And what of Sir Thomas? Has he left as well?"

Clarissa's visage paled. "I have no idea." Her aunt moved the platter of cold meats and a loaf of bread onto the table.

As they sat at the table and unfolded their napkins, Jane said, "Are you ever going to tell me about Sir Thomas, Aunt?"

"I have told you. He was a suitor many, many years ago. But I left London and he married. And I am sorry to say that he insists on tormenting me. I am sorry, too, Jane that he most likely awakened you last night. But I am not sorry he came, because we spoke and now he will torment me no further." Clarissa looked up from her plate, and Jane saw the glitter of unshed tears in her aunt's eyes.

Jane excused herself from the table and reached into a cupboard for the half-full bottle of wine and two glasses. She poured the richly colored liquid into the glasses and gave her aunt time to recover. "Aunt, I have made a decision today. I have written to Harry and will go to Cornwall next week or in a fortnight at the latest. I have trespassed long enough on your kindness." She put up a hand as Clarissa started to speak. "Please don't ask me to stay. I know I can never return to London. But Cornwall is so far removed from the eyes of the Upper Ten Thousand that I will feel comfortable living there."

"But where will you live?" asked Clarissa.

"With Harry's family, I hope." Jane paused before rushing on. "We will be married . . . if he will have me, that is."

"Jane! Please don't be impetuous. Think more carefully what it will mean. It is the rest of your life you are speaking of."

"I have never been more rational in my life. For years I have done as bidden by my elders. I even married my father's choice of a husband. But not again. I am going to do, for the first time, what I want. My only regret is you. My father's estate shall surely crumble, and so too will your allowance. But we shall figure out a way, one step at a time," Jane concluded.

Clarissa's wide eyes searched Jane's face. She nervously smoothed her graying hair and rearranged her tattered brown shawl. "How will you travel? Please don't say by your horse."

"Have no fear. I will go very respectfully, by the mail coach," Jane said with a smile.

"Oh, but, Jane, you haven't a maid. It is entirely improper," Clarissa said with a wail. Her aunt stood up and began pacing the floor. Silence filled the room save for the creaking of the floorboards. "I shall accompany you, then."

The idea had crossed Jane's mind, so she urged her aunt to take the trip. "I will be honored to have you near my side when I wed," she said as she leaned forward to kiss her aunt. "Thank you for granting me one of my fondest wishes."

A cold, wet day found Jane and Clarissa boarding the mail coach, with their two bandboxes stowed on top. Jane had entered the coach after checking at the inn to see if Harry had sent a letter. Empty-handed again after nearly two weeks of impossible waiting, Jane felt her spirits sag.

"Are you sure he will be there?" asked Clarissa again.

"Yes, yes. I told you he was expected home from university this last month. His studies are complete. All will be fine," Jane answered with as much certainty as she could muster. "We will go to the manse as soon as we arrive. He might even be waiting for us in Land's End. I told you I sent him another letter to announce our arrival."

Clarissa held her tongue, though Jane was certain her aunt longed to chastise her for writing letters to unrelated gentlemen. Clarissa's arguments against her plan had had no effect. Jane reflected that following the rules of the *ton* had brought little happiness to either one of them.

The two ladies jolted forward as the driver set the team to their paces. They were quite lucky to be alone in the coach save for a thin, elderly gentleman who had a very yellow mustache and teeth that were even more yellow. He hiccoughed once or twice and promptly nodded off. Clarissa spent the time reading her niece's latest three chapters, and made encouraging sounds.

Jane's anxiety refused to be kept at bay as she looked out the window laced with raindrops.

A change of horses and a cold luncheon at an inn four hours later did little to ease her worries. The old gentleman was replaced by a beautiful governess with cloying perfume who was also headed toward Cornwall. Almost all of Jane's and Clarissa's conversation halted as soon as they discerned that the governess was trying to eavesdrop. The rest of the two-day wet journey was completed in near silence, with each of the three women privy to her own thoughts. The mud slowed their progress and dampened even further their already depressed spirits.

In due course they arrived in Cornwall. The sharp cry of seagulls announced their arrival. The rain had finally abated, and the sun's first rays bounced off the shiny, wet whitewashed houses of Cornwall. Colorful primroses peeked over the tops of some of the village's window boxes as the ladies descended onto the village square. The coachman tugged the bandboxes from their moorings and bid the ladies a good day.

Within moments, it became clear that no one was there to meet them. Seeing Jane's disappointment, Clarissa suggested they have a bit of tea at the nearby inn. Clarissa had already formed a plan, as she had had less faith that someone would meet them. While walking toward the inn, her attention was caught by a dilapidated old carriage being driven too fast.

Clarissa turned in time to witness the amazing transformation of Jane's face. Her happiness seemed to pour out of every fiber of her body. Despite the impropriety of it, Jane cried out, "Harry, Harry!" while flapping her arms over her head. Harry's team clip-clopped onto the square, and he tossed down the reins to a stableboy from the inn. He grabbed Jane around the waist and whisked her around in circles.

"Am I glad to see you again, Duck! It has been forever!" exclaimed Harry as he popped a kiss on her forehead. A lock of unruly hair fell into his light brown eyes.

"I knew you would come. I just knew you wouldn't let us down," Jane exclaimed.

"Let me guess. Miss Fairchild wasn't as trusting, I take it?" retorted Harry while showing Clarissa his boyish grin.

"It is nice to see you again, too, Mr. Thompson," responded Clarissa in her most prim voice.

Harry laughed and asked the ladies if they would join his family at the manse for supper. Jane answered in all happy eagerness, failing miserably to bring her emotions under control. During their ride to the manse, Harry regaled the ladies with tales of his college years. Clarissa's even temper allowed her to roll her eyes only once during the journey. She did try to judge Harry's heart, however, to better benefit her niece. As far as she could tell, Harry seemed to be in his typical good humor, with as many pranks to tell as always. He hid his feelings quite well.

Supper at the manse turned out to be a complicated affair. The Reverend Thompson was flanked by his wife, his two sons, and three daughters. In addition, Harry's youngest sister, Fanny, had asked "her dearest friend in the world" from school, a "delightful" girl by the name of Kitty Dodderidge, to spend a few weeks in the country with the Thompsons. The large party of ten crammed into the smallish dining parlor of the manse. Mrs. Thompson's shrill voice shouted directions to the serving girl as the reverend's booming voice sallied through every conversation. It was always like this at the Thompson household. Clarissa had forgotten how difficult it was to carry on any rational conversation. Each person clamored for attention, and family members cut into conversations and switched topics faster than the notes of a piano concerto. When the cacophony reached a particularly loud pitch, Jane eyed Clarissa and smiled.

At that moment Harry stood up. "Hear, hear!" he exclaimed. "I would like to make a toast to Miss Jane, er, excuse me, Mrs. Lovering." A hoot of laughter followed this exclamation. "And to Miss Fairchild for coming back to Land's End to celebrate my return from university." He continued as he eyed Jane with a big grin on his face. "I can't tell you how happy you have made me."

Everyone cheered. Clarissa's discerning eyes were quick to notice the less than eager applause by Miss Dodderidge and the look of adoration in her eyes when she gazed at Harry. With a sinking heart, she looked at Jane and wished again that the events of Jane's and her own life had turned out far differently.

She turned her attention to the burnt pudding and resolutely began to consume the politic amount.

Jane's feelings were so very far removed from her aunt's. She was exhilarated by being in the same room with the man she loved. She was on familiar ground again for the first time in a very long time. The years spent with Cutty, and the months since his death, seemed to be of another lifetime. She was home. Cornwall. The land of her childhood. The land of her mother. She longed to have Harry to herself and to converse privately with him, but knew it was impossible for the moment. He looked so young, so openhearted, and so full of joy, as always. So different from Cutty and the Earl of Graystock. She shook her head slightly as she looked down at the burnt pudding and pushed it around her plate a few more times.

After the early supper—for the Thompsons kept country hours—Harry proposed a game of badminton in the side garden. Miss Dodderidge jumped at the idea and forwarded that she would like to be on Harry's team. The sides formed naturally—Harry and Miss Dodderidge were joined by two of Harry's sisters, Lillian and Fanny. Harry's older brother, William, was left with Jane, Clarissa, and Sarah Thompson. The game commenced with much giggling and Miss Dodderidge falling into Harry. He laughed and when doing so looked to Jane with almost a request for reassurance.

The game was suspended when darkness overtook the group. Jane was frustrated again when Miss Dodderidge took Harry's arm to go inside for coffee in the music room. She had hoped to detain Harry to speak privately with him. But it was not to be. Clarissa intoned her opinion that it was time for her niece and herself to say good night. Harry offered to bring around the carriage, but was stopped by Miss Dodderidge again. With a slight blush, and a batting of eyelashes, she insisted that he must stay to play charades. Before Harry replied, William said he would be delighted to take the ladies to Pembroke, as he had no interest in charades. With pursed lips and downcast eyes, Jane accepted his offer and said good-bye to the Thompsons and their guest. Harry winked at her and said he would pay a visit on the morrow.

Chapter Six

The surprised stares of two bleary-eyed servants greeted Jane and Clarissa the next morning in the kitchen as they saw to their own spartan breakfasts. The few remaining servants at Pembroke Manor had been enjoying a break from their duties and should have been somewhat put out by the sudden arrival of the two ladies. Yet the maid-of-all-work and the assistant cook burst into smiles and effusive greetings.

"Ah, Miss Jane, the new head groom will be 'appy to see you. He's been 'aving the devil—ah, excuse me, Mum, but he's been 'aving a bad time with most o' the young 'uns!" said the young cook.

"Nelly, it is good to see you, too! Will you send word to the stable that I'll come around within the hour?"

With a quick bob, the servant left. Jane had hoped she would not have to set foot in the house, as her father would be furious. She had expected Harry would meet her at the village square with a proposal and a plan. But at least the news of her removal from her family had not reached Cornwall. She fortified herself with the knowledge that Harry would rectify everything within a day or two. And she prayed her father would send George back here to watch over the stables.

To relieve her sense of unease, Jane informed Clarissa of her intention to ride that morning. Clarissa said she would write to her brother to inform him of her temporary invasion of the family home. Jane's domicile was to be left vague in nature.

Jane breathed deeply as she entered the large, well-kept stables beyond the gardens of her family's home. There was something achingly familiar about the scents of pine and hay, and the sounds of horses munching on their oats and molasses, that brought a great sense of peace to Jane. She hugged herself and almost cried with the sheer joy of being home. She took great pleasure in talking to the head groom. A three-year-old bay gelding was chosen for morning exercise.

After a fast trot across the first meadow, she urged the young horse over a small stile separating two fields on their property. The strong sun of early summer was producing a fast rise of wheat in an adjoining field. Everything felt so right that Jane relaxed and enjoyed a long gallop before crossing the bridge leading toward the manse. This was where she belonged—on a great horse, in the gentle summer of Cornwall. She felt in her bones everything was going to be all right. London and Littlefield were far behind her. Her future with Harry beckoned.

She halted when she saw the small party coming into view of the opposite bank.

"Hey ho," cried Harry as he moved ahead of the ladies beside him and waved. "We've just been coming to see you."

Jane laughed and replied, "I've saved you the trouble."

"Oh, but we still have to have our walk, and the ladies do so want to see the famous Pembroke stables," insisted Harry, brushing the lock of brown hair from his eyes of the same color. He was wearing his ancient boots that were too short and a rust-colored coat patched at the elbows. Dear Harry!

Miss Dodderidge scurried forward to reclaim his arm. He looked down at her impish face containing a wide mouth that seemed a bit rouged if Jane's eyes did not deceive her.

"Do not let me keep you from your mission," replied Jane with a smile. "I shall meet you there in a half hour's time."

Jane trotted back toward the stables and tried to think of a plan to have a private interview with Harry. She had always shared so much time alone with him when they were younger that she could not understand why she was unable to corner him now. Why had he not come around to the house alone? Her sus-

picions lay in the direction of the pretty, petite Miss Dodderidge.

Jane refused to worry about the young miss. Jealousy was
not part of her character. She was in a serious situation, which
Harry knew about from her letter, and he would marry her.
There was no question. He was a gentleman's son, and he had
been her best friend ever since they were children roaming the
high cliffs together. She was uncomfortable because, well, because there were so many things left to be settled and so much
to say.

She wondered if it was right to marry Harry without baring
all her secrets. She reasoned that gentlemen had secrets—secrets about mistresses—that were never divulged. Certainly
there were things that one kept to oneself and never discussed.

As Jane's horse trod on the withered daffodil stalks in the
last field before Pembroke, she thought about Lord Graystock.
His eyes had dilated when she had whispered his name that
dark afternoon. She remembered his beautiful hands, and capable fingers. His palms had been smooth except for the hard, callused places defining an avid horseman. She visualized what
his hands had done to her that day. He had touched her breasts,
and her face, and the most sensitive recesses of her body. She
shivered in the morning sun and wondered where he was at that
moment. And she hoped she would never have to face those
steel-colored eyes ever again.

Halfway to London, he had wondered for the hundredth
time if he should go back to her door, or onward to her father.
On the one side, he had a niggling premonition that she would
reject him outright despite the circumstances. In fact, he was
sure she would delight in refusing him. He also knew that accepting her refusal would be the coward's way out of this dis-
concerting turn of events. On the other side, she was a widow
and thus had the right to determine her own future.

But she lived with her father. And why was that? Why had
Cutty not left her a large independence? He had been quite
well-to-do. Cutty Lovering had had one of the largest houses in
Mayfair and a rich seat in Northhampshire. It was true Cutty's
son had inherited the lot of the entailed holdings.

Rolfe knew the younger Mr. Lovering as well as or as little as he knew many other young bucks at White's. Mr. Lovering's name appeared regularly in the betting books, but he was not one of the notorious gamesters who played fast and deep. The virtuous Mrs. Lovering should have been well cared for by her deceased husband or her stepson. Perhaps the stepson who looked as if he matched Jane in years had tried to force himself on his stepmother after the old man's demise, and Jane had removed to her father's house. Rolfe cursed. Now he was fabricating stories, a character trait that had never surfaced before.

There was something about the way Jane had acquiesced to Rolfe's advances despite her innocence that infuriated him. She had not been a skilled courtesan, but she had not hesitated in her liaison with him. Or had she? She had started to insist he stop when he asked her if she wanted him to stop. A gentleman would have desisted, but he had not. He had taunted her, knowing her pride would not allow her to show any fear.

But he had not known she was chaste. And even when he had discovered her innocence, he had not been able to pull back from the cusp of deflowering her. His complete lack of control disgusted him.

As Rolfe stopped at a watering trough in one of the numerous small villages en route, he removed his gloves and brushed the dirt off his coat. After a few minutes' rest, he continued past the last edges of the town. He had contemplated stopping for nuncheon, but had realized he had no appetite for food. He pulled a small flask from his saddlebag and drank deeply. The half bottle of brandy he had consumed the night before and the liquid fire in the flask had not dulled the guilty feelings he desired to obliterate. If anything, the spirits made him even more keenly aware of his predicament.

It was back to the business at hand—or rather at foot, that of leg shackling. An ill feeling settled in his stomach as he remembered his first marriage, to Constance. She had been a mere child—so petite, so lovely, with her deep auburn hair and large green eyes that always sparkled with mischief.

That had been before their marriage. It was not that she had not had any feelings for him. She had adored him with every ounce of her being. In fact, she had worshiped him. Watching her perish, and the child as well, had scarred Rolfe's psyche in a way no battlefield scene afterward could. The oft-played scene revolved in his head—the endless flow of blood, Constance's pitiful pleas for help and for her mother, and her almost blue face at death matching that of the child, a little boy with black hair. Overnight, it had seemed, the old earl's hair had turned white and the entire village had gone into mourning.

He shook his head and brought his mind back to the immediate future. There was a meeting to arrange behind the walls of one of the oldest houses in Hanover Square, the house of Lord Fairchild, his future father-in-law. He rehearsed in his mind all possible scenes toward the successful outcome of his suit. But then, it should not be difficult, given his rank and his wealth. It was just his reputation, which would bring pause to any devoted father.

Rolfe was well aware of the rumors that circulated each time he surfaced in town. One older, flirtatious widow from Brussels had had the audacity to whisper in his ear with a coy French accent that she would like to "make love to the dark murderer from the countryside." She had scratched the back of his neck as she giggled behind her fan to hide her insidious, cavity-filled mouth. And while his paltry handful of acquaintances were eager to join him in gentlemanly pursuits, such as fencing, riding, and breakfasts at White's, those same gentlemen almost never invited him to private entertainments in their houses, let alone introduced him to their female relatives. It was when he realized this that he had closed the door on forming any attachments to other human beings. He had become ruthless in his aloneness. In seven years he had become as cold and as impersonal as a judge at sentencing. He could have easily disputed the allegations by exercising his considerable diplomatic skills, but by his inaction he had chosen his course.

Jane Lovering caught one of her booted heels on the lower rail of the fence as she studied the paddock full of horses. She leaned into the fence, removed her hat, and handed it to the groom along with her riding crop and gloves. She squinted as she appraised the new crop of babies. This was one of her favorite activities. It was funny. Some of the gangliest foals could turn into marvelous three-year-olds. But they seemed to grow in spurts. First the hind end would grow, followed by the front, or possibly the neck would mature before the rump. But the two things she prized most was a certain look in the eye and a straight stance. She was just picking out her favorite, a black colt sure to turn gray like his dam, when the party from the manse made their appearance.

Harry moved behind her. "There you are—as always!" he exclaimed. "Picking out a new favorite?"

It was one of the reasons why Jane loved him. He had always been able to read her mind. "Of course," she replied. "Over there by the gray mare. The smallest one. Born just two weeks ago, I think. He is a beauty, isn't he?"

"Quite the looker," responded Harry as he turned to address his sister and her friend. "Look, girls, come see the newest additions to the famous Pembroke stables."

"Oh, they are quite pretty," exclaimed Miss Dodderidge, gazing into Harry's eyes.

"They are more than just pretty. A fine fortune they will fetch," said Harry. "That is, if Jane—or I should say Mrs. Lovering—has anything to do with their training. A finer horsewoman does not exist," he continued, looking at Jane. He had mentioned her married name with humor in his melodious voice.

Jane felt the warm cloak of praise and was filled with happiness. He still loved her, she was sure. Jane motioned the group past the pasture toward the house.

"I would be honored if you would all join us for refreshments inside. I will give Miss Dodderidge a peek in our library if she is interested in the history of our family's stables," she said with a friendly air.

"Oh, I would be delighted, Mrs. Lovering. Quite delighted to hear everything about you and your husband's progress," responded Miss Dodderidge while eyeing Harry.

It amused her really, this young lady's flirtation, Jane thought as Harry clarified Jane's status as a widow. Miss Dodderidge's flutterings of apology were met with a smile and assurances of forgiveness. The first inklings of Harry's friendship with Jane marred the forehead of Miss Dodderidge.

At the entrance to Pembroke Manor, Clarissa greeted them, carrying a woven basket full of cut flowers. Jane caught her aunt's attention discreetly and nodded toward the side of the house. Her aunt sighed in exasperation, but smiled her assent.

With fairly good acting, Clarissa insisted, "Oh, Jane, I almost forgot. You must take Harry around to the garden first. The butterfly bush has just come into bloom, and there is quite the buzz about it." With only one cry of protest from Miss Dodderidge, and the insisting arm of Clarissa to persuade her otherwise, Jane was able to whisk Harry to the side garden.

Harry's warm brown eyes gazed at Jane as they strolled to the far corner of the garden past the roses. He patted her hand, resting on his forearm. "It is wonderful to see you again, Jane—may I still call you that?" Harry asked with his usual grin. "It is impossible to think of you as Mrs. Lovering."

"Of course. Unless you insist I call you Mr. Thompson, that is," Jane answered, laughing.

"Ah, it has been so long. Too long—six years. I'm afraid we have grown up and must make an attempt at being proper after all."

This was it. He was going to edge his way into a proposal of marriage. Jane was excited but relieved beyond measure. She had dreamt of this moment for so long but had not really believed it would happen.

"Look at this, will you," exclaimed Harry with awe. They had arrived at the pale lavender spikes of the butterfly bush, which reached the height of a man. White moths covered almost every bloom on the plant, making it look surreal.

"Snow-white Linden moths, a member of the Geometridae family. They must have just emerged. They are a bit late, of course, but see how they are not flying—they are drying their wings. What a rare opportunity," Harry said.

"They are lovely, Harry. Shall you take one for your collection?" asked Jane with just the smallest hint of sadness.

Harry seemed lost in another world as he admired the delicately winged moths. "No. I have specimens enough of these."

"Well, then," Jane said while clasping Harry's hand in hers. There was an awkward pause. She noticed his hand was not as large as the earl's and it was uncallused and just the slightest bit moist. She brushed these thoughts away and realized she was not the only one embarrassed and nervous. For some inexplicable reason, she suddenly felt old beyond her years. Harry looked so young, free of all the serious worries of life. She longed to feel the same way. "Did you consider my letters, Harry?" she asked, eyes downcast.

"Why, yes, I did," Harry answered with a smile. "Quite thought-provoking, indeed," he continued.

Jane reached to brush the wayward lock of hair from his eyes and noticed that they were exactly eye level to each other.

Harry blushed and took her hand in his. "Jane . . ."

With a pause, she responded, "Yes?"

"I am sorry I didn't write to you straight away. I actually just received the letters. I arrived but five days ago from London, where I went to look into the possibility of joining an expedition to Mexico," he said, rushing through his explanation.

"How exciting, Harry!" Her eyes willed him to continue.

"I want to help you, Jane. I won't stand for what your father has done to you. It was very wrong of him. But before I can offer myself to you, you must understand the position I am in," Harry said with an innocent glow on his face.

"It doesn't matter, Harry. You know I will accept you."

Harry looked very embarrassed. "Jane . . . Please just listen. I have very little to recommend my suit. As one of five offspring of a clergyman of a small parish, I must earn my keep now. I was fortunate enough to finish my studies by being adopted as the assistant to one of the professors when he invited me to live with his family. Do you understand, Jane?" he paused, then continued before she could speak. "If we are married, I will forgo the expedition and, I suppose, return to apply for a post at the university. Would this type of life appeal to you?"

Without stopping to think about what she was doing, Jane leaned forward and kissed him. For a moment, Harry's lips remained passive before he tentatively moved his lips into hers and awkwardly embraced her. His moist hands cupped her neck.

"Are you sure, Jane? That this is what you want? You will not be unhappy living on sixpence a year when you are used to something altogether different? Will you not miss your horses?" demanded Harry, finally losing his ever present grin.

"Are you trying to persuade me to change my feelings for you? Will you be happy with me as your wife? Do you still feel for me the same way you did six years ago?" questioned Jane.

"Of course I do. A gentleman's feelings never change," Harry responded, looking at his feet on the pebbled pathway.

"Oh, Harry, you do feel differently now. I can see it in your face."

"That's not it, Jane. That's not the point."

"Then what is the point?"

"The point is that you are unaccustomed to the life my wife must accept. Your father is a viscount, your husband was a rich gentleman, your servants vast, your hardships few."

Jane grew exasperated as she wondered how she could explain the inner hardships she had faced. "Harry, all your worries are groundless. I do not dread taking on the role of your wife, and that of the mother of our children one day. I don't care if I have to 'live on sixpence a year,' as you said. In fact, I don't want you to give up your dream of an expedition. I could go with you."

Harry blanched and paused. His eyes lost all their expression as he brought Jane's delicate hand to his mouth and kissed the back of it. "That would be quite impossible. But if life as the wife of an assistant professor is what you truly desire, then you shall have it," he intoned as he closed his eyes. "How should we go about announcing our plan?" he queried.

She felt light-headed and almost numb with a feeling akin to fear. "I don't know. I haven't thought about it. I was so anxious to see you before anything else." She paused and bent down to breathe in the fragrance of the butterfly bush. "Will you let me think about this? The next step? Let us not divulge this happy news until we have formed a plan. Do you agree?"

Harry covered Jane's hand again, and she noticed the color had returned to his face. His grin reappeared. "Your wish is my command, Mrs. Lovering."

Jane sighed in exasperation and shook her head, smiling.

* * *

With displeasure, Rolfe sat in the leather-bound chair in his library. He was bone-tired, exhausted from the long journey, lack of sleep the night before, and no substantial nourishment for an entire day. He smiled when he realized he had just spent a day similar to strings of days spent on the front. He closed his eyes as he fingered the curved glass containing the heavy amber liquid. His head was splitting, and yet he could not keep himself from thinking about her. He really would just like to get his fingers around her beautiful, long neck. He laughed harshly and threw the glass into the fire. The flames hissed and smoke flew forward as he lurched to his feet and strode toward his upstairs apartments.

The evening had started off as planned. His butler, Jenkins, had greeted him at the door to his townhouse upon his lordship's arrival with nary a whisker of surprise. After a warm bath and a new outlay of clothes, he felt a renewed sense of purpose.

His ornate carriage had taken him the short distance to White's, where he had hoped to dine in comfort and possibly learn with the utmost discretion any gossip concerning the Fairchild family. His evening had met with some success, although "success" was not exactly the term he would have used. While dining alone, he had chanced to hear a group of young bucks arguing about the choice of a gaming establishment.

"Querkson's it is, I say," interjected a carroty-haired youngster of no more than eighteen years of age.

"But it's so dry, deary," jeered another. "No ladies, don't you know. Not at all like the Fox's Den." A round of laughter crashed around the group as another of their party spilled a drink and fell to the floor.

Rolfe shook his head while watching them. He thought that a day—nay, a month—spent on the battlefield would cure their idleness. He wondered if it was not groups of exasperated fathers who invented wars every few decades or so to test and strengthen the integrity of the next generation. Now, he thought cynically, he was thinking like a graybeard. He was awakened from his reverie by the intonation of the very name he sought.

"Fairchild said he would meet us at the Fox's Den," quipped a young man with a bit more polish than the rest. "Come on, you dolts, let's go."

That had been enough to get Rolfe to his feet after signaling a member of the serving class. His driver had shaken his head when instructed to drive to the latest gaming hell.

The son of Lord Fairchild was deep in his cups when Rolfe arrived. The randy group of young gentlemen had managed to precede the earl's arrival and had surrounded young Fairchild, regaling him with the latest on-dits.

Fairchild's face was flushed, due no doubt to alcohol, although his speech had not yet reached a slurred quality. His gaze darted around the room with agitation. His teeth were stained from tobacco, and he had a sad look of innocence lost about his person. But clearly, noticed Rolfe, he was a popular member of his circle.

As the evening wore on, Fairchild won, lost, and regained a small fortune. His friends slapped his back through the losing and the winning. Rolfe had joined Fairchild's game after watching from afar for a half hour's time. All of Fairchild's friends had departed the game at certain times in the company of willing females, who led them to private salons upstairs. Fairchild was not one of them. He remained glued to the game.

Rolfe noticed with a sick sense of disgust the basic ebb and flow of the game and the resulting excited and nervous twitches of the players. He had tried to lose himself in gambling when he had first appeared in London soon after Constance had died. He had been lucky that his commission had forced him away from the gaming hells.

But it wasn't until Rolfe donned his hat to leave that he heard a friend of Fairchild's utter a most interesting piece of information. "I say, old friend, are you going to repay the old man with your winnings, or pay off your lender?"

Fairchild replied with as much loftiness as he could muster, "Oh, nothing as boring as all that. What's say we go to next afternoon's race?"

"But you can't, old boy. Much too populated. One of your father's acquaintances is sure to see you and turn you in."

Fairchild's green eyes were filled with red veins. He appeared acutely awake, as if he hadn't slept for weeks. "Freddie, you are altogether too much the coward. Come on—stop your fretting."

It was not much, but it was a clue. But then, all young gentlemen were known to overextend themselves upon sampling the intoxicating delights of London the first season or two. Rolfe had, his father had, and many generations before and after had and would.

The following late afternoon, it was with a sickening sense of dread that the Earl of Graystock watched his calling card, with one edge crisply folded, borne away on a silver tray held by Lord Fairchild's butler. With flattering speed, the man returned and ushered Rolfe into Lord Fairchild's study.

The older lord extended his hand for a firm shake and motioned to an ancient-looking brown leather chair. Rolfe noticed just the slightest bit of decay around the room, a frayed bit of trim on the draperies and faded fabric on two cushions. But the overall taste and design of the room were of the first quality.

"Delighted to see you, Graystock. Last saw your father several years ago in town," Fairchild said with a crooked smile.

Rolfe noticed that Lord Fairchild clipped the pronouns off his sentences, just as Rolfe's grandfather had used to do. "I'm sorry to inform you that my excellent father died two years ago, sir," replied the earl.

"So, it is so, I understood. So sorry," continued Lord Fairchild. There was an discomforting pause as Fairchild waited to hear why he had the honor of the earl's call and Rolfe struggled to express the reason for his visit.

The air in the room was filled with dust, as revealed by the late rays of light filtering in through smudged windows. "I have come to ask for the hand of your daughter in marriage, Lord Fairchild," Rolfe stated. He stopped to see the effect of his words on the older gentleman.

Jane's father smiled and raised his hands in surprise. "What is this? What are you about, sir?" exclaimed Fairchild.

"Just as I stated, sir. I have come to arrange the terms of a marriage between myself and your daughter," he restated. "And, of course, to receive your blessing," he added with just the slightest bit of haughtiness.

Lord Fairchild rose from his seat and moved to look through the dirty window. Without turning he asked, "I may assume you have discussed this with my daughter? She knows you are here?"

"I am aware of the rules of convention, sir," he responded.

Both Rolfe and Fairchild knew that this answer was in truth no answer at all. The stooped gentleman was shrewd enough to guess the real answer. Rolfe had decided to take a chance when he deduced that the other's manner did not suggest an overly fond relationship with his daughter. If the father had truly cared for his daughter, Rolfe knew, he would have summoned the courage to confront him with the rumors concerning Constance.

"I am well aware of your daughter's circumstances, that of the misalliance with Mr. Billingsley. This means nothing to me," continued Rolfe. He added, almost under his breath, "And I am aware of your family's financial circumstances as well."

Lord Fairchild turned from the window and stared at him. Rolfe could see the man's pride warring with his greed. His intuition had proved correct, and it was now time to dangle the proverbial carrot.

"If Mrs. Lovering is engaged to me, I will of course endeavor to ease any of your family's present financial difficulties, if I am allowed the privilege," Rolfe added with only the smallest hint of irony.

"Your offer is most generous, my lord. But forgive me if I ask again if you have had a private audience with Jane, er, Mrs. Lovering." Before Rolfe could speak, Lord Fairchild put up a staying hand. "You see, I must ask you this, sir, as my daughter has an independent mind—her mother's fault, really. But I am sure you must have noticed this if you have spent any length of time with her." Lord Fairchild smiled. "Perhaps we should speak in terms of 'what if' for the time being. Supposing Jane did marry you, what would be your proposition, Graystock?"

Rolfe wondered if Mr. Billingsley had endured the same quarter hour with the same dialogue less than two months before. Rolfe could now sympathize with Jane. Her father gleamed with anticipation. He could guess she had suffered for her refusal to marry that fop. She could at least be said to possess integrity.

As a gentleman, he would restore her name and her family's

finances to ensure the forgiveness of his lack of control one late afternoon. After the marriage, he would remove himself from Hesperides for 360 days a year, returning only for the fall harvest and festival when necessary. He would also offer his future wife the option of the periodic use of the townhouse in London. Rolfe would travel, and possibly even settle in a new city. These thoughts flew through his mind as fast as the fly buzzing in the room from the window to the base of the candlestick on the desk.

"I would send my secretary around to discuss your family's financial needs with your solicitor, if that is acceptable to you, sir. You will be offered a lump sum payment, or a smaller series of sums at regular intervals if you prefer," Rolfe said.

Lord Fairchild had stopped pacing and now wandered toward his bookcase filled with volumes covered by a thin layer of dust. A strange half-strangled sound came from his direction. Rolfe turned to face Fairchild's back, which had recovered an erect posture.

"I'm sorry, sir, did you have something to say to me?" queried Rolfe.

"No, no," said Lord Fairchild, turning to Rolfe once again. "Your offer is most generous. I daresay Jane is one of the luckiest girls alive this day. You are most welcome into this family, Graystock." While Rolfe guessed it was in Lord Fairchild's nature to be more exact in determining the sum he could expect to receive upon the betrothal of his only daughter, his lordship refrained from minute questioning. Surely it was because the Upper Ten Thousand correctly surmised Graystock was richer than Croesus. Not in his wildest dreams could Fairchild have plotted a better answer to his family's travails.

Suppressing a cynical smile, Rolfe walked toward the older gentleman. "May I suggest that we refrain from announcing your daughter's betrothal at this moment? With the affairs as of yet incomplete, I would prefer to wait. However, you have my word as a gentleman of my intentions," added Rolfe. He offered his gloved hand to Lord Fairchild. His lordship grasped the younger man's hand, seemingly afraid to lose it.

"I shall write to your daughter, with your permission, sir, to inform her of our happy conversation," Rolfe said.

"I am certain she will receive both your and my correspondence with the utmost delight," responded Lord Fairchild with a little less certainty in his voice.

Rolfe almost laughed at the absurdity of Lord Fairchild's pleasantry. As Rolfe voiced his good-bye, he noticed the door to the study opened just a fraction of a moment before he arrived at the exit. The balding butler frowned at him as he accompanied Rolfe to the front hallway. He had the strangest impression that the man wanted to speak to him. Shaking his head, he turned his back on the butler and footman and departed with a feeling of emptiness in his person.

Chapter Seven

Thomas was bored. He cursed his boredom within the confines of his room at Hesperides. He had shot every last grouse in this corner of the world, and surely he had caught enough trout to feed a ballroom full of guests. He reasoned that he had been a good guest and had done what was required of him. It had been more than two weeks since the earl had departed, and three days since Clarissa Fairchild and Jane Lovering had left Littlefield. Through discreet questioning of tradespeople in the village, he had learned that the two ladies had set out for Cornwall.

God help him. He had vowed never to set foot in that godforsaken part of England again. And he would not. As he packed the last few remaining items into his traveling bag, Thomas felt a bit guilty concerning the cowardly fashion of his imminent departure. He had left a note for the dowager countess begging off her insistent hospitality. Vague estate problems, he forwarded, forced him to continue his original journey home. He had hinted in a way that could not be construed a total fabrication. He was sure to have a pressing problem or three upon his arrival in Chichester.

Thomas finally grabbed his hat from the desk and found himself performing a most ungentlemanly tiptoe down the main stair before he forced himself to tread normally. He gave the footman stationed at the Hall's entrance the letter for Lady Graystock and murmured the required civilities before leaving.

While riding to the end of the village road, Thomas marveled at his good luck. He had not been stopped by the dowager countess or anyone else. He was free. Free to leave this place that had witnessed the opening of old wounds. The last three and a half weeks had seemed an eternity. He was tired of facing old emotions in the country, where time was heavy. After a brief visit home, he would return to the gay life of town, where amusements could divert the mind.

He was a confirmed bachelor at heart. His dealings with women had proven to him without a doubt that the fairer sex had been put on earth to torment him. For these reasons, it confounded Thomas to find himself heading toward Cornwall not more than three hours into his journey. He rode kicking and talking to himself the entire way. He wanted nothing more than to turn back toward Chichester. But the small, constant voice of his conscience urged his mount further southward. By the time he arrived at Land's End, he would have a plan.

The letter from the earl reached Jane the same day two letters arrived from her father. One was for Clarissa, the other for herself. With unease, she accepted the missives from the footman and set out for the copse in the side garden. Her steps became more agitated as she neared her destination.

She had thought the earl would leave their business be. It had never occurred to her that he would pursue the matter. The cream parchment weighed heavily in her palm. Her fingers traced Graystock's red wax seal. She could feel a flush rising from her collarbones as she opened the first letter.

Dear Mrs. Lovering,

It is to be hoped that you open this letter without too much trepidation. You must have known I would write to you at the earliest possible moment to resolve the circumstances of our last encounter. I am only sorry that affairs in town prevent me from immediately flying to your side to discuss our future in person. Any flutterings of affection must wait until we see each other in the near future.

I have had the pleasure of an audience with your good father this afternoon. We have reached an agreement regarding a betrothal. With your permission, I would suggest our marriage take place within a fortnight, in Littlefield or Land's End, whichever is preferable to you.

Be not alarmed that I will require your presence in the future. I am familiar with your feminine sensibilities. You will be given the choice of living in town or in Littlefield during the different seasons of the year. I am sure my grandmother will be delighted by your presence. I will not interfere with your life as you so desire. I would insist only on modest decorum on both sides.

I do not require nor desire any children from our union. My brother's child will ensure the continuation of the line.

I bid you good day and assure you of my arrival within the next ten days. I hope beyond words that you will accept my visit and my proposal. I thank you in advance for your kind welcome.

Yours sincerely,
Rolfe Fitzhugh St. James

Well! Of all the puffed-up audacity. It was unbelievable. Jane reread the letter a second time to ensure that it was as bad as she had thought on first perusal. Horrid, arrogant man! The letter commanded her obeisance. It was sure of itself, and even sneering in passages. It was insulting, too. It was as unflattering as the gentleman himself. She longed to obliterate every line from her memory.

She broke the seal of her father's letter without any curiosity. She already knew the contents. It would be filled with flattery about Jane's great conquest. It would welcome her back into the family with grace. And it would contain all the falsehoods of an unloving father's feelings toward his only daughter. It would not question her response to the proposal. Oh, when would her father ever love and accept her for her true self? But then, her father had never accepted anyone. He had dictated everyone's affairs his entire life. He was so sure of the path to happiness. It was by following the rules of society and maintaining a level of prosperity necessary for living in said society. There was to be no deviation from these standards no matter how much unhappiness ensued.

The letter confirmed her thoughts. But her father had surpassed himself in the use of compliments toward the earl. He must be providing her father with more gold than Lord Fairchild had ever conjured up in his fondest dreams. Jane's stomach clenched with disgust.

She envisioned the earl's bronzed hand composing the letter with little more effort than ten minutes' time. She could almost guess that he had been smiling cynically while he composed it. His dislike for her flowed between each line. Well, she would relieve him of his duty with pleasure equal to the obvious pleasure he took in tormenting her.

Jane walked back to the house through the wet grass and the daisies that were just now sprouting. She stopped as she spied a giant silk moth hidden in the shadows of the sidewall stones of the house, well camouflaged by its brown markings against the branches of a dog rose bush. The "eyes" on its wings were hidden among the many folds of the retracted wings. The large moth would fascinate Harry. She contemplated capturing it to show him but could not find it within herself to trap the creature. Something about the killing of these moths repulsed her. The forced spread of the insect's wings and the pins through the thorax reminded Jane of crucifixion. With her hand, Jane tugged and released the slim branch to force the moth to flight and its freedom.

The Earl of Graystock had chosen the written mode to announce to Jane the news of their betrothal with good reason. He was convinced that by writing to her he would give her the chance to huff and puff about the idea, be furious with him, and then accept the plan as the only viable means for her future. He really had no desire to endure her gyrations. Feminine arguments bored him. But he was curious about the state of Mrs. Lovering's mind. He felt quite generous in his offer to arrange for the marriage to take place in Land's End or Littlefield. He had condescended to give her a choice.

It had also become clear to him that the root of all of the Fairchilds' financial woes lay in the sweaty palms of the

youngest Fairchild, although certainly, the father held some of
the blame for not tempering the actions of the son. The sums of
money that had slipped through the clutched hands of young
Fairchild were absurd. By Rolfe's estimation, the family had
lived beyond their annual income of six thousand a year by at
least the same amount. The names of every moneylender Rolfe
knew of and many he did not headed the notes in his hands. His
secretary was silent before him with eyes downcast.

The secretary cleared his throat and asked for instructions.

"Pay them. And I will draft a note to Fairchild, the younger,
requesting his presence at dinner tonight. Tell Jenkins to
arrange for a guest at my table. And see to it that Lord Fairchild
receives a copy of our agreement and the bank draft on the morrow," he commanded while sifting through the agreement.

"As you say, my lord," said the secretary.

"And another thing, Mr. Christian. I will not tolerate discussion of the terms of this agreement with anyone. From this moment forward, it will not be discussed, nor referred to when my
future countess takes residence," Rolfe insisted, looking over
the tops of the pages.

"Of course, my lord," intoned the secretary in a well-
practiced monotone as he reviewed several sheets of paper.

Rolfe stared at the young secretary until Mr. Christian raised
his eyes to meet his gaze. Mr. Christian tried to maintain the
stare but was unable and finally lowered his eyes to his hands.
The ticking of the clock became very loud.

"That will be all, Christian," the earl stated with the icy cor-
diality and finality of all his orders.

Jane spent the morning bent over her foolscap. She wondered which character should move the story along. There
seemed to be too many important characters. Untangling the
maze was like pulling a comb through a windblown head of
hair. And the two main protagonists were not in enough scenes
together. Worse, she was having trouble immersing herself in
her work. Thoughts of Harry, and of her father and the earl, kept
popping into her mind, making writing a coherent sentence impossible. What to do? As she forced her characters into unnat-

ural actions, Jane wondered about her future and how it would unfold.

She was mostly apprehensive about the task itself, that of getting married. Harry could not arrange for a special license, as he was a gentleman without title or money. The banns would have to be read for several weeks in the neighborhood church. And of course, of all the luck, Harry's father, the rector of Land's End, had gone to Bristol to help his ailing brother, another rector. She and Harry had not been able to envision running off to Gretna Green, as had so many other desperate couples. That seemed only for the truly reckless, and it was so far away. So they had decided to maintain the secrecy of their betrothal. They had agreed to go to Scotland only if Jane's father or anyone else tried to disrupt their plans. Jane longed to confide in Clarissa, but embarrassment prevented it.

The Earl of Graystock's letter added to her discomfort. Each day that he did not appear, her temper, alternating with relief, rose a notch higher. The audacity of a written proposal and the certainty of its acceptance galled her to no end. Again she envisioned his large hand writing the proposal in businesslike efficiency and was disgusted. She suddenly remembered the feel of those same callused hands caressing the inside of her thighs. A shiver ran through her shoulders.

A more awkward dinner was hard to imagine. Two gentlemen, strangers to one another, one young and one older, dined alone under the gaze of four elegant footmen. Rolfe did not make the smallest effort to entertain his guest, Theodore Fairchild. A single arched eyebrow rebuffed most of Mr. Fairchild's stabs at conversation. By the time dessert was served, all attempts at dialogue had ceased along with the younger gentleman's appetite.

"We will forgo dessert, Jenkins, I believe. Mr. Fairchild and I will retire to the library, where we do not wish to be disturbed," Rolfe said with finality.

"Yes, my lord," replied the butler.

Theodore's face, already pale, seemed to turn a shade whiter.

The gentlemen decamped to the polished library. The slight

scents of saddle soap and lemons permeated the dark room filled with books on shelves, floor to ceiling. Two rolling ladders leaned against opposite walls, facilitating the retrieval of the uppermost volumes. Rolfe motioned to his guest to help himself to the brandy in the nearby glittering decanter. When Theodore turned from the table, he almost dropped his glass. Rolfe stood, legs wide apart, holding a riding crop in one hand and tapping it into the palm of his other hand.

"Would you care to explain the papers beside you?" Rolfe questioned as he nodded toward a stack of notes on the side table adjacent to Theodore's seat.

"Now, see here, my lord, you have no right to question me," replied Theodore with as much hauteur as he could muster.

"Oh, I think I do. To put it very plainly, Theodore—I may call you Theodore, then?" he asked without any doubt of the reply. Rolfe knew Theodore was much too embarrassed to do more than nod in the affirmative, even though he probably had no desire to be called by his given name. "I have every right to question these exorbitant sums. I want to understand what I am paying for."

Theodore avoided Rolfe's direct stare and found his seat. He nervously placed his glass on the small table and picked up the sheaf of papers. In an offhanded manner, Theodore answered, "Well, let's see here. This one is for the racing curricle I plan to use to win the races at the fall meets. And this one is, ah . . . for a lady's, ah, how shall we say . . . favors. And this next one is to settle—" Theodore stopped as he saw Rolfe's hand rise into the air.

"That, dear boy, is not the question I asked," Rolfe said. He placed the riding crop on the table and walked around the corner of the desk. Leaning against the edge, he crossed his arms. "Now you will tell me why you would conceive to spend these sums, which neither you nor your father possesses."

"My lord, you do not frighten me. You have paid these bills, and you are to marry my sister. And you've saved my father from becoming a bankrupt. But you are not entitled to know the answer to your question."

"You have a choice, then. I will ask you again, and you will answer, *Theodore*, or you may have the thrashing you deserve," he finished. "Actually, I prefer the thrashing technique. It allows me to vent my anger, and to make certain that you would not consider an idiotic repeat performance of your ability to accumulate debt. Yes, corporal punishment works very well, I have found," he concluded, picking up the crop again.

Theodore jumped to his feet. "You wouldn't dare. You are to marry my sister, we are to become . . . brothers."

Rolfe strode to within two feet of the young gentleman, and paused as he raised the crop. "Given your current habits, I do not think I will choose to call you 'brother,' " he replied. "Besides, I already have one dissolute brother. I don't need another."

Theodore slitted his eyes and dared him. "You won't do it."

Rolfe brought the crop down with all his force against Theodore's shoulder and chest. He viewed the cub's shocked expression with disdain and raised his crop again. Changing his mind, he grabbed him by the scruff of his neck and shook him.

"All right, all right, I'll tell you. Just stop—"

"I'm not letting you go until I hear your pitiful excuses."

"I don't know why I did it. Why I spent all this money."

Rolfe tightened his grasp on the neckcloth.

"All right, I'll tell you. Let me go . . . please."

Theodore sagged into the seat as Rolfe leaned against the desk once more. He allowed the boy to sob into the handkerchief he'd provided before probing again.

"Come now, be a man. What is this all about?"

"I suppose it all began as a way to punish my father. And I suppose I can tell you the truth, as you will be part of the family. But I must warn you that Jane knows nothing of this, and you must swear you will not tell her. I have been a good brother to her of late, but I do love her, and I want none of this to hurt her. She has suffered enough."

"I will not swear to anything until I know all the facts."

"Oh, all right." Theodore paused to blow his nose noisily. "It started five years ago, when my mother died. You know of course that it was an accident. A hunting accident—my mother was shot by a stray bullet that was meant to fell a stag." Theodore stopped to organize his thoughts. "Of course it was a shock. My father immediately packed us all off to London 'for

a change of scene that will do us all good,' he said. I don't think
Jane and I felt the way my father did. He was always controlling in the extreme. Anyway, it gave me a chance for the first
time in my life to get away from him. It was easy to disappear
in town with all its diversions. I made friends. We made merry.
I spent the family fortune, plain and simple."

"You spent your family's fortune to punish your father because he was too controlling? I think not. If your father was too
controlling, he would have sent you away—or at least back to
the country once he saw your excessive habits."

"But it was not just that," continued Theodore.

"What was it, then?"

"Well . . . You are forcing me to tell you something that not
a living soul knows except my father and me. . . . He killed my
mother. He was the one who shot her." He wiped his brow and
stared at his lap.

"You saw this? You are certain?"

"Well, yes. I was in a different position than my father in the
wooded area. I heard a shot. And I found my father standing
over my mother, a short time later when I was crossing to the
place where I had just downed a stag. My father insisted our
gamekeeper had fired and killed her by accident—but my sire
held the discharged gun."

"You must have confronted him, asked for the truth," he
said.

"You don't know my father. He would of course tell me it
was an accident, especially if it were not. And he did not tolerate my mother at all in the end. I think he always resented the
fact that it was my mother who brought the estate, the stables,
and the fortune to their marriage. He hushed up the whole murderous business by paying off our gamekeeper to take the
blame for her death. That man was happy to take the money and
tell his story when he did not have to go to jail after the inquisition to confirm the accident."

"So, you punished him in the only way he cared—you spent
his fortune. It took you five years, but you did it."

"Well—it didn't take five years, it took a little more than one
year," admitted Jane's brother with embarrassment.

"But then what did you all live on the last four years? Oh, wait, let me guess. Cutty Lovering's money?"

"Well, yes."

"And Jane knows nothing of all this?"

"No," responded the young man.

"You allowed your father to marry off your sister to an old man to pay for your debts? Yet you have the temerity to say you have been punishing your father?" he asked with anger.

"Yes, well. Appearances are everything to my father. Old Puff Guts has the audacity to want to become part of the prime minister's cabinet. I'm very sorry for Jane. More sorry than I can say. I had no idea he would have Jane marry Cutty to get himself off the hook. I had thought Jane's beauty would assure her a good marriage, and so she did not enter into my considerations.

"But at least Cutty was an old family friend. One of Jane's favorite people in the world. I do not think she minded much marrying Cutty. He was at least better to her than our father. And now she is to be a rich lady. She will find her happiness with you," he challenged Rolfe.

"You seem so certain for one who has brought so much dishonor and unhappiness to your family. And how can you be so sure your father killed your mother?"

"Well, why did he not disinherit me or disown me when I spent our fortune years ago? I'll tell you why. It is guilt."

"I am ashamed for you and for your father. I will discuss with him your circumstances. For now, I will have your solemn promise not to exceed the monthly stipend I have allowed for you. Not a farthing more shall find its way to your pockets. And if you ever do decide to 'punish' me or any member of your family again in a similar fashion, I will have you shipped to India to work in my family's tea holdings. Do you understand?" Rolfe grasped the young man's chin and tugged, forcing Theodore to look him square in the face. "Furthermore, I task you with figuring out a way to atone for your ill-natured deeds. Have I made myself clear? There will be no second chance with me."

Chapter Eight

Rolfe's carriage made its way toward the entrance of the Fairchild estate in Cornwall. His mood had not been improved by the heat and the dirt of the journey. He did not feel very charitable toward any member of the Fairchild family, and in his darker moments he hoped Jane was as upset as he was angry.

A lone footman emerged from the brightly lit small mansion as the carriage approached. He held up a lantern to aid Rolfe's descent. As the carriage creaked out of sight toward the stables, Rolfe inquired about the ladies of the house.

"They be at supper, my lord. There are guests with them from the manse," replied the footman. He proceeded to mount the stairs to the entrance. "But who may I say is calling, my lord?"

"There's no need. Mrs. Lovering is expecting me. I shall present myself," he said, tapping his cane on the doorframe.

He moved through the doors as the footman trotted to keep up with him. Faint laughter guided his steps toward the double doors past the entrance hall.

Rolfe entered the dining salon and encountered a remarkable number of young people at table. He had expected an ailing minister and maybe a wife. But here was a jovial scene with much laughter, which stopped abruptly as he walked in, save for one errant giggle from a particularly silly-looking girl.

The table featured two young men and four young ladies in addition to Jane and Clarissa. The giggling chit modeled a strange garnet-colored hat with five butterflies dancing in the black netting. He stared at the young woman.

"I am delighted to see you again, Lord Graystock," Clarissa said after she had recovered her manners. She stood up and offered her hand to Rolfe. "I'm so sorry, we were not expecting you so soon. You have caught us celebrating the birthday of Miss Dodderidge. Please allow me to present to you Miss Thompson and her sisters, Miss Fanny, and Miss Sarah along with Miss Dodderidge, of course, who is wearing a gift from the Thompson family," she added, smiling. After he nodded curtly to each of the ladies, Clarissa continued, "And this is Mr. William Thompson, and his younger brother, Mr. Harrison Thompson." To the gathering, Clarissa sobered. "May I present to you all, the Earl of Graystock?"

The murmurings of proper greetings were executed along with the requisite curtsies and bows. Then quiet enveloped the room.

Jane ventured to look at him. He was elegantly attired in a blue dress coat, snug-fitting doeskin pantaloons, and highly polished white-tasseled Hessians. He had removed his high-crowned beaver hat and was holding it under his arm. He looked the veritable bridegroom surrounded by a roomful of country cousins! She had lowered her gaze to her lap after the momentary shock of seeing him walk through the door. While she had known he was to appear at Land's End on any given day, she had not been prepared for the embarrassment of seeing him again. Furiously, her mind worked at her predicament.

Jane had not told Harry about the earl, even after she had received the letter, because she had not wanted to further complicate matters. She had hoped that luck would be on her side, at least this one time in her life, and that she would be safely married to Harry before he arrived. She had very much doubted he would "fly to her side."

She had also avoided the topic with Clarissa, who had surely received the same effusive prenuptial letter from her father as Jane had. She had rebuffed Clarissa's two attempts at discussion, calling her father's plans "ridiculous."

The earl apologized stiffly and said he would retire to the rooms prepared for him before rejoining them all after dinner. He refused Clarissa's insistence that he join them at the table.

As he departed, Jane motioned to a maidservant and asked her to provide a hot bath for the earl and a tray in his room. She had not said a word to him, nor had he once looked at her.

Upon his departure, a general buzz circulated around the table. "Who is he? Why is he here? How long is he to stay? And is he married?" were questions asked by the people from the manse. Clarissa responded, as Jane was unable to speak.

Jane had never known that Clarissa had such an excellent capacity for evading the truth with half-truths and out-and-out bounders. Clarissa had the good-hearted temerity to explain that his lordship was here from London to oversee the selection of several new horses for his stable. He was the special guest of Lord Fairchild, and in his absence Clarissa had been asked to prepare for the earl's visit. To Miss Dodderidge's delight, she answered that Lord Graystock was indeed not married. The three young ladies from the manse fairly cooed in appreciation.

"Oh, what a fine addition to our local society," murmured Lillian Thompson.

"Did you say he has over thirty thousand a year? That's almost unheard of," remarked Fanny.

"A fine catch indeed," added Miss Dodderidge as she removed the winged headpiece.

"Aye, indeed—that's if you want to be murdered in your own bed," responded William Thompson with a wink.

A general roar met his statement, which required William to explain his outrageous remark. "When I was in London years ago, I overheard two mamas at Almack's talking about the infamous Earl of Graystock. They called him a murderer. He apparently killed his wife in cold blood, in her bed. She had been carrying the unborn child of her lover, and in a jealous rage he killed her. The mothers said that they wouldn't introduce their daughters to him if he had two hundred thousand a year . . ."

Jane raised her head in shock. "That can't be true, Will. Lord Graystock might have an unpleasant character, but surely he did not murder anyone, especially a defenseless woman."

"Now, Will, we will have none of that kind of talk at this

table. Not when the earl is a guest here. My brother would be provoked by your remarks," added Clarissa.

Harry burst out laughing. "Suit yourselves, but don't say my brother didn't warn you, when we find you all stiff as doornails, dead in your beds."

"Harry, you must guard against misjudging people. Please remember that the earl is my brother's acquaintance," responded Clarissa with anger. It had the desired effect of making everyone stop talking about the gentleman in question.

As gaiety was restored to the mood of the party and a strawberry tart was served in Miss Dodderidge's honor, the general banter resumed regarding Harry's plans for the fall.

"But I thought you were going to go on that exciting exploration tour of Mexico," said his favorite sister, Fanny.

With a look toward Jane, Harry shook his head. "No, no, my plans have all changed. I will do that another year. I have applied for the position of assistant to my old professor of Sciences at Oxford. With any luck, Mr. Melure will take me."

"But why are you giving up your trip? It was to be such an adventure. Something you dreamed of for so long," said Fanny.

"Yes, I know. But this too is an opportunity not to be passed up," responded Harry, darting another glance at Jane. She could feel a blush creeping up her neck as she tried to turn the subject.

"Why don't we all remove to the front room?" she suggested, standing up to signal the end of the meal. She had lost her appetite when the earl entered the room, and now Fanny's comments were leading her even further toward indigestion.

The game of charades was in full swing by the time the earl appeared in the main salon of the house. Surprisingly, he agreed to participate in the game without hesitation. He joined the team comprising Jane, Mr. Harry Thompson, Miss Dodderidge, and Miss Fanny, who had lost their first two rounds. Mr. Thompson on the other team urged him to be the pantomime for the next round. With solemn face, Graystock accepted the challenge. After choosing one of the folded pieces of paper in the crystal bowl, he opened it and stared at the scrap of paper for a full minute.

At the prompting of Clarissa to start the pantomime during

the two-minute allotment of time, the earl dropped to his knee in front of Jane, grasped her hand, and looked at her.

Jane's heart raced as all her worst imaginings took over. He was about to propose to her, publicly this time, ruining her plans with Harry.

"Why, it appears that his lordship is on the point of propos- ing . . . is the word 'wedding'?" Miss Dodderidge tittered.

"How about 'love'?" Harry jumped in.

"How about 'madness'?" queried Fanny with a giggle.

The entourage laughed heartily. He shook his head and then removed his signet ring and slipped it onto Jane's finger before she could draw her hand away. The large gold ring swam warmly on her ring finger. She could see the Graystock crest of a knight and slain dragon on a domino background imprinted on the dark bloodstone. This was the ring he had used to seal the wax on the letter she had received. Suddenly the scene began to swim before Jane's eyes, and she excused herself as she ran from the room.

Rolfe watched her leave. The laughter died away, and an awkward silence filled the room. William Thompson coughed once.

Miss Dodderidge fanned herself and preened. "Perhaps, you could do the pantomime with me, my lord," she giggled.

Harry Thompson glanced at him and the door once or twice.

"I beg your pardon, miss, but I believe we must forfeit," Rolfe replied. "The word you were all to guess was 'pro- posal.' "

"Your time has expired, my lord," Clarissa responded. "And your team has lost another round." She offered the crystal bowl to William next. As that gentleman began his pantomime, Rolfe left the room quietly to avoid notice, if that was possible.

He took the front hall steps two at a time, disregarding the footman's glance. It was easy to determine which room was Jane's, as a slight flicker of light emanated from beneath the closed door in the otherwise darkened hallway. Furthermore, he could hear sounds when he cocked his ear to the door. He knocked and heard a cessation of noise, and then the rustling of feminine skirts.

From beyond the door Jane responded. "Yes?"

"I want to speak to you," he replied in an urgent whisper.

"My lord, we have nothing to discuss. Leave me in peace."

Rolfe sighed and shook his head. "Jane, don't be difficult. Please open the door."

"It is unseemly for you to be trying to enter my chamber. Now please go away," hissed Jane.

Rolfe leaned his body against the doorframe and crossed his arms. "I will not go away until you open this door. I am happy to wait here all night if necessary."

Before Jane could respond, a second set of footsteps could be heard running up the stair. Rolfe moved from the doorway into the shadows beyond the windowed alcove in the hallway.

A young man, one of the two gentlemen from the manse, tapped on her door and whispered, "Jane? Jane, are you all right? It's me." Jane opened the door just wide enough for her to look both ways down the long hallway.

"I'm fine."

"What the dickens? Why did you run away? And where is the earl? The footman informed me that he went racing up the stairs. I was afraid for your safety," Harry said, out of breath. "You didn't let the bounder in, did you?" he continued as he tried to peer inside her room.

"No, of course not," she replied as she pushed him back, stepped out of her room, and closed the door.

"Come on, Duck. Tell me?" Harry asked.

"There's nothing to tell. . . . Oh, Harry, please let us return to the salon and try to appear that everything is normal. I'll explain it all in the morning." She linked her arm with Harry's, and they walked down the hall toward the stair. As she moved away, Rolfe moved forward to hear her last words, "Meet me next to the footbridge on Mr. Gordon's property before church tomorrow. Will you?"

"Of course."

Rolfe turned to Jane's door and hesitated before opening it. A pale blue muslin dress with various undergarments lay on a beautiful old bedspread. A small leather trunk lay open on the floor next to a pair of riding boots and a hat. The earl frowned and closed the door before moving to his own chamber.

Even a simpleton could see that she planned to flee. As Rolfe strode to the bureau and poured cool water into the white porcelain basin, he wondered where she would go. Obviously she could not go to London, or to Littlefield. Did she have some remote cousin or boarding school friend she would go to? It was preposterous. She was behaving like a trapped fox, chewing off her chances for a decent future. He was prepared to give her a life of ease and luxury. One she and her family could ill refuse. But when he eyed his harsh features in the dull mirror before him, he hesitated. She clearly fancied the young gentleman from the manse. He sighed and wondered again why he put himself through this aggravating exercise. Since when had he played by society's rules? Oh, yes, maybe once long ago. But that was a long, long, *long* time ago.

Jane arranged the dark folds of her riding habit around the sidesaddle as she headed toward the footbridge. Her horse could sense her stiff, uneasy state of mind and reacted accordingly by nervously tossing its head. Dismounting, she looked anxiously on the other side of the bridge to see if Harry had arrived. But she knew no one would be there. Harry was late on all occasions.

"Hello, Mrs. Lovering," the earl said as he came up behind her.

Whirling around, Jane felt herself blush. "Lord Graystock . . . Sir, you surprised me."

"I can see that." The earl tapped the side of his boot with his riding crop as his gaze bore into her eyes. "Jane, I am loath to make small talk. You will tell me now what is going on here. And why are you avoiding me?" Graystock insisted as he moved to within inches of her.

"I am not." She looked at the ground as she was overcome by the intensity of the earl's eyes. "Well, maybe I am. But I do not want you here. I told you in Littlefield that I would not marry you. I don't know why you insist on persevering."

"Perhaps it is because I am a gentleman. And gentlemen are true to their honor. Jane, I must marry you. And you must marry me. Or are you impervious to all sense of propriety?"

Jane looked around the earl toward the bridge. In vain.

"He is not coming," Rolfe said.

"Whatever do you mean?"

"A note was sent to the manse explaining that you were unable to keep your engagement with Mr. Thompson."

"You did what?"

"It is not appropriate for a female to meet a gentleman surreptitiously."

"By your reasoning, it is inappropriate for you to be here now. I am not engaged to you, nor am I answerable to you, my lord."

"I will not force the issue. I shall give you time, Jane. But I urge you to choose your path with care. And I ask for your word that you will not run away from your problems. That is the coward's way, you know. Your problems will only follow you wherever you go," he said with one eyebrow arched.

"I shall not promise you anything. But I do assure you I am not a coward, my lord."

"I had not thought so. Now, please tell me you will not leave Cornwall without a word."

Jane looked at the ground, and her heart pounded with confusion. She was angry and flustered that he had managed to guess her plans.

The earl took the last step toward her and lifted her chin with the warm cup of his hand. The intensity of his steel-colored eyes unnerved her. With a rush, his lips met hers, softly and then more firmly as he folded her into his body. Jane did not resist his embrace, as she felt numb from the shock. He stroked the side of her breast down to her waist with one hand while exploring her mouth. Jane realized that she was holding her breath, and inhaled sharply as he deepened the kiss. It stunned her to feel and smell his masculinity again.

He pulled back and looked at her. "Well?"

"Yes, well," Jane replied with a slight hitch, "I cannot promise you anything, my lord."

Jane pushed him away from her. She felt the cool morning air and shivered. She had been drugged in the warmth of his embrace. And her acquiescence to him had been at complete odds with her intentions.

"Please, stop," she whispered, looking off to the side. "Your attentions are unwelcome, and I have told you this must go no further. Really, there is no reason to worry about my virtue any longer. I am to be married shortly. Actually, very shortly."

He let out his breath. "I see. And who is to be the lucky gentleman? No, let me guess . . . could it be young Mr. Thompson?"

"Well, yes, it is he."

"And you are in love with him?" he asked, his eyes hooded.

"You have no right to question me like this. But if you must know, the answer is yes," she said, lifting her chin.

"And your father and his family approve of the match?"

"No. For that reason, I ask your forbearance in not revealing our engagement at present. This is much to ask, but at least it must relieve you of all your moral obligations to me."

"Jane, stop calling me 'sir' and 'my lord' when we are alone. It is preposterous after we have lain together," he said as he reached for her hand. "Now, I must ask you to think carefully of what you are about. Are you certain Thompson will give you the kind of life that will make you happy? And your father—he is most enchanted with the idea of our marriage."

"I can very easily picture his countenance when you offered for my hand," she said. "How much would it have cost you from the Graystock coffers? Ten or more thousand?"

He regarded her and did not answer.

"It is as I thought. The price for my hand has seen new heights. My father will be vastly disappointed, I am sure."

Graystock stepped close to her once again. He cupped her face in both of his hands and stared into her eyes. "Are you sure this infatuation with Mr. Thompson is not a passing fancy? Will you not be miserable with a man who is unable to match . . ."

Jane removed his hands from her face. "Excuse me, but do not presume that since we have, have *lain together*, as you so aptly described it, you know everything about me and what will make me happy. Harry will make me happy. You will not." She stomped her foot once. It was infuriating to have to explain her feelings to the earl. He had no right to question her.

He moved to stroke her hair and once again leaned to kiss her, with all restraint lost. His proximity tormented her body and her mind. When he pulled away, she could not stop her tears.

"Damn you!" she said as she turned to remount her horse. Her last shred of dignity was removed when she was forced to request his aid.

"It would be my pleasure," he responded with a huge smile. "I live to be at your beck and call," he continued glibly.

Rolfe still felt the imprint of her delicate form on his chest and remembered the sweet, warm scent of her flaxen hair. He smiled. He could at least be glad that she had allowed him to kiss her. A promising sign in itself. And he felt confident that she would not secretly hasten away. Everything else was not to be counted on, for he was quite sure they would never, ever be of one mind on any subject! It was a great tax on his forbearance.

Chapter Nine

A light summer rain tapped against the windows of the
Fairchilds' main salon that afternoon. Girlish laughter filled the
room as two spirited games of cards began in earnest after tea.
Jane had excused herself from play to face the dreaded task of
composing a letter to her father.

This was it. She would go through with it. Following a
painful interview with Harry's father yesterday, in which the
latter had refused to grant the couple's wishes without her father's consent, Jane and Harry had made covert plans to travel
to Gretna Green despite her conversation with the earl. Seeing
the reverend's fright, springing from his idea that Jane's father
would turn him out of the living, she knew that they would have
to remove quickly. They resolved on departing in two days'
time via Harry's dilapidated version of a carriage. Jane had two
days to pack and write letters to her father and Clarissa. Her efforts to assure Lord Graystock that he had no further responsi-
bility in her corner had failed, as he had made no plans for his
departure from Pembroke. She sighed, knowing she must speak
with him again to prevent any possibility of his trying to follow
them. An examination of her conscience also made her realize
she must also pluck any remaining guilty feelings she felt toward her family out of her heart. There was only the smallest
voice inside her head echoing doubts about the intelligence of

her plan. A louder demon reminded her constantly about the future plight of her aunt and the rest of her family.

Sitting at a small writing desk at the front corner of the room, she gazed out the large windows to take in the beauty of the vista. It pained her to know she was likely to never again be in the house once she married Harry. But what was that, compared to life with the man she loved?

She turned and looked at Harry's profile. He grinned as Miss Dodderidge's hand covered his own. She begged him to help her with the intricacies of the game of Hearts. Between Harry and Miss Dodderidge sat Clarissa, with the earl opposite, dressed in a severe black superfine coat that emphasized his broad, hawkish physique. Jane glanced to the second table of card players when she felt Graystock's cool gaze turn toward her.

The other table featured William and his three sisters, Sarah, Lillian, and Fanny. Much arguing erupted from that table, as family members were guaranteed to fight amongst themselves when the formality of manners and small titles such as Miss and Mr. were unnecessary and forgotten.

Jane twined the fingers of one hand as she wracked her brain for verbiage. She was on the point of quitting the room to seek the solitude necessary to compose her difficult letters when she spied from the front window Sir Thomas Gooding, riding up the pea-gravel lane in front of the house. His hat was misshapen from the wet, and he handed the ribbons over to a groom, who hurried in the direction of the stables. Jane tried to capture Clarissa's attention as she rose from her desk to stand before the double doors. Clarissa looked at her with a doe's innocence.

The doors opened, and a footman introduced Sir Thomas, who stood brushing the last of the raindrops from his coat, which had been mostly protected by his greatcoat. His short dark brown hair was matted where his hat had failed its duty.

Jane moved forward to clasp his hands. "Sir Thomas, how delightful to see you again, sir."

"Thank you for your welcome, Mrs. Lovering. I am sorry to drip all over you."

"Nonsense, sir. We are so happy you have come for a visit."

She knew without glancing at her aunt that it was Clarissa's turn to feel as ill at ease as she herself had felt the night before, when the earl had arrived unannounced. The necessary effusions of greeting and introductions were well under way when Graystock, with laughter in his expression, slapped his friend on the back.

"What brings you to Cornwall, my good man?"

"I should ask you the same, Graystock. I thought you were in London on pressing business."

"Yes. Well . . ." The earl was at a loss for words for once.

William Thompson blurted out, "Why, Lord Graystock is here for a look at the famous Fairchild horses, of course."

Sir Thomas grinned. "I see. The stallion has not learned his lessons well? I, then, am come to seek a horse as well."

Jane interjected, "Where are you staying, Sir Thomas?"

"At the Tabard Inn."

"You are very welcome to stay with us, of course," Jane said as she looked at Clarissa's ashen, downcast face.

Gooding paused and looked toward Clarissa as well. "You are very kind, but I would not impose."

"Oh, come, come, Gooding, let us have none of that," replied the earl. "Mrs. Lovering has invited you, and you must accept if for no other reason than to even out the numbers at mealtimes."

"If Miss Fairchild is not inconvenienced, I would be delighted to accept the invitation," he said quietly.

Clarissa looked up when she heard her name mentioned. "You are very welcome, Sir Thomas," she said.

"It is settled, then," Lord Graystock said with satisfaction as Jane handed Sir Thomas a cup of lukewarm tea.

Never one to miss the opportunity of meeting someone new, Miss Dodderidge giggled and asked Sir Thomas if he would like to join their table. Still glancing at Clarissa, Sir Thomas declined and walked to stand by the fireplace to dry his damp boots. Jane dispensed with the idea of composing a letter and moved to converse with Sir Thomas.

"May I inquire about the health of your family, sir? I presume they are all well?"

"Yes, very much so. Or so I believe. I received a letter from my uncle, Lord Rushmore, the day I left Littlefield," responded Sir Thomas, his smile reaching his brown eyes.

"I believe I had the pleasure of meeting your uncle a few years ago. He was a great friend of my husband's."

"Oh, yes, I remember. Uncle Willie used to invite Mr. Lovering to come for the superior foxhunting found on his estate. They would mount up every autumn whether conditions were favorable or not," he said. "When I was there during holidays as a boy, I used to beg and beg to go with them. But they never would consent until I reached the advanced age of fifteen. They decided along with my father that that would be a suitable age for me to break my neck!" Sir Thomas added with a laugh. Jane took Sir Thomas' empty teacup and placed it on the mantel.

"I was sorry not to be at Cutty's funeral, Mrs. Lovering. He was a great man."

"You must have been following Wellington at the time, dear sir. I am sure my husband's family never expected you. But your words are very kind," Jane responded. "Your uncle traveled a good distance to come, as did your wife."

Sir Thomas pinched his eyebrows together. "Ah, that must have been just before our divorce, when Lucinda was still trying to keep up appearances. Pardon me, Madam." Sir Thomas added the last under his breath.

Jane had had to bend her ear closer to catch it all. Shocked, she turned to look at her aunt. Clarissa's face was white as she stared at Sir Thomas and then back at her cards. Jane did not doubt that it took all of Clarissa's strength of character to remain seated and continue playing the game. She noticed her aunt's hands were unsteady.

"Sir, please let me offer you my condolences," Jane said. It was amazing that in the small circle of society in London, she had not known about the divorce. The scandal of divorce was an event requiring many hours, days, months, and even years of speculation by the *ton*. But then again, Jane's small circle, more Cutty's older male acquaintances than her own, gossiped less than their female counterparts, especially in her hearing. Jane could list all the illnesses and deaths that plagued her husband's friends' families, but she was ignorant of the worst offenses of their sons and daughters. In addition, she had closeted herself in the country away from *ton* events and the cutting tongues of London, where she had suffered a miserable first season followed by a much-gossiped-about marriage.

"It is quite all right, Mrs. Lovering. I am reconciled to the fact," responded Sir Thomas, eyeing the intricate mantelpiece.

Jane, a little embarrassed, changed the subject. "Shall we send a message to the inn, sir, to retrieve your belongings? It is too wet to go back, really. May I send a footman and groom to collect everything?"

"That would be most kind of you. Yes."

Graystock turned to him. "Do tell us about the success of your hunting and fishing schemes on my property, Gooding."

"You will be content to know your larders are stocked to the gills," Sir Thomas responded. "And by the by, your grandmother, when I left, was busy adding more names to the invitation list for your house party this fall."

Clearly irked, Lord Graystock did not reply.

With much amusement, Jane observed that Miss Doddridge's attempts to draw the earl's attention to herself had failed miserably. She smiled as Sir Thomas spoke to her once again.

"Will you visit your aunt for the festival, Mrs. Lovering? I will be there, as well as the Kellerys and the Smiths. And if her grandson does not return soon, I'm sure the dowager countess will invite many other people you would know from town."

Jane glanced at Lord Graystock. He seemed to be quite still, listening for her answer. "I think not, sir. I have accepted other engagements this fall that preclude a visit." Clarissa drew the attention of everyone in the room at the conclusion of the hand in play. "Will you all excuse me? I must have a word with Cook, and with our housekeeper, if you please."

The male cardplayers all nodded as they pushed the cards to the center of the felt-covered table. Miss Dodderidge protested and then snuggled up to Harry by clutching his sleeve as she looked at the earl. "Do let us play charades again, Mr. Thompson and Lord Graystock. It was such a lark last evening."

Jane noticed Lord Graystock made no effort whatsoever to conceal a pained expression. When Miss Dodderidge continued to pester the group, the earl stared at the chit with such a black expression that Miss Dodderidge was dampened into submission.

Clarissa's heart pounded so desperately that she was sure everyone in the room had noticed. As she rushed into her room, she held her throbbing temples in her hands and lay on the bed. She closed her eyes and replayed scenes with Thomas in her head until her mind swirled and she thought she would go mad.

She remembered his youthful face, before the war, when he had proposed to her on bended knee with laughter in his eyes. He had been in such good humor when she had nodded her assent, his face glowing with a look she had seen but once or twice many, many years ago. She remembered the shock of seeing him again in Littlefield—his anger, his bad manners, and his reproofs. And she also remembered the scene at Littlefield in her cottage, late at night.

It had been a repeat of the conversation at the seashore but with even less civility. But never once had he mentioned his divorce, an almost impossible event. And now, for the sake of propriety and pride, she would be required to maintain a calm demeanor, suppress any hopes, in the face of this news. She wished more than anything to throw herself at his feet, beg his forgiveness, and pray for a renewal of his attentions, but she knew in her heart it was too late. There was just the smallest of voices in her ear whispering, "Why did he come?"

She fingered her old lace cap in agitation and forced herself off the bed and into the kitchen to inform the housekeeper of Pembroke's newest addition.

The morning dawned cool and sunny, a fortuitous event for the foursome at Pembroke and the party at the manse. A visit to Porthcurno had been proposed the evening before, and most of the young members of the set had embraced the plan with enthusiasm. Jane awoke from a restless sleep with the realization that this would be her last day at Pembroke. Tomorrow, early, she and Harry would leave as fast as his ruination of a carriage would take them. At least they would have adequate horseflesh until the first posting exchange, as they would borrow horses from her family's stable.

She had finished at midnight all the letters that would be posted upon her departure, and she had packed a small trunk and pushed it behind all the gowns in her armoire. All that was left to do was to get through this day without anyone learning of her plan. And without losing her mind.

As she finished fastening her practical dark blue riding habit, she felt guilty for not selecting her black mourning. But that would mean forgoing the pleasure of riding—and she had such few pleasures. Jane looked at her small escritoire and saw the earl's ring, which she still possessed from that dreadful game of charades. She had to find a private moment to return it to him. She had been safekeeping it in her pocket but had put it on the escritoire while she wrote her letters. She took the few steps back and slipped the heavy gold ring into her pocket.

The last of the picnic was being handed to the pretty occupants of an open carriage as Jane approached from the stables riding a young bay mare. The gentlemen, all astride, nodded to her as she took her place behind the earl, Sir Thomas, and the two brothers. Her mount was full of spirits and threatening to bolt at the smallest provocation.

"You are going to have a lively time of it, Mrs. Lovering. Are you sure you wouldn't prefer to switch horses?" Mr. Harry Thompson asked, while looking longingly at the beautiful horse.

Jane smiled at him as she leaned over the mare's shoulder to pat her. "Ride old Boots? I think not!"

"He might be gray around the whiskers, but he can still give some young ones a run for their money. Come on, let's switch," teased Harry.

"I believe Mrs. Lovering would as soon take your suggestion as she would ride in the carriage," drawled Lord Graystock.

"Whyever would you say such a thing?" Jane asked.

"When have you ever taken a gentleman's suggestion?" replied the earl, with one eyebrow arched.

Harry hooted with delight. "Hear! Hear!"

Jane tried not to sound defensive when she answered, "It isn't that. It is just that I'm bringing this mare along slowly and she requires a delicate hand."

Harry laughed and broke in, "This gets worse and worse. Are you insinuating that I will maul your dear creature?"

He was smiling and of such a good nature that Jane knew even an insult from her would do little to bother him. Wishing to prove the earl wrong, Jane dismounted and offered the reins to Harry. "Of course not. If you really want to switch . . ." She raised the stirrup and unbuckled the girth as she added, "Old Boots and I will have a dandy time of it, I'm sure."

Harry arranged her sidesaddle on his aged horse, laughing the entire time. He then moved to her spirited animal and was successful in his endeavor of placing his saddle on the young mare only after Jane moved to soothe her.

The party trotted eastward toward the beach of Porthcurno following the winding dirt path through Pembroke's fields and hedges. Two miles further brought them to a small fishing village, where large, disassembled timber balks marked the outskirts of the parish. These were laid across the small harbor during winter to block the worst of the winter gales. Jane was explaining the practice to Sir Thomas when the carriage drew parallel to the mounted group. Miss Dodderidge called out to them and waved her bright handkerchief. The exercise of the morning had failed to dampen the spirits of the skittish mare, and the sight of the handkerchief set the horse into a dead run. Poor Harry had let the reins dangle freely as they walked through the village to give the animal a rest.

The group watched helplessly as Harry's mount galloped through the treacherous cobblestone streets of the village, slipping as she bucked and swerved. Jane knew that going after him would only further frighten the mare. With fifty feet of slippery cobblestone left before the dirt path resumed on the far side of the village, the horse lost her footing and went down with Harry astride.

Jane had already dismounted, along with William Thompson and the earl. As she ran toward Harry she felt as if time moved forward too slowly and that a tunnel had formed between her and a quite motionless Harry. She reached him just as the horse was trying to right herself, pushing her front legs into a position to be able to stand up. An oath escaped Harry's lips. With a soothing voice, Jane spoke to the mare and rapidly disengaged Harry's foot from the stirrup, which had been lodged beneath the horse.

He was pale and barely conscious as Jane urged the mare away from him. William took the reins and walked the shaking animal to the earl before returning. Jane listened to Harry's shallow breathing, patting his hands and calling out to him as he slipped into unconsciousness. She noticed, with a wretched feeling, that Harry's ankle lay at an unnatural angle. A babble of female voices, marked by the high-pitched shriek of Miss Dodderidge, moved closer. Jane glanced at the earl, who intercepted the group and insisted on their restraint.

"Oh, but, my poor, dear, brave Mr. Thompson," wailed Miss Dodderidge.

"Pray, Miss Dodderidge, please attempt to keep your wits about you," Lord Graystock said dryly.

"Oh, but I must go to him, this instant."

"No, my dear, you must not," he responded as his arm intercepted her wrist.

"Miss Dodderidge, please stay back and comfort Harry's sisters," Jane insisted without looking at the foolish girl.

Sir Thomas had joined Jane to feel Harry's neck and head, when his eyes reopened. Jane brushed the hair from Harry's forehead and spoke to him. "It's all right. You fell off the mare. Don't try to move just yet."

Harry groaned and tried to sit up. "Really, I'm all right, I think. It's just this cursed ankle." He lay back down and closed his eyes. "Just give me a few moments, please."

William came forward from a nearby inn with a pitcher and glass. "Harry, do you want some water?"

Jane retrieved a handkerchief from Harry's coat and dipped it into the pitcher of water. She cleaned his dusty face and the small cut on the side of his brow.

"I've really gotten us all in a scrape now, haven't I?" Harry said as he propped himself up on his elbows.

"Not for the first time," Jane responded. "Do you want to try and get up?" Sir Thomas and William moved into position and hooked their arms under Harry as he stood on his one good leg.

"How do you feel?" William inquired.

"Like I've just been trampled, thank you," he said as he straightened his dirty, patched coat. "But I'll survive."

"Dr. Coopersmith should see that ankle," William suggested.

"Let's send word to him right away," Sir Thomas said as he motioned to the pub's serving girl standing nearby.

"No, no, I won't ruin our outing. Dr. Coopersmith is only half a mile from here, right next to the beach where we had planned our picnic," Harry insisted.

"Harry, don't be ridiculous," Jane said. "We're taking you back to the manse, straightaway."

"No, no, I'll not be the cause of spoiling all our fun. Just help me into the carriage. Come on. I want to show our guests Logan Rock as promised."

Jane noticed that the earl had been watching the scene unfold without a word. Color had returned to Harry's face, and his body movements proved that only his ankle had been affected by the fall. Sir Thomas had signaled to her and the earl that Mr. Thompson's head appeared undamaged. Lord Graystock moved forward and told the carriage driver to tie the reins of Jane's mount, Boots, to the back of the carriage and arranged for the saddle to be switched to his horse. Harry was placed between Fanny and Miss Dodderidge amid much cooing. After checking the nervous mare's legs and flanks, Lord Graystock swung onto her back with practiced ease.

Jane swallowed her desire to insist that she ride her own horse. Instead she mounted the earl's gelding with Sir Thomas' assistance and followed the carriage the rest of the way, enduring the feminine nonsense trailing the vehicle.

The doctor confirmed what everyone suspected and prescribed immobilization of the badly sprained ankle for several weeks. The doctor splinted the ankle while Harry's face remained tight and pale. As Clarissa herded most of the group toward the door, Jane had a moment to lean toward Harry.

"I'm sorry, Jane," he whispered.

"I'm sorry too, about your ankle. Does it hurt dreadfully?"

"No, not really. But, Jane, this needn't change anything. Don't worry, we'll find a way."

"You're not to think of that right now. We'll make a new plan. Let me think a bit," Jane replied. Her head throbbed as she massaged her temples. She looked up to see the earl watching her beneath hooded eyes. She didn't care. Really, she didn't. She didn't even care if he had heard their entire conversation.

The earl walked over to her. "Mrs. Lovering, would you like the doctor to give you something for your headache?"

"No, thank you, sir. I do not have the headache."

"Are you always this contrary? Or do you just insist on favoring me with this behavior?" he said just loud enough for her ears only.

"No, sir. I was unaware of your misconception of my behavior. I shall endeavor to ensure that your opinion of me changes for the better," she said with a false smile.

"I say, my stomach is rumbling. Shall we proceed to the cliffs for the picnic?" Harry said with a smile.

Miss Dodderidge rushed forward and clung to Harry's hand. "My dearest friend, I shall find the choicest morsels for you. Please allow me to do this little thing for you," she insisted while batting her eyelashes.

"Of course, my dear, " Harry said, favoring her with a grin. The earl and William assisted him to his feet and his crutch. His bandaged lower leg was impressive enough to ensure repeated girlish fawnings for at least the duration of the outing.

Upon reaching the small cliffs overlooking the sea, the gentlemen helped Harry navigate the short distance to the site. The ladies arranged the blankets and the picnic, and as promised, Miss Dodderidge stationed herself next to the injured man to fuss over him. At least Harry seemed to be enjoying the attention.

Jane sighed and walked to the cliff. She stopped and closed her eyes, breathing in the fresh, moist scent of the Atlantic Ocean. She looked below the palisades and watched the swirling surf crash into a huge solitary rock below. Winding up the less steep portion of the cliff, a path twined like a pale serpent.

Lord Graystock moved next to her and shaded his face with

his hand. Jane noticed the wrinkles around the corners of his eyes and the whiteness of his teeth as he squinted. His starched white linen cravat contrasted with his bronzed, angular face.

He motioned to a promontory point and asked, "Is that the famous Logan Rock? "

"No, my lord. It is just over there, near the jagged ridge. The large roundish rock."

"Oh, yes, I see it now. Shall we walk over to examine it?"

Reluctantly, Jane walked toward the rock, taking the earl's offered arm. She could feel the outline of his coat and where the shirtsleeve poured out of it. His arm was broad and firm. Her fingers rested on the familiar, strong hand with tanned skin warmed by the sun. She felt awareness of his body prickle her skin as she shivered involuntarily.

"May I offer you my coat, Mrs. Lovering?"

"No, thank you, my lord. The sun is quite hot, actually."

They walked the short distance to the landmark in silence, neither one of them capable of maintaining the flow of conversation. They stopped in front of the huge boulder. Lord Graystock passed his hands over the face of the rock and pushed. As discussed the night before during supper, the rock moved from side to side.

"Amazing," he said in surprise.

"It is said to weigh sixty tons," added Jane.

"And no one has dared push it off its base? A remarkable feat of restraint."

"Yes, we Cornish are a restrained lot. No one from here would dare disturb this landmark."

"Are you a restrained creature?"

"I would not know. That is for my acquaintances to decide." Jane was embarrassed, given events of the recent past. He exhibited remarkable self-control by not voicing a cynical reply.

Rolfe turned to the horizon and motioned toward the faint trace of an island. "What is the name of that small island?"

"That is not an island. It is Lizard Peninsula, the most southerly point of England."

"I had thought Land's End held that distinction."

"No, Land's End is the farthest point west." She guessed he

was trying on his best manners in an effort to make her less uncomfortable around him.

"I should very much like to see it," he said.

"It is a good thirty-mile trip, my lord."

"Well, perhaps we could organize an early-morning expedition with those from the manse who are interested."

"Hmm," replied Jane. She had little desire to plan an outing of this nature when her hopes to fly to Gretna Green had just been postponed.

"That is an answer that displays admirable restraint, Mrs. Lovering. You are in danger of revealing your Cornish nature," Lord Graystock said in a mocking tone.

"Yes, I suppose I was. Is that also what I revealed by allowing you to bully me into relinquishing a green horse to Mr. Thompson?"

"Ah, we get to the heart of your pique today."

Jane made an annoyed noise. "I am not piqued!"

"The lady doth protest too much."

"Why do you insist on staying on?" Jane changed the subject, for her anger had taken hold.

"For the pleasure of your company, my dear."

Jane snorted. "I think not."

"Well, then, to ensure that you choose the best path, Mrs. Lovering."

"I have been out of leading strings for this age, my lord. You insult me by insisting that I am not capable of finding happiness on my own."

"You will be doing a poor job of it indeed if you elope with Mr. Thompson."

Jane paused and tried to organize her mind before speaking. It seemed that there were no words to reply that would be appropriate, so she said nothing.

"Do you deny it? It is no use, you know. You have left a trail of evidence more obvious than a snake shedding its skin."

"Ah, now you compare me to a snake!"

"No. I compared your packed trunks to a snake's skin. And I still haven't heard your denial."

"And now you are entering my chambers and spying on me. How dare you!" Jane could tell that she had finally punctured his armor by the fierce anger she could see in his dark gray eyes.

"I won't deny it. Will you deny you are planning to hike off?"

She tried to calm herself by taking a deep breath. She knew enough of him to know that if she continued to goad him, he would interfere further. "I won't deny it. I have nothing to hide from you. I told you I would marry him," she said. "I would ask, if you have any regard whatsoever for my feelings, that you would not expose my plans to anyone." She brushed the hair from her face and gulped as she grasped his hand in her own. He appeared surprised by her bold action. She forced herself to look deep into his turbulent eyes. "I am begging you. Please do not betray me. This will make me happy. It is what I have wanted for almost ten years. I love him. Please don't allow anyone to take this one dream away from me. Aren't I allowed one fulfilled dream in my lifetime?" It pained her to beg this gentleman.

Lord Graystock appeared discomforted. "I would not deny you your dream, Mrs. Lovering. I had only hoped it would be a dream that had a chance of ending happily," he said in a gruff voice.

"But it will."

"And this is a dream held by Mr. Thompson as well?" he asked, nodding toward Harry, who sat far in the distance.

Jane shaded her eyes and looked at the groups on the blankets, spotting Harry surrounded by his sisters and the ever present Miss Dodderidge. He looked so young, and full of laughter, as the latter popped a grape into his mouth. Lord Graystock's eyes narrowed as she turned back to him.

"Of course it is," she answered, embarrassed.

"Really? I have not noticed a preference, to be very blunt."

Jane mounted her defense in much annoyance. "Harry is careful to conceal his feelings because of our delicate situation."

"I did not know young gentlemen were capable of concealing their sensibilities. Most write bad poetry in their drunken passion and litter a lady's person with their comical musings."

"Yes, well. Harry is Cornish as well."

"Ah, the famous restraint."

"So, my lord, do I have your word—that you will not reveal our plans?" Jane finished with the hope that she could end this nightmarish conversation.

"Yes," he said in his deep voice.

"Thank you, sir."

Jane walked away from Graystock toward the general party. A recent habit forced her to feel for the earl's ring in her pocket. All at once she paused, then continued walking. She was frustrated that she had again forgotten to return his ring to him. But nothing could make her go through the further embarrassment of returning to his side. She would just have to remember during the next opportunity. It annoyed her that she didn't feel more exhilarated from having convinced him to let her live the life of her own choosing. Instead, she felt deflated as she turned her eyes away from the sea and toward the blankets where her future and her past lay.

Rolfe scanned the coastline, his eyes coming to rest on Lizard Peninsula once again. He knew he should just leave this miserable part of England. He did not want to be here. Jane did not want him here. In fact, the only person who seemed to be happy with his presence was Miss Fairchild, for some unknown reason. For the last few days she had gone out of her way to ensure his comfort by conversing with him and arranging events that would tempt him. But he knew what had to be done. He would leave as soon as possible for London. He had done his duty. And now he would keep his promise to Jane. He would not meet with her father until after she and Mr. Thompson had eloped. For the rest of the summer he would reside in London. Society would be thin at the end of summer, and that was how he liked it.

He was tired of all the idle chatter and frivolous activities. He would do a thorough review of all the estates' holdings by calling all seven of his stewards into town. Then he would tour several properties if necessary on his way back to Hesperides prior to the fall season. The plan was sound, and he itched to leave. He felt a dark mood penetrate his being, not unlike the ones suffered before and after a hard battle. He longed to retrieve his horse and ride back to the house, but decorum dictated otherwise. He cursed the fact, as he moved toward the others, that even being an earl did not excuse one from performing distasteful acts of socializing.

Sir Thomas spied the brooding expression on the earl's face and proposed a walk down to the beach to give Graystock a small chance at solitude. He felt his own opportunity for happiness was improving, while his great friend's was diminishing. Sir Thomas looked at the even profile of Miss Fairchild and noticed that despite the faint lines on her face, and the ridiculous white lace cap, she was still lovely. One could almost forget the plainness of her brown wool dress when noticing the feminine, proper arch of her back as she sat perched on a rock. He had renewed his hopes for them since arriving at Land's End. After four days filled with trivial talk, he was at least perceptive enough to know that perhaps Miss Fairchild would not repel his advances.

Thomas offered his hand to Clarissa, and she rose from the ground gracefully. With the exception of Jane, Miss Dodderidge, and Mr. Harry Thompson, the group managed to wend their way down the cliff with only a stumble or two.

Once on the narrow strip of beach, the group separated not unlike a strand of pearls breaking. Graystock refused to be anywhere near the party. Fanny and her two sisters, in their maidenly white muslin dresses, created a lovely picture of innocence as they held hands and laughed while running ahead. The girls kicked off their boots and walked in the foamy water's edge. William Thompson endeavored to chastise them on their unladylike behavior while Clarissa and Thomas followed the young girls at a distance that promised a measure of privacy.

"Your friend does not seem to be enjoying his stay here in Land's End," remarked Clarissa.

"A certain lady is to blame," Thomas responded. After a brief dozen steps, Thomas glanced at Clarissa's profile and began again. "Why must you wear these caps? Have you given up all signs of youth? They do not become you." He reached over to finger the lace on her modest white cap. In a swift movement, he snatched it from her head, removing half the pins from her hair in the process.

Clarissa gasped and reached for her worked-muslin cornette. "Sir Thomas, I implore you . . ." She appeared very self-conscious as her wavy brown hair fell to her waist.

"It is a crime that so much time has been wasted, Clarissa." She inhaled as she heard him speak her given name. Her pale blue eyes darted to his face and looked away.

"You know why I have come, do you not?" Thomas asked. Clarissa hesitated. He pulled her into the shadow behind a large rock embedded in the sand. "Come, come, you mustn't play the shy maid with me," he continued, grasping her chin with one hand.

She looked at him finally, and the wind blew strands of her unconfined hair across her face. "I am sorry. I do not know."

Thomas brushed the hair from her face and kissed her cheek as he whispered in her ear, "Because I love you. I still do, you know."

He grasped her head between his hands and met her lips with his own. Thomas could feel tendrils of her hair dance between their faces. He sensed her breath on his cheek and felt like crying out for the sheer joy of it. "I'm sorry it has taken me so long to rein in my anger," he continued. "I'm afraid I said some dreadful things to you."

Clarissa reached up to touch his face, "What did you say that was not deserved? I am sorry I did not have the courage to defy my brother, and that I lacked trust in your feelings."

"My love, I realize now that it was more a lack of confidence, made worse by an overbearing brother," Thomas mused with sadness.

"You know not how closely you guessed what happened. I must tell you all. My brother, feeling all the power of the family title newly bestowed on his questionably sturdy shoulders, deemed the son of a clergyman in a smallish parish to be unworthy of his sister."

"As I would have done if you were my sister," said Thomas with a smile.

"I pointed out more forcefully than ever in my life that it was unlikely anyone would ask for me again. But he held firm in his belief that the life of a well-provided spinster was better than that of a poor wife disowned by her family. While I would have chosen the latter, my brother offered further argument by insisting you were solely interested in my dowry."

"It is as I thought. If you had been in possession of a greater degree of confidence in yourself, perhaps you would have dismissed his word."

"Yes. However, eight unsuccessful seasons had rendered me quite unable to muster enough vanity to disagree. I had also seen you waltzing and smiling on several occasions with Lucinda Vandermay, whom everyone knew was an heiress in search of a husband. So, after much insistence by my brother, I agreed to reject your suit with two conditions."

"Ah, and what, pray tell, were the conditions, my love?"

"First, that he would conduct the final audience with you alone, as I could not bear the thought, and second, that I would be allowed to immediately quit London to retire as a spinster and end the painful and fruitless search for a husband. I know Edward wanted to argue the second point, but in deference to my tears he relented to my request. After a long visit to an old childhood acquaintance in Bath, I was to go home to Land's End in Cornwall. It was while taking the water cure in Bath that I decided to make a life of my own apart from my brother and his family. Hence, the wind had blown in the direction of Littlefield, and I resided there quite simply and peacefully until you arrived!" she explained.

He brought her hand to his lips and kissed it.

"I didn't know you had divorced until you mentioned it to Jane the day you arrived. I am so sorry," Clarissa said with her eyes averted.

"That is what made me come to see you. Graystock's grandmother made a comment about Lucinda the day before I left, which made little sense. It came back to me as I rode toward Chichester, and I suddenly realized she didn't know of my divorce. I turned toward Cornwall when I hit upon the thought that perhaps you did not know as well. I had assumed that everyone in England knew. But I had forgotten the remoteness of the country." He pulled her further behind the tall rock and kissed her again as he grasped her thin hand in his large palm.

"With much difficulty, I obtained from the Church and then Parliament a divorce five years after Lucinda departed with a baronet while I was in uniform. It seems her love for me dimmed considerably after she realized a knighthood was not as exalted a position as she had thought. And of course, in her case absence did not make the heart grow fonder," said Thomas as he gripped her hand. "Her generous and infatuated lover was quite insistent on shouldering the outrageous expenses to legitimate his child by her, and I was the grateful cuckold. It was all quite civilized despite the wording of the petitions." Thomas kissed Clarissa's hand before he concluded, "They live in Brussels now, well away from the cold shoulders of British society."

"I thought you married her for her fortune," admitted Clarissa.

"Actually I married her for two reasons. First, because she was desperate for a husband and begged me. She had failed to attract anyone during several seasons, and life with her parents was a misery. And second, I was very angry with you and decided a marriage of convenience would suit me, especially with someone who would be eternally grateful." He paused and leaned down to pick up a rock. As he hurled it into the sea, he continued, "What I had not counted on was her fickleness and her poor character. As to her fortune, it was considered quite larger than it was, as the reverse is now true with my own."

Clarissa did not respond. Instead, she stared down at the sand. A great fear grew in the pit of his stomach as he spied tears form in her eyes.

Thomas raised her chin again. "What is it, my love? Please don't cry. Everything will be all right. Don't you see? You will marry me, won't you?" he asked hesitantly.

"Thomas, how can we marry? I am too old for you now. I may never bear you the children . . . the son you must want."

"Tut, tut, Clarissa. Now you are overestimating the size of my estate. There is no need to continue the 'prestigious' Gooding line! And while I would welcome any children our union might produce, it is the very last concern I have. What I truly want is you by my side, always."

Tears flowed down her face now as she stared at him. With a sudden flinging movement, she boldly embraced him. He was overwhelmed that all his dearest, heartfelt wishes had been granted in the space of a very few minutes.

Clarissa snatched her lace cap from him and threw it into the sea as he laughed.

"I shall consider that an acceptance to my gauche proposal," he whispered as he fished out his handkerchief and handed it to her. Clarissa clung to his arm as if she would never let go, and he kissed her once more.

Clarissa was still glassy-eyed when they returned to the threesome at the top of the cliffs. She and Thomas had spent the last few minutes discussing marriage plans in a cloud of happiness. The larger group appeared behind them a moment later.

"I must beg for your congratulations," Thomas directed to the group as they approached the grassy knoll. "Miss Fairchild has made me the happiest of men and consented to become my wife." He grasped the waist of his beloved possessively.

Jane jumped to her feet and bounded into her aunt's arms. "Oh, Aunt Clarissa, I am so very, very happy for you. And Sir Thomas," she continued as she looked at him over her aunt's shoulder, "I will be so pleased to have an uncle as kind and good as you! I had hoped and hoped this would happen!" She disengaged from Clarissa and embraced her soon-to-be newest member of the family. "And where is the wedding to take place? It will be from here? Yes?"

"I think not," Clarissa said, blushing. "Sir Thomas and I were just discussing the thought of having Reverend Gurcher marry us in the church at Littlefield. My home has been there for so long, and it feels better, the idea of marrying there."

Thomas prayed the distance would preclude her brother's attendance.

"Then you must have the wedding breakfast at the Hall," insisted Lord Graystock.

"You are very kind, Graystock," stated Thomas in acceptance after seeing the small nod from the lady at his side. "I had hoped you would do me the great honor of standing up for me."

"Of course. It is without question," Lord Graystock said in his usual dismissive manner.

During this exchange Mr. Harry Thompson remained seated due to his injury, but he grinned and shook the couple's hands.

"Ha, ha, Miss Fairchild, Cupid's bow has finally pierced your hardened heart. A feat I had doubted would ever happen," teased Harry unmercifully.

"Young man, I do not look kindly on comments meant to ruffle the feathers of my future bride," Thomas said, smiling.

Jane laughed and nudged Harry's backside.

Miss Dodderidge just giggled and prayed she would be next.

Chapter Ten

Jane tethered her horse to the shrubbery separating the field from the side of the manse the next morning, determined to have a private word with Harry. It was quite early. Even the purple morning glories had not bothered to open their faces toward the hazy sun yet. Jane crept up to the manse and counted the fourth upper window on the right. She picked up a small stone and threw it at the glass, as she had done so many times in her youth. It had been their custom to head off on fishing or butterfly expeditions in this way. William's head appeared at the window, his hair sticking up in a comical fashion.

"Whatever do you want at this hour in the morning?" asked William, none too pleased.

"Please tell Harry I'm here," whispered Jane loudly.

William yawned and shook his head as he disappeared.

Harry's head appeared moments later, and Jane noticed he seemed to be fully dressed. "Hello, Duck. Thought you would sneak by. Be right down," he said, wearing the same cheerful, open countenance of his youth. She doubted he would ever grow up.

Jane walked and Harry hobbled on his rude crutch to the other side of the thick hedge, which afforded a view of Pembroke's more lovely acreage.

They sat on the large trunk of the fallen chestnut tree as they had so many times while planning their expeditions years ago. Harry plucked a long stem of grass gone to seed and put the end in his mouth as Jane remarked on a new tear on his shabby brown coat. She examined it and shook her head.

"Oh, Harry. I feel so discouraged. What are we to do now?"

Harry took her hand in his warm one and rubbed it. "Come now, Duck. I told you it will be all right."

"No, it won't. It will take days to reach Scotland, and we haven't the means to hire a coach, and it will be too painful for you to drive with your foot pressing on the dash all the way."

Harry just stared into the distance.

"Although I guess I could drive most of the way, when there would be few people on the roads to notice," Jane added, pleased to have thought of a possible solution.

"As we figured before, it will probably take at least a week to reach Gretna Green," noted Harry.

"But with any luck the return trip to London will only be a few days," Jane said. "After a bit of rest there, we can go on to university."

Harry still stared into the fields. Jane studied his profile. He squinted at the sun as he chewed on the grass stem.

"All right," he said. "I think I can manage in two days' time. Would that suit?"

Jane's dual concerns waged war within her. She was made uneasy by Harry's injury, but she was also alarmed that Harry's father might have sent a letter to her father informing him of their desire to wed. She knew all too well how fast her father would find his way to her.

"Are you certain, Harry?" she asked. Before he could respond, Jane changed the subject. "At least I shan't have to worry about my aunt any longer. I know Sir Thomas will make her happy. They waited even longer than us to find happiness."

"Then there is hope for us yet," said Harry with a grin. "Now, I say we go about this in a hugger-mugger fashion."

"I just hope everyone at the manse hasn't guessed our plans yet," she said.

Harry looked away.

Jane sighed. "Whom did you tell?"

"Just William. I will need help with the carriage and horses and my bags, of course."

"Of course. Now let me think—a plan. A simple plan always works best."

"Middle-of-the-night escape?"

Jane laughed. "No, no. I say we plan a trip north to Lizard with the whole pack of us day after tomorrow. That way you can bring your carriage to Pembroke and no one will notice if I slip a trunk in along with a picnic and blankets and everything. That's it. And Lord Graystock asked about going on an explore there just yesterday."

"And we'll just wave to the group when we all stop there and then say, 'Tallyho, we're off to Gretna Green'?" asked Harry, laughing.

"No, of course not, you simpleton. We can be the last to leave on the return trip, and we can say we want to have the wheel checked in town because we fear a crack or something."

"Or something," Harry replied, rolling his eyes.

"Do you have a better idea?"

"No. But do you really think someone like Graystock is just going to leave us stranded?"

"Don't worry about that gentleman. He will understand."

"He knows, doesn't he, Jane?"

"Yes," she said, avoiding his eye.

"Did he somehow guess, or did you tell him?"

"I'd rather not discuss this," she replied. "We have so many more things to arrange." Searching for another topic, she rushed on. "Have you received any news from university?"

"Yes. Mr. Melure sent me a very jovial reply. He asked who my 'intended' was and when he could expect us."

"Oh, that is wonderful news. We will be rather short of funds after our journey. Cutty's solicitor informed me in a letter that the funds he forwarded were the last of my husband's gifts held in trust for me. We won't be able to linger in London for more than a day or two. Only long enough to rest."

"And enjoy our honeymoon," added Harry, smiling.

Jane looked at him and inhaled sharply. She hadn't thought at all about a honeymoon. "Oh, Harry, will this work? Please take me in your arms. I am nervous about all of this deception."

Harry stood awkwardly and gathered Jane and his crutch in his arms. He kissed her on the forehead. "Duck, this is for the best. We'll make it work."

Jane felt little comfort. She shivered for a moment in the cool morning air. She wondered why she was not more relieved. With the problem of her aunt solved, she should feel much less guilty than ever before. Instead she felt high-strung, more nervous and unsure than at any other time in her life.

Jane returned to her family's house and found Lord Graystock alone in the dining room. He rose from his seat and bowed as she nodded slightly. She observed he was wearing impeccable, darkly conservative riding attire, which complemented his omnipresent aura of assurance and command. She helped herself to the sideboard's offerings of scones and sausages and accepted tea from the maid just arriving from the kitchen.

"You are late rising this morning, my lord," Jane teased with a smile.

"Yes. You know how I detest the morning air. Bad for the lungs," he replied.

Jane spied a bit of tracked mud on the carpet. "I guess it is not bad for the horse you rode this morning."

"That, I suppose, is also true," the earl responded. She bit into her scone as he continued, "I am to relay to you that your father, brother, and the rest of your family's household in London will be returning this evening to Cornwall. Your aunt had a letter from your father this morning."

Jane choked and tried to retain a measure of dignity.

"I also have decided to depart," he added.

Jane's mind raced with the news. "Oh?"

"I must settle some affairs in London," said Lord Graystock as he put aside an old newspaper. She noticed the faint smudges under his eyes, signaling lack of sleep.

Jane was so unsure of what to say, she held her tongue. She felt Lord Graystock's gaze move over every feature of her face, waiting for her reply. In agitation, she pushed aside her plate, and her hands arranged and rearranged the knife and fork on the white-and-blue-patterned china.

"I shall take my leave day after tomorrow. That is, if it is convenient for you. If you would prefer that I depart prior to your father's arrival, I can of course arrange for my removal by this afternoon."

Jane found her voice. "Oh, no, my lord! Please, do not leave so soon, I beg of you. Your original plan suits. In fact, several of the people at the manse, as well as you yourself, indicated a desire to visit Lizard Peninsula. Perhaps, if you agree, we could all go the morning of the day of your departure. After nuncheon there, you could continue northward to London."

The earl gave Jane a measured glance. She looked away. "How delightful," the earl answered, one eyebrow raised with hauteur. "Your plan seems most providential." He accepted another cup of coffee from the maid. When she had departed, the earl continued. "Jane, surely you have not forgotten your dear father. How do you propose to settle our betrothal with him?"

"I do not want to quarrel with you or him again, my lord. My family really is no concern of yours, except for the large debt we owe you. My father will have to repay any and all monies you directed to him. Obviously, this may take some time. I only wish I had had the chance to stop you before you gave a farthing to him. My father has the uncanny ability of allowing our fortune to slip through his fingers at an alarming rate."

The earl narrowed his eyes. "Have you never wondered why?"

"Of course I have. I have argued with him till I am blue in the face. Our stables are some of the finest in England, and yet . . ." She stopped. "If I had been left to manage our estate, it would not be in the hubble-bubble fashion it currently is. However, it is a woman's great misfortune to have been born into her sex. I daresay servants have more control over their destiny than a mere female born of a nobleman."

"Jane, you obviously have made a decision regarding how you will break the unfortunate news to your father concerning the ending of our betrothal. I shall not interfere." He paused here. "You may relate to him at the same time that I will desire, or shall I say require, a meeting with him and his solicitor after he has a chance to consider the future."

Jane nodded. The earl stood up and pushed the chair to its proper position. He placed his palms on the back of the chair and leaned forward. "May I offer you my best wishes for your future happiness, Jane? I mean that with all sincerity. I shall not see you again, I fear, after the next two days. I wish Godspeed to you and your Mr. Thompson."

Jane could not meet his gaze. She heard his departure in the soft click of his heels on the wooden floor and the sound of the door closing. The plate in front of her swam before her eyes, and she felt ill. She had rarely felt so miserable in her life.

Her stomach churned as she wondered what was the impetus behind her father's drive down from London? Could he have learned of her refusal? No, that was impossible. Or had the threatened letter from the reverend found him? Dare she wait to find out? Or should she flee with Harry this very morning?

With a sigh, Jane knew her anxieties would prevent the planned, needed escape to her writing this afternoon. The manuscript had reached a plateau and would need every ounce of her concentration for the completion of the next passage. And all she could think of was the two men, her father and Rolfe, who had caused her to feel such negative emotions—anger and guilt.

In those moments at the table, Rolfe had known that he loved her. It struck him with a quiet force. As he mounted the stair toward his rooms, for a second he stopped breathing and grabbed for the banister. With sudden realization, the irony of his situation hit him. For twenty-nine years he had never, ever loved another human being in the way he did Jane. And yet he must leave her. He realized that the feeling had been growing ever since he had left Hesperides for London. No, he admitted, it had begun the first day he had seen her, when he had hugged her body close to his and breathed in the lavender scent of her silky blond hair, while she had been forced to share her horse. He doubted he would ever be able to forget her expressive eyes, her delicate beauty, and most of all her proud character. He had tried to exert his will over her. Tried every method he knew. But the fact of the matter was she had no interest whatsoever in him.

*   *   *

The next two days passed with surprising ease. Jane's father and brother arrived, along with the household servants who traveled between the houses. She was agitated by the idea of their first meeting, considering the unfortunate circumstances of her departure from London. But she had forgotten her father's considerable happiness over her supposed betrothal. There were so many effusions of joy on his part that few responses were required on her side.

Upon his first sight of her, her father shook her hand and even kissed her on the cheek! He told her he was proud of her and complimented her on her great good fortune. He even laughed and accused her of being a "sly thing"!

Jane was grateful the earl was not present during her father and brother's arrival. He had retired early and requested a light repast in his apartment. Theo teased her until she could bear it no more and excused herself. Clarissa had gone into town to take herself away from the critical eyes of her brother.

The following morning was busy with guests from the manse and plans for the trip to Lizard, which was scheduled to take place the following day. Lord Fairchild was late in rising, so Jane did not see him until luncheon. While the foursome ate, the father dominated the conversation with gossip from London.

Midway through the meal, Theodore Fairchild could not stop himself from bursting forth with Clarissa's good fortune. "Father, what do you think of Aunt Clarissa's excellent news?"

Clarissa put down her fork and knife. Jane hushed her brother and gave him a look.

Lord Fairchild, whose spirits seemed boundless these days, smiled at his sister. "What good news, Sister?"

"I am to be married, Edward," she responded.

"Well, who would have thought? You and Jane have been busy this summer. Who is the lucky devil? Mrs. Thompson hasn't dropped off this mortal coil, has she? The Reverend Thompson is looking for a new wife, is he?" he asked, laughing.

"No, it is Sir Thomas Gooding."

"Gooding? Gooding? Not poor Mr. Gooding from so long

ago? The second son of a clergyman, with no prospects? I forbade you long ago to marry the pauper."

"Why, yes, it is he. But it is Sir Thomas Gooding now."

"I stand corrected. So Gooding improved his lot in life, did he? Do tell."

"I shall most certainly not tell, Brother. For it does not matter to me if he were still poor 'Mr. Gooding.' And furthermore, I will no longer allow you to impose authority over me. I made a mistake many years ago, and I shall not make it again." Clarissa stood up and placed her napkin on her plate.

Jane guessed it was the first time in Clarissa's life she had stood up to her brother.

"I have some letters to write. Please excuse me." Clarissa left the room with her back very straight.

George, the butler standing unobserved by the door, smiled at Clarissa as she left the room. He leaned forward and whispered, "My humble best wishes to you, ma'am."

She looked at him and smiled. "Thank you."

"Harrumph," Lord Fairchild grumbled as he cut into his overcooked roast mutton. Jane surmised that he did not want to show it, but he was in all likelihood secretly glad to be relieved of the burden of providing for a spinster sister.

"Do tell Cook I am most displeased with the roast, George," Edward Fairchild said without looking at him. Silence entered the room when the butler left.

Jane picked at an invisible piece of lint on her sleeve. Theodore looked like he was trying very hard not to laugh.

"And what are you laughing about?" Lord Fairchild demanded. He held his cutlery in his fists on either side of his plate.

"Ah, nothing, sir. Nothing at all."

"Good. And where is Lord Graystock? I have not seen him a'tall, I swear. Has he gone into hiding, Jane?"

"No, Father. He is at the inn, seeing Sir Thomas off."

Sir Thomas had refused to stay at Pembroke upon the news of Lord Fairchild's arrival. His bags had been packed, and he had spent the night at the Tabard Inn prior to a departure for London to make several arrangements before the marriage.

Clarissa and Sir Thomas had talked with Jane before his

leave-taking. Clarissa's desire to stay with her took precedence over his desire for Clarissa to return to Littlefield, where they could see more of one another under the generous hospitality of Lord Graystock. All of Jane's arguments for Clarissa to follow Sir Thomas had been ineffective. Clarissa had refused, yet she agreed to meet him in a few weeks' time in Littlefield.

"Well, I hope Graystock graces us with his presence tonight. I have a few questions for him," said Lord Fairchild.

"I believe he will return shortly, Father," Jane replied.

"Good. Now, have you settled the date of your wedding? And will it be here or at Hesperides Hall?"

Jane forced herself to continue eating. She swallowed her bite and answered her father. "We have not discussed a date."

"Glad am I to have arrived, then. Left to your own devices, you shall lose him, girl. Don't you know that unless you fix a date immediately, cold feet can set in?" Jane, unresponsive, drank deeply from her water goblet. Her father grunted and continued, "And why are you wearing widow's weeds again? I thought we had put an end to that nonsense. You'll scare him away, looking like an old crow!"

George, who had returned, could not help but snort at the vulgarity of the advice.

Edward Fairchild turned to him with haughty disdain. "You may leave us now." After the butler had departed, her father continued, "And take George with you when you depart for the wilds of Littlefield. I have put up with that man's insolence for almost three decades because of a promise made to your mother."

From lifelong experience, Jane held her tongue. She knew her father was well aware that George was indispensable to the running of the entire estate, especially when Lord Fairchild was away on his long stays in town pursuing his political ambitions in the House of Lords.

"Aunt Clarissa will be wed in Littlefield this September," Theodore added, turning the subject.

"Hmmm, interesting. Perhaps we could impose upon the earl to make it a double wedding. Save on all the expense of a wedding breakfast for half the county of Cornwall, we will!" her father responded with a smile. He had yet to understand that his acts of economy would be unnecessary, given the earl's benevolence.

Jane could feel her brother's probing glances. She remained silent and ate everything on her plate without comment. She watched the scene at the table almost as if she watched a play in progress. She became sad when she remembered the calming presence of her mother. That lady had been the proverbial glue in the family, making her husband laugh even at himself at times and showering Jane and Theo with love and devotion. Without her mother, there was a lack of harmony, and no healing balm.

"Come, Jane, shall we take a ride down to the beach? It has been so very long," her brother suggested.

Jane looked up in surprise when she heard the sincerity in his voice. "What a delightful idea. I shall meet you in the stable as soon as I change," she responded.

The siblings looked toward their father expectantly. "Go on, then, with you both," he said. With an air of disgust, he continued, "George informed me I must see our neighbors regarding a faulty irrigation ditch."

Jane stopped and turned toward her father. "No need, Father. I spoke with them this morning, and they agreed to clear away the debris on their property." The father shook his head and returned to his paper.

The bracing salt air refreshed Jane as she galloped in the sand beside her brother. They separated when large boulders did not allow both to pass through side by side. The palisades grew higher in the direction they were headed. Her young gelding bucked and bolted past Theodore's beast when a flock of seagulls squawked their disapproval and rose en masse in front of them. Theodore laughed and urged his more seasoned mount to catch up to Jane's. After a bit, she managed to calm her animal and bring it down to a fast walk. She patted the horse on the shoulder and looked toward her brother as she tried to catch her breath.

"Good show, Jane!"

She smiled and enjoyed the exhilaration that a good gallop always brought her. The speed and the edge of danger always excited her and made her feel alive. There was nothing quite like the feel of two tons of powerful horseflesh under her and the sensation of two hearts, one equine and one human, working together as one. That was on a good day, on a good horse.

"Nothing like getting the butterflies out of the young ones, is there?" added her brother.

Jane shook her head in accord. "I'm glad you came home, Theo. It has been so long since I last saw you." She paused to tuck under a lock of hair that had escaped from her hat. "I declare I have seen you only two times in the last three years, once at my wedding and again at Cutty's funeral. You are running with a popular set, are you not?"

She looked at her brother's face and saw a masculine version of herself and her mother. They all had the same hair and eyes and mouth.

"The joys of London are not to be missed—don't you remember how Father insisted? But I have missed you too, Jane," he added. He drew abreast of her mount and smiled. "And I have come in person to witness your newfound happiness."

"How noble of you, truly, Brother," Jane said with a laugh.

"I speak not in jest."

"Then you shall be surprised by the object of my happiness."

Theodore looked at his sister, and all sense of a smile dropped from his face. "What do you mean to say?"

"As I am sure I can trust in your confidence, I will tell you. I am betrothed to Harry, not the earl."

"Oh, good Lord, no, Jane! Not Harry Thompson? He's as likeable as the next bloke, but for God's sake, what are you about? You cannot throw your life away with him!"

Jane stopped her horse and regarded her brother coldly. "You sound remarkably like Father, Theo. I have never deemed it appropriate to tell you how to live your life. Please do not start to tell me how I must live mine." Jane lowered her gaze to the water lapping the sand. "Certainly I have earned the right after my first marriage." It was the closest she had ever come to complaining about her first marriage.

"Yes, you have," he admitted. "But I have met Lord Graystock, and he is so much more than good old Harry."

"Oh, yes, he has a fortune, to be sure. But he cannot make me happy," she said. "How came you to know him so well?"

"In London. We met several times." Theo paused to dismount and grabbed the reins of Jane's horse. She looked at him for a moment and then dismounted. His strong arm went about her waist as they strolled along the beach, their horses on long reins following with droopy heads.

"I must beg your apology, Jane."

"Whatever for?"

"For not being a good brother to you. All these years, you have thought it Father's fault you had to marry Cutty Lovering. But it was not his fault. It was my fault. I gambled our fortune away."

"What nonsense are you spouting, Theo? You are not the gambling sort. Whyever would you protect Father? You dislike him as much as I."

"That is true. Actually, I hate him more than you. But it is also true about the gambling. I've lost our fortune twice over. On purpose."

"But why? Oh, why did you do such a thing?"

"To punish him, of course. We both know that elevation in politics and rubbing noses with people of good *ton* is all he cares about. Whereas position means nothing to you and me. By taking away his fortune, I took away his standing and his chances for advancement in the House of Lords."

"But why were you punishing him?"

Jane halted her steps in the sand. She looked behind her and watched the incoming tide wash over their tracks. Theo took her hands, encased in kid gloves, and looked away.

"He killed our mother, don't you know," he replied. Jane strained to hear the spoken syllables. She sucked in her breath.

"No, it isn't so," Jane whispered behind tightly closed eyes. She felt the warm breath of her horse as it nudged at her pocket for the promised bit of sugar. Jane pushed the horse's head away, but not before it left a long green spittle stain on her riding habit.

"It is."

"But she died while out taking some air. The gamekeeper, Harstead, shot her by accident. She was wearing her dove-gray-

and-brown-wool dress that cold morning. I remember it so well. And Harstead mistook the movement and the fabric for a stag. I heard him tell the inquisition authorities myself."

"Yes, and when I saw my father and Harstead just after the accident, will you tell me why Har's gun was cold and clean, while my father's was dirty? When he wasn't looking my way, I checked, and the gun had been fired without being reloaded. He killed her and he is a liar."

"But why did he do it? It must have been an accident. And why would he lie?"

"Because it wasn't an accident. You and I both know they almost hated one another the last few months. He refused to let her live here alone with us while he went to London. And she hated the city. Instead, he made us all miserable with his controlling presence here. Why they had become estranged I don't know. But he found a convenient, ugly way to get rid of the problem so he could live a life of ease in London. You, of all people, know how he is. If he can't control you, he wants to get rid of you. And he hasn't had the nerve to say one word to me about the gambling, which is against the grain of his character. It proves he knows that I know what he did."

"You should have told me. And I am not at all sure you are correct in your assumptions. You know very well there could have been a mix-up with guns or any other number of things."

"I didn't want to burden you. That is why I chose not to tell you," Theo argued.

"So instead, I was forced to marry Cutty. Thank you very much, but I would have liked to have known so I could have had your hide whipped. George would have done it for me." Jane moved to the gelding. With difficulty, she mounted the horse, bouncing several times on the tips of her toes to gain the necessary momentum to hoist herself into the saddle. She looked out to the sea. "I don't know if I can ever forgive you, Theo. You should never have presumed to know what type of punishment to inflict on our father. That was for the authorities to decide."

"But Jane, having our father tried before the House of Lords and possibly hanged would have brought unbearable attention to our family. I could not choose that path."

"And so you guard and control the family name almost as much as he does, Theo? I didn't know you were capable of this level of pride. You have proved yourself your father's son— tenfold!"

Theo scratched his head and searched for an answer. "You speak of familial pride, Jane? You have it in good quantity yourself if you do not give in and marry Graystock. You speak of control. Do you not desire Harry for the simple reason that you would never be able to control Graystock, yet Harry will bow to your every whim?"

"I don't think I will ever be able to forget what you did, keeping a secret of this magnitude from me and then causing my improvident marriage. I loved Cutty, as a daughter loves a good father. But that is not the type of marriage I sought. Your actions brought unhappiness more to me than to our father. You should be ashamed." She urged her horse into a gallop without a backward glance.

"Jane, Jane," he called out to her. "You will not go to the authorities with this information, will you?"

Theo watched Jane gallop away without responding to him. He let out his pent-up breath and shook his head as she disappeared around a bend on the beach.

He did not go after her, as he did not want to suffer further abuse, even if he did deserve it. He had gotten off lightly. If she had been a man, he was sure he would have been challenged to pistols at dawn or, at the very least, fisticuffs. But his soul felt lighter by the admission. Maybe he would sleep better this night, far from the madding crowd of London and the devils that plagued him. He vowed to do everything in his power to ensure the future happiness of his sister. He would move heaven and earth for her.

Chapter Eleven

A fortuitous excuse arrived by courier in the form of a letter from Rolfe's solicitor in London. He was even spared the unpleasant duty of informing Lord Fairchild in person of the necessity of his hasty departure, as Fairchild was still abed when the party assembled and departed for Lizard Peninsula in the morning. A simple written note would do. Graystock had avoided Jane's father all day yesterday, with the exception of the dinner hour. His lordship had been so much in awe of his future son-in-law that he had been better behaved than usual. And while Fairchild had been unable to refer to the upcoming nuptials less than three times in an overfamiliar way, Rolfe's monosyllabic replies had stopped his further comment. The older gentleman was probably reasoning with himself that he should curtail his caustic remarks at least until his daughter was safely married. What joy then!

It was under gray skies and a cold westerly wind that the party of ten departed for Lizard in three carriages—one regal and polished, the second large and serviceable, and the other small, rusted, and chipped. Harry took up Jane and Clarissa in his deteriorating equipage while Lord Graystock invited William, Fanny, and Miss Dodderidge to join him in his ducal traveling carriage. Theodore Fairchild brought up the rear with

Lillian and Sarah Thompson rattling around in the large conveyance meant for six passengers.

Jane refused to look back at Pembroke as they departed. William had discreetly loaded her trunk next to Harry's smaller one behind the picnic baskets on the back of the old carriage. Jane took comfort that they were finally on their way as they moved northward from the bustling town of Land's End.

"You're leaving, are you not, Jane?" Clarissa asked.

"I will not lie to you, Aunt."

"Oh, are you sure, Jane? Do nothing rather than make a mistake. Your happiness is my only concern, my dear."

"And yours, mine. I am so happy for you. Sir Thomas is everything I could dream of for you. With your betrothal, my last remaining doubt is removed," Jane said with emotion.

"But Jane, you change the subject. Why not wait a bit? Things will right themselves. You have been so happy back here, among your horses and in the country."

"Father would toss me out on my ear if he knew I had refused Lord Graystock. No, I must make my own way, and it is with Harry. Oh, but please don't let us argue about this anymore. Let us just enjoy this last day with each other. It may be many months or even years before we have the means to visit again." Jane reached for the handkerchief in her pocket lest the tears she felt forming in her eyes should spill over. "I shall miss you, Aunt. And you must promise to visit me at university if you are ever inclined. That is, once we have a place to call our own—or rather, if we can afford a little place. I am afraid we will be staying with Harry's mentor in the beginning. An assistant's income is but a pittance. But I do have high hopes, too, for my scribbling." Jane twisted the handkerchief in her hands and avoided her aunt's sympathetic gaze. "While I haven't quite finished the third part of the manuscript, I know I will be able to finish it once we are more settled. I shall send it to you first, you know."

Jane felt impelled to argue her case further. She tried not to sound defensive. It made her sad to have all of the people she loved feel pity for her. For that they undoubtedly did. One could read it in their eyes if not hear it from their lips.

She took a deep breath and faced the concern in her aunt's

pale eyes. "Oh, Aunt, I am happy. I love Harry. I always have."
She gazed up at Harry's profile in front of her. His hat was
askew, but he was trying to make a show of formality by wearing his only "good" coat, made of faded black wool with un-
fashionable narrow lapels. It was marginally better than his
brown patched everyday coat. He was humming as he focused
on driving the team. She turned once again to her aunt. "He is
the one for me. I care naught for finery, property, and jewels, or
especially for the haute *ton*. I shall be happy not ever again to
have to mingle among the society ladies with their sharp claws
and even sharper tongues. They will be pleased by my formal
removal from London as well. I am sure that my unexceptional
marriage will delight them."

Her aunt raised her eyebrows. "You will send me your directions once you have settled, Jane? Promise me that, at least."
She moved to hold Jane's hand. "And I shall promise not to reveal them to my brother if you request it." Clarissa leaned forward and brushed her other hand against Jane's cheek.

Jane struggled not to cry.

"And promise you will write to me if you are ever in distress
or in want. I know your prideful ways will fight against this, but
if you care at all for my sensibilities, you will honor me and
your mother, by promising me."

"I promise," said Jane, looking across the grassy cliffs to the
sea beyond. She could not deny her aunt this assurance.

The occupants of the second carriage were arguably more
agreeably engaged. Miss Dodderidge was at her best, preening
before William and Lord Graystock. She had arranged to be
seated next to the earl and had not given him a moment's peace.
He tried to focus his thoughts elsewhere, but with little success.

Miss Dodderidge presumed to entertain him with trite stories of her girlhood hidden between self-serving little smiles
and fluttering lashes. It was many minutes before he realized
she didn't have a fan, but used her gestures in a manner not unlike a coquette's favorite device. She asked no fewer than three
times for his lordship to rearrange the summer blankets to better protect her pastel dress, trimmed with too many flounces
and bows. Rolfe sighed in exasperation during the last request

when she exclaimed his lordship must not be shocked by her ankles, which she had "mistakenly" revealed. Graystock cursed the plan that had put him in this ridiculous scene, and he was grateful that he would have nothing further to do with young people apart from this one last afternoon.

The two sisters occupying the third carriage looked rather irritable. If only the heir had not insisted on driving the carriage himself, they would have been much more cheerful in his company.

The party from Land's End was quite famished by the time they reached their destination. They found themselves on a small cliff not unlike their picnic site of just a few days ago. The sea oats swayed in the cool breeze and framed the larger fishing village and port in the distance. Most of the fog had burned off the coastline during their advancement. After the luncheon of cold meats, cheeses, and a large plum pudding that had survived the ordeal of the trip, the group was unanimous in the desire to inspect the rock wall below. Miss Fairchild explained that the area was famed for the dark green rock veined with red and white. Harry added that Lizard was home to many rare species of plants and minute reptiles.

"Many an afternoon was spent here in my youth chasing down butterflies and lizards," Harry said with a smile. He continued almost to himself as his smile faded, "I shall miss it."

"But, Harry, you will be back during your breaks at school, shall you not?" Fanny inquired.

"No, Fan. Maybe every now and again in the next decade. But you know it is too much to undertake very often."

Miss Dodderidge picked several spores of spent dandelions from Harry's sleeve as Jane smiled at him. He glanced back at Jane and grinned. Then he caught at Miss Dodderidge's hands and tickled her under the chin.

"You must stop picking at me, Miss Dodderidge. This will not do. This job is for my mum, not for a dainty young miss like you.

"Oh, I don't mind," Miss Dodderidge said with a coy smile as she wiped a small spot of pudding off of Harry's chin. "You know I am only too happy to help whenever I can."

Fanny giggled and leaned against William in her post-meal fatigue.

"Come, Miss Dodderidge, let us lead the way on an expedition to the grotto on the beach," Harry ordered as he hauled himself up with his cane and offered an arm to the young lady.

"Is not your ankle too weak for the descent?" Miss Dodderidge asked.

"Oh, my, no. I shall be fine with your steady arm."

The group paired off, as the small path was just wide enough for two to pass comfortably. Lillian and Sarah Thompson were left to descend without the aid of a masculine arm as Fanny grasped Theo's arm, their elder brother assisted Clarissa, and the earl, Jane.

Jane was not comfortable in the disquieting presence of Lord Graystock, but their earlier communication, which had cast away all of her doubts concerning his continued pursuit, had also removed almost all of her anxiety regarding his possible actions. But his hawkish features, when she dared peep at him, were imposing and serious, which made her feel self-conscious. Aside from a cautionary word or two from the earl during their climb down, not a sentence was uttered.

Finally they were on the narrow beach, and they fanned out to examine the walls of the grotto at the end of the strip of sand. Small pools of water were trapped in the rock formations during low tide. The water further illuminated the intricate patterns of colors on the unusual rock. Water dripped from the low ceiling. Farther back, the grotto divided into two tunnels. Harry and Miss Dodderidge disappeared into one tunnel, laughing, followed at a slower pace by Clarissa, William, Theo, and the three sisters.

The earl pointed to the other tunnel. "Where will this side lead us?"

"Well, the other winds around and ends on a beach the other side of this cliff. This path goes straight into the cliff but is illuminated at the end by a natural blowhole."

"Ah, shall we see it, then? It sounds most intriguing."

"As you wish."

Lord Graystock took the lead and moved forward along the

damp passage. He grasped Jane's hand when she stumbled in the shadows. His hand was so large, and her fingers felt so small in his warmth. They reached the end of the tunnel after forty yards. A small shaft of light pierced the darkness above them.

All at once Jane felt nervous. "I think we should return, my lord. The others will be wondering about us."

"That is true," the earl said, grasping her other hand in his as well.

In the half-light, he faced her and looked down into her eyes. Waves of light danced on his face, illuminating the pale silver irises of his eyes. A damp mist clung to his black hair. He dropped her hand and smoothed her hair with his palm.

Jane's heart skipped a beat while she stared up at his rugged, dark face. She could hardly breathe as she noticed the taut muscles of his cheek. The confined space suffocated her and robbed her of her senses.

His head dipped forward to within inches of her lips. He hesitated. Then his hand reached to cup her neck as he brought his lips to hers. His tall, powerful frame engulfed her.

She did not resist at all. In the great silence of the grotto all that could be heard was their echoed strained breathing and the far-off roar of the waves breaking. Jane lifted her arms around Rolfe's massive shoulders and drank in his kiss like a lost soul finding solace at an oasis in the desert. His essence permeated her senses. He smelled of soap, salt air, and a cologne she had only ever noticed on his person. The whorls of his fingertips teased her earlobe, and she shivered. She did not care what he would think. She was leaving, and this was to be her good-bye.

She was attracted to him, without a doubt, but he was not for her. She struggled to remind herself that he was too domineering, too demanding, and altogether too vexing. Most of all, she forced herself to remember, he certainly did not love her. He needed a docile woman who would mold herself to his autocratic ways. Jane would never allow herself to be controlled by anyone again.

Rolfe brushed aside the black lace covering the front of her mourning gown and trailed kisses from her neck to the delicate skin touching the lace. Without thinking of what he did, she found he had untied her sash and unbuttoned her back buttons to push down her gown. Jane's breath surged from her as the earl lowered his lips to the tips of her breasts. He kissed one breast, then took the other between his lips. Jane felt a hard, tugging sensation in her womb and between her legs when she pulled him closer. His arousal strained against his breeches as her hand brushed his thighs and finally pushed at his chest.

"This mustn't go any further, please," she mumbled. He kissed her gently while he arranged the gown back in place.

His eyelids were heavy when he faced her now. "Yes, you are quite right. What must have I been thinking?" he said.

He turned her around and rebuttoned her gown. He retied her sash, but made the loops far too big. Jane's most private places were throbbing with desire, and she placed her fingertips to her temples to try and bring herself under control. Her hands instinctively went to her pockets when she lowered them to face the earl. The cold, hard outline of his ring reminded her of the last act she must perform before leaving with Harry.

"I must return this to you," she said, withdrawing the ring from her gown. The bloodstone looked black in the dim cave.

"Ah, my ring. I had forgotten."

He cradled her delicate hand in his larger one and closed her fingers over the ring. She looked at him with bewilderment.

"It is my hope you will keep it, Jane. Before you say no, I hope you will listen to my reasons," he said. She did not protest, so he continued. "You have refused my hand, my name, my protection, and my help. I will take a small measure of comfort knowing you have this one last possession of mine. Use it to send for me if you are ever in need. I could not bear to ever think of you in desperate want. You can seal a letter to me and I will come at once. Or you could sell it. But I don't want it back."

Jane looked at the faintly visible etching of the knight and dragon on the ring and then turned her gaze to him. "As you wish, I shall keep it. But I shan't sell it. Never that." It was the first time she had ever acquiesced to a request of the earl's. She wondered if he would plead his case one more time, to insist that she go away with him rather than with Harry, to kiss her until she relented, but his expression bespoke a negative answer.

He released her hands. "Thank you," he answered. He moved past her and felt along the passage walls back to the harsh, bright outside world. He did not offer the guidance of his hand to her again.

When Jane and Graystock returned, the group was at work, repacking all the food remains in the wicker baskets and folding blankets. William was putting everything into the storage area on the Fairchilds' carriage.

At the end of the carriage ride from Pembroke, Miss Dodderidge had given up all matrimonial hopes of securing thirty thousand a year from the earl, for while she was an insipid girl, her primary nature was quite practical. Worse yet, she had been unable to attract even a single glance from Theodore Fairchild during the course of the afternoon.

As her departure from Cornwall approached at an alarming rate, she had decided on the moment, while in the grotto, to fix the interest of Harry Thompson without dangling after the other impossibilities. He was the only one who showed any promise, she decided with resignation. She was sure his family was good for at least five hundred a year, given the size of the living.

And his family did boast of an ancient connection to the aristocracy. A third cousin four times removed or so. Her coal merchant father would be impressed if she could attract a gentleman, even a poor one. And he really did give her butterflies in her stomach. No one had ever done that to her, no matter how determined she had been at flirting with her victims. She retied the bow of her hat under her chin when she saw everyone moving to their respective carriages. The loss of thirty thousand a year was really too bad, she thought, as she eyed the earl. But then again, her insides jumped when she moved to Harry. He really was divine, even though he was poorer than a church mouse.

She sighed and walked toward Clarissa Fairchild to detain her. Perhaps she could switch places with the aunt on the ride back? Miss Fairchild arched her brow and gazed at her.

"I think not," Miss Fairchild said firmly. "As a matter of

fact, I had hoped to have a conversation with you and Fanny during the ride home. Would you mind if I joined your group?"

"But Fanny and I could join your carriage."

Harry turned around from the back of the equipage. "Ah, but that would ruin our plan," he said to her with a wicked grin.

"Oh, I just love plans. What plan is that? I insist on being included," Miss Dodderidge said petulantly.

Jane, seated in the carriage, sighed and closed her eyes, too weary to play her part. Harry glanced at her, winked, and turned to Clarissa.

"I shall tell you all about it, my dear, in the other carriage," Clarissa said. "It is a secret we can rely on you to keep safe. But you must depart with me now."

Miss Dodderidge looked first at Harry, then at Clarissa, and finally at Jane. She stomped her foot just the smallest bit and addressed Harry. "All of you are in the know except me. It is most unfair, I insist on hearing what is going on this instant, Harry—er—Mr. Thompson."

Harry raised her hand to his lips with a flourish and kissed it. "Miss Fairchild will explain it all on the ride home, my dear," Harry said.

Miss Dodderidge lifted her chin a notch higher and flounced off in a huff, mumbling something about rudeness.

At the last moment, Clarissa reached for Jane's hand and stroked it. She looked as if she would begin to cry if she uttered a single word. Jane squeezed her aunt's hand and whispered, "I will miss you so," before Harry pulled himself into the seat and urged the horses toward Graystock's coach.

No one remaining on the ground knew how to say good-bye to Lord Graystock, who looked as unapproachable as always. But he entered his large ducal coach before the others could find their manners and their tongues. A brief raise of his arm and a nod from the shadowed window was all they saw. Jane turned in the opposite direction and fiddled with her reticule.

The overcrowded Fairchild carriage took the lead and veered westward after a mile or so down the sandy track. Graystock's coach continued northbound, followed by Harry and Jane. The excellence of the earl's coach and horses allowed their inadequate conveyance to be outstripped within a few miles.

The air was heavy with moisture as they lumbered along. Harry's brother had drawn back the stiff and misshapen bonnet of the carriage prior to their departure. Jane dusted off the cobwebs in the corners and shook the blankets off the side. She noticed that the padding under the cracked black leather seats had disintegrated a long time ago. She would be spending quite a few hours in this poorly sprung little cage, and she would feel better if it was a little cleaner. It also gave her something to do instead of worrying away the time.

But worry she did. It was funny, her mother had always told her to chase away any fears or worries, as they were useless, godless emotions. She had always obeyed her mother, but during the last month or so she had been unable to keep her worries at bay. Flipping the last daddy longlegs from the door, Jane peered into the little grove of pine trees bordering the road. She couldn't even hear the clopping of the earl's horses ahead anymore, and so she straightened her spine and finally faced forward. She looked at Harry's bent form. His brown hair peeked out from under his hat, and he was chirping the team along. She drew in her breath and exhaled. Peace, glorious peace, at last.

There being but one inn in the ensuing thirty miles, Jane was unsurprised to find a groomsman polishing the shiny lacquer finish of the earl's coach when she and Harry stopped just past dusk at the Two Swan Inn. Jane had had a growing suspicion that this might be the embarrassing end of her grueling first day toward Scotland. But there was no other place to retire for the night. Inquiries had proved that the next accommodations were thirty miles further, and the weather seemed uncertain. That distance was out of the question. Jane was sure Harry's ankle throbbed, although he complained little. Her spirits sagged as low as the dusty brim of her bonnet. She was anxious, knowing her father had certainly been informed of their elopement by now. What if he came after her? She and Harry had discussed this possibility while driving and agreed to go at least sixty miles each following day, barring any accident.

The first growl of thunder emitted from the sky accompanied sparse, fat raindrops. Jane and Harry hurried into the inn to escape a drenching. The public space was filled to overflowing with revelers at tables, toasting the rain. A quick perusal brought a sigh of relief from Jane—the earl was nowhere to be seen. Harry returned from speaking to the innkeeper and escorted Jane to the last remaining table, jammed into a dark corner near a dirty, smallish window. Waving to a dour-faced serving wench, Harry ordered two portions of supper and ale. Jane shook her head, protesting the ale, but Harry stilled her.

"You will need it when you hear what I have to tell you."

"What, pray tell?" asked Jane with her lips compressed.

"There are no rooms available."

"Goodness, now what are we to do?" She paused, deep in thought. "Did you offer a greater sum of money?"

"Yes. It is not that," he said loudly above the din.

"What is it, then?" Jane inquired.

"His lordship took the last room, an attic space usually reserved for the serving maid. Seems the earl was none too happy about the accommodations, but he reserved it nonetheless. And his servants have taken up all the space in the stables."

"Well, we will just have to make do. We will have to stay at this table until first light."

"Jane, I can't bear this. It is unseemly for a lady to spend the night in a pub."

"Yes, well, what are we to do? I will be fine, as you. I am more concerned about how we will stay awake tomorrow on the road after a night here."

At a nearby table, two men who had imbibed too much began leering at Jane.

"Mate, w'd ya lookie here, a fancy lady and her gen'leman friend," said the first.

"Dunno, friend. Methinks it's not 'er husband. Don't see no ring," joked the other. Several other tables of men broke into laughter.

Jane paled as Harry became flustered. She scanned the room and knew the scene would become worse rather than better.

"Let's see if the little lady needs a bit more protection from the hooligan," the first added with a toothless grin.

As the two started to rise, a tall figure stepped in front of them. "The lady has no desire for your company. I would suggest you enjoy what is left of your meal," the earl said in a deep baritone.

Harry stood up, his chair falling backward at the same time. He came up behind the earl and peeked sideways. "His lordship is right, mates. My, er, sister does not need any help from you. I thank you for your concern, but we just want to be left in peace."

The men settled back into their chairs, eyeing Lord Graystock with deference and ignoring Harry completely.

The earl turned his back on the laborers after a final dark look and pulled up a chair to sit uninvited with the pair. The sour-faced maid bobbed several times and asked him if he cared for any refreshments. He waved her off without a glance.

"I took the liberty of commanding the last room in the inn for you, Mrs. Lovering. I thought it wise, as I knew we were traveling the same route."

"You are very kind, my lord," Jane responded. "However, I cannot rob you of the last room. Mr. Thompson and I will do very well here. We shall leave before first light, in any case. Perhaps we shall even leave as soon as the storm abates."

"My dear Mrs. Lovering, I knew your pride would not allow you to accede to my wishes readily, and that you would prevail to try to change my mind, and so I shall tell you my plans," the earl said. "I shall retire to the luxury of my coach, which is far superior in comfort to the attic room of this modest inn. Mr. Thompson is welcome to join me, as there are two long well-padded benches and adequate room. Or he may choose the dampness and conviviality of this . . . ale room."

Much to Jane's surprise, Mr. Thompson accepted the earl's gracious offer. He was a young man who did not look gift horses in the mouth. Jane guessed that the small amount of pride Harry possessed was often swallowed because of his less fortunate birth and his easy humor. She was horrified that he had acceded to Lord Graystock's plans so readily.

"But we will be . . ."

The earl, looking as aloof and as confident as ever, interrupted her. "Surely you are not going to waste our time discussing this ad nauseam, when your husband-to-be has already agreed? Have you forgotten the vows you will soon be making, those of honoring and obeying?" he said in mocking tones.

"I have not forgotten. However, I am not married at present, and it is unseemly for us to accept your generosity."

"But, Jane, dear, you must admit it is the only solution," Harry said. "I for one must thank you, Lord Graystock, for your attention and generosity." Harry shook the earl's hand.

Jane lifted her chin a fraction of an inch and narrowed her eyes. The earl stood up abruptly and bowed to her. "I shall see you when you are ready to retire, Mr. Thompson," he said as a manner of leave-taking, and he turned away.

The evening had passed as uncomfortably as the day had begun. Jane had escaped from the creeping glances of the common laborers in the tavern soon after the earl's departure. She had resigned herself to going to bed early in an effort to put as much distance between herself and her father as possible on the morrow. It was an easy decision, as the innkeeper had grudgingly provided a single tallow candle half spent. They would leave an hour before dawn, and she had left strict instructions with the innkeepers to awaken her.

The coarse gray sheets of the bed itched. She noticed the bed was nothing more than compressed old straw that smelled moldy in certain places. It was the first time in her life she had suffered these conditions, and she almost felt sorry for herself. After two hours of tossing and turning, she rose from the tormenting bed and pulled open the latches of her small trunk. She dug out her ink and quill, as well as some precious paper. If nothing else, the time spent wrestling with the covers had at least inspired her with a solution to the mess the heroine faced in her manuscript. She wrote without pause until the candle guttered and she lay exhausted on the foul-smelling bed.

Chapter Twelve

The hour before morning was cold and damp, a harbinger of the day ahead. Jane wore her warmest undergarments and prayed for clear skies. She and Harry decamped in good time, with only the mud slowing their progress.

Harry's ankle had swelled, so Jane insisted on taking the ribbons. She urged the pair on with a sense of dread and excitement. From time to time she turned to see Harry's patched and rumpled form sprawled on the old leather seat. He seemed to be in a brown study, without hint of his perpetual happy nature.

This was finally it. She would marry him in just a very few days. For love and for a lifetime of harmony. She had Harry's family as an example of the kind of domestic bliss she craved. A bit uproarious at times, but warm and happy. His parents adored one another and their entire brood. Of course, Jane was sure she didn't want a brood quite as large as that of the Thompsons, but dreamt of the deep well of love reflected in the reverend's and his wife's eyes each time she saw them together.

Her parents had been the opposite. They had fought for years before her mother had stopped crying during every loud argument. Jane had asked her mother about the change. It was simple, she had explained. One stopped crying when one stopped caring. She had tired of her husband's controlling, bullying ways and had learned to avoid him as much as possible. She had refused to live in London, the city her husband loved. She had insisted on remaining at Pembroke with her two children, amid the animals and nature she and her children adored.

Jane turned to see Harry swat at an invisible gnat and belch. Mumbling an apology, he laughed and told Jane to direct her attention back to her driving. At just that instant, the wheel caught a deep, muddy rut at an awkward angle. A crack, signaling breaking wood, filled the air. The left side of the carriage sagged, and Jane gripped the reins in one hand and the underside of the seat in the other as she calmed and stopped the pair. Harry popped up from his slump and looked over the side.

"It's done for," he said.

"As I guessed," she said with a sigh.

Jane pulled on the brake and descended from her perch. The wheel lay next to the rut, which concealed two jagged quartz rocks that had caught and twisted it. It could be fixed, but not without time, labor, and more precious coins.

"I'll ride on ahead to find help," Jane said.

"It will be faster to go back to the smithy near the inn."

"How do we know that? Besides, I didn't particularly like that village. No, I'll ride on ahead."

"We'll go back together. I can't let you go alone, you know that, Duck."

"Please stop calling me that."

Harry looked at her and scratched his head. Suddenly Jane was reminded of her brother's angry words. That she would always control Harry as much as her father had always controlled her mother. That Harry would always be under the cat's paw. "Why don't we ride together, then, to the next village?" she asked.

Harry nodded his assent as she unhitched the horses. A rotted fence nearby provided the leg up they needed for each to ride bareback. Jane's black gown barely concealed her knees, let alone her ankles. She shrugged and sighed. She prayed no one would see her. In her heart she knew she wanted to avoid the other village because it would entail an encounter with Rolfe, as they had departed before the earl.

Harry and Jane alternated between walking and cantering

the next several miles. Her horse's prominent withers dug into her body until she was forced to stop for rest. Under the shade of an oak tree, Harry leaned over and massaged his leg.

What she had forgotten was the earl's superior equipage. Just as they turned their horses' heads toward the road once again, she heard the rumble of a conveyance behind her. The team of four was going almost full out, just short of a gallop, when they rounded the corner. The carriage's tall coachman pulled the horses to a stop as they neared. Jane's eyes widened when she saw it was Rolfe who drove the team. A short, embarrassed coachman with compressed lips sat beside the earl.

Rolfe vaulted off the seat as Harry moved closer to her.

"Are you hurt?" Graystock inquired with urgent concern.

"No, no, we are both unhurt, my lord," Jane responded. She watched the earl's eyes trace the shape of her leg from her exposed knee to the tip of her slipper. She felt herself blush and raised her chin a notch higher.

"We would be grateful if you could inform the smithy in the next town of our predicament, my lord," Harry requested.

"Better yet, I shall convey you both there posthaste."

Jane was about to insist that it was unnecessary and they could see to themselves, when Harry for the second time interceded on their behalf and accepted the offer with a grin.

Jane snapped her mouth shut and turned the horse away from the prying eyes of the coachman on the ducal carriage. But no matter which angle she tried, she knew it would be difficult to dismount without exposing more of her person. Suddenly, strong hands grasped her waist and eased her descent.

"Here, Mrs. Lovering, do allow me to help you from your perch," Lord Graystock said. His powerful arms lowered her to the ground, his face half a foot from hers. Gray eyes revealed an arch expression.

"We meet again, my lord," Jane said, looking at the ground.

"It seems we are ill-fated in our good-byes, Mrs. Lovering."

Jane raised her eyes to the snowy folds of his cravat and blinked, avoiding his discomforting gaze.

He removed his hands and Jane felt bereft.

"Come, let me escort you into the coach," the earl suggested. A groom had already helped Harry dismount and remove his tight boot. The liveried man placed pillows under Harry's leg on one bench of the coach while Rolfe and Jane were forced to sit beside one another on the other side. Lord Graystock leaned forward and asked if he could be permitted to examine the ankle. Harry acquiesced and admitted it seemed more swollen than the night before and the various shades of purple were spreading instead of fading. Jane looked at Harry's strained face and then at the earl as he manipulated the ankle. Lord Graystock descended the steps of the coach, and the two occupants heard murmurings from the earl and coachman outside.

"Harry, this looks much worse than the last time I saw it," Jane said in a shocked whisper.

"I know."

Harry looked tired and defeated. Jane silently chastised herself for pressing on.

"We'll call for a doctor and rest in the next town," Jane quietly insisted.

Lord Graystock's powerful frame filled the doorway as he stepped inside. Little was said on the journey. Harry was in pain, Jane's mind was filled with a necessary revision to her plans, and the earl stared at Jane's profile or at the passing scenery in the window beyond her. It was hard to tell which. Each time a bump in the road caused Jane and Rolfe to jostle together, they moved away from one another with a rapidity of motion indicating heightened awareness of each other's person.

A scant two hours later saw the equipage turning from the main road onto a narrow lane. The spent blooms of horse chestnut trees littered the ground as the graceful arc of the branches provided blessed shade from the hot sun. Rolfe was at least glad the heat would help dry up the cursed mud that had been their undoing. He failed to draw Jane's attention away from a gatekeeper's house as they passed through a large set of stone columns with crested black wrought-iron gates. The gates swung open with precision as the earl nodded to the keeper. A large brick Palladian mansion stood at the crest of a long hill.

"Where are you taking us, my lord?" Jane asked in a mild, shrewish tone.

"To a place where Mr. Thompson can rest in comfort." He looked at her, challenging her to refute the wisdom of his words.

"But where are we?"

"Seaton, the estate where my brother resides."

Jane looked as if she was about to protest, but instead she swallowed the retort and looked at the immaculate floorboards of the coach. Lord Graystock suppressed a smile. He could imagine how bitter a pill pride could be when swallowed. And obviously, Mrs. Lovering had rarely, if ever, found herself in circumstances where such medicine must be taken. He was relieved he would not have to argue the point.

"I must apologize for the inconvenience."

"It is not an inconvenience. I had planned to stop over here this evening in any event. There are chambers enough in this house for the entire Thompson family and their many cousins. You are both welcome to stay here for as long as it takes Mr. Thompson's ankle to heal properly. If he does not take care, he will suffer from it every day of his life."

Jane looked too embarrassed to meet his gaze. "You are an expert on these matters, are you?"

"I have had enough improperly cared for injuries to know of what I speak."

Rolfe was astonished that he had admitted any frailties to her and resolved to remain silent.

"I can't tell you how delighted I am to see you, Brother," stated an ill-kempt, blond version of the earl. "How long has it been? I tried to calculate it last evening when I received the message you would be arriving. Afraid I was too deep in my cups to figure it." There was a slight slur to the dulcet tones, and his gray eyes were red-rimmed and watery. "Ah, a lady present. I do apologize, ma'am," he said as he bowed unsteadily.

"Mrs. Lovering and Mr. Thompson, may I present to you my brother, the Honorable Frederick St. James?" the earl inquired.

The greetings and thanks were given and received in tones most politic. When the full extent of Harry's injury was made known to the earl's younger brother, a physician was sent for and the foursome adjourned to the saloon in the front of the establishment. The earl excused himself thereafter to the comparative privacy of his chambers.

As he mounted the carpeted grand staircase, Lord Graystock pondered his brother's state of affairs not for the first time. Frederick resided at this particular estate for the better part of each year. However, Rolfe had never trusted him enough to deed Seaton, which was unentailed, to him. Despite his slow physical ruin from drink, Frederick at least showed a spot of the same dark humored cynicism as his father and brother. Rolfe wondered that his brother's wife and son were not in evidence.

Harry could feel the pain in his ankle worsening. All he wanted to do was lie down and find out if laudanum could be produced from somewhere within this monstrous mansion. And all Frederick seemed capable of doing was prolonging the agony.

"As you can see, Mrs. Lovering and Mr. Thompson—I may call you Jane and Harry, may I not?"

Surprised by the familiarity, they replied, "Of course."

"As you see, then, my brother has a great disgust of me. I have been a disappointment to him, and to really my entire family. The proverbial black sheep, I believe I am called, don't you know? I apologize for my presumption and bluntness, but as you will be our guests here for a while, it is as well you know the circumstances."

Speechless, Jane and Harry looked at Frederick. For probably the only time in his life, Harry's lighthearted wit eluded him, and Jane's manners were lacking.

Frederick continued, "May I offer you both refreshments? I shall pull the cord and Wiggins will bring us all something. A little stronger than tea, I suggest. Harry's ankle and all that."

Jane found her voice and manners. "You are very kind, sir, but I think I shall avail myself of one of the guest chambers you have so graciously provided and take a bit of a lie-down. It has been a long journey."

"Of course, my dear. Harry and I will settle in for the duration. That is, until the good doctor arrives."

Harry was sure he did not want to remain in the present

company, but looking at his throbbing ankle, he sighed and decided a bit of brandy might be just the thing, as the requested laudanum had not materialized.

"You're looking rather hipped, Harry. What is it, old man? Worried about facing the gluepot in Gretna? Nothing to the old marriage business. You just need a little of my specialty, 'Kill Devil,' just in from the colonies. Superior flavored rum. What do you say?" A portly butler entered and waited patiently.

Looking at the man, Harry nodded and Frederick continued, "Wiggins, old chap, bring in the firewater, say."

When the butler had departed, the earl's brother continued, "Good chap, even though he might try to put on airs from time to time. But then he draws in his horns when he oversteps."

When the so-called firewater had been consumed, which proved indeed to live up to its name, Harry realized he needn't have been concerned about keeping up his end of the conversation, as Frederick was so deep in his cups he would never notice or remember on the morrow.

In good time the doctor came and examined his ankle. A private audience, with Jane and the earl included, proved what Harry had dreaded. He must keep the ankle elevated for at least the next two days to bring down the swelling, and then the doctor would visit again. The doctor thought that the ankle was probably broken and would need to be immobilized if there was to be any hope of avoiding a permanent limp. Jane looked disheartened and again thanked the earl for his generosity and hospitality.

Dinner was a strained affair, with Frederick wavering between a modicum of lucidity and drunken collapse. The earl, reserved and pale, said not a word. Harry seemed to be the only soul willing to make an effort toward any type of conversation. Jane's uninspired remarks were ill rewarded, as she felt all the awkwardness at being the only lady surrounded by three gentlemen. She excused herself soonest, and left the threesome to their port.

It was still early when Jane returned to her chamber to get her scribbling box. Upon asking a footman for the location of a room where she could write undisturbed, she was directed to a small sitting room where an escritoire sat facing double doors. It was a cozy room, and Jane soon found herself lost in her work.

A good hour had passed in a haze of writing when Jane chanced to glimpse outside the French doors. She was surprised to see the garden ablaze with light. She rose, nudged the doors open wide, and walked to the edge of the Wentworth railing, where a footman walked down a line of terrace lanterns, lighting each one with a small torch. A strong breeze teased the first of late summer's leaves from their heavy branches. The footman turned toward her after lighting the last lantern.

"Why are you lighting those? Is some sort of celebration planned?" she asked.

"No, ma'am. The earl ordered them lit, as he is wont to do when he visits the estate, especially when guests are about." The footman blew on the charred remnants of the torch. "I told him you were in her ladyship's sitting room."

Jane nodded her head and thanked the footman. "'Tis a pretty sight to behold." The young man bowed and walked away.

White blossoms, amid the cloak of darkness in the vast beyond, beckoned her. She leaned forward and breathed in the sweet scents of roses and jasmine. The sight of so many white flowers piercing the night amazed Jane. Intrigued, she ran down the steps onto the lawn and beyond to the pea-gravel path. As she walked along the phlox border of the flower bed, she heard a crunching sound mingling with the rustling of her silks.

Turning, Jane found herself face-to-face with Lord Graystock.

"My lord."

"Mrs. Lovering."

He offered his arm and an excuse as they continued to walk. "I see you have discovered the moon garden." He bent over to snap off a fragrant bloom and handed it to her. "My mother was quite fond of all-white gardens and arranged for them to be planted at each of our properties."

"Most unusual. I have never seen a garden quite like this." And after a pause. "Where are your brother and Harry?"

"Mr. Thompson has taken himself off to his chambers, to elevate his leg. And my brother, I should think, would be in the library at this time, capable only of babble, I am sure."

Jane paused before answering. "I am sorry."

"About what? Being forced to be a guest here? Or my brother's utter lack of control?"

"All of it, I guess."

"There is no need to apologize. We know each other well enough by now to avoid formalities."

He looked fragile. No, "fragile" was not the word one would associate with the earl. Rather, he seemed to have peeled off some of the layers of reserve he generally wore. His tanned, rugged visage looked pale gray in the moonlight as his dark eyes searched her face. Jane stopped and reached toward him, cupping his high cheekbones.

The gentle action softened his eyes further. It was the first time she had initiated an embrace, and she felt tentative and unsure—acting on instinct alone. She stroked his cheek and brushed the hair from his temple. He closed his eyes and moved his face to press his lips into the palm of her hand.

"I want to show you something," he whispered. He reached for her other hand and tugged her arm down as he began walking the length of the parterre. Jane's gait matched his stride.

They stepped through a large archway, heavy with white roses, into a walled garden replete with a gurgling fountain and lighted lanterns in the center. Everywhere, the scent of roses perfumed the air. White blooms surrounded Jane and Rolfe.

"Out of all our estates, I think this was my mother's favorite corner of the world."

"It is not difficult to understand why." Jane leaned forward to inhale the heady scent of one large bloom. "You have never spoken of your mother."

"She was beautiful, with light blond hair like Frederick's," he said, grimacing. "I take after my father."

"I don't agree. You both look very similar, apart from the color of your hair."

"Ah, but I did not inherit my mother's charm and ever present kindness and good humor." Rolfe led Jane to the stone bench and sat down. "She died of the influenza when I was young—eight years old."

"I am sorry. I cannot imagine losing a mother at that tender age. It was difficult enough for me at eighteen to lose my mother. I hope your family was able to provide the love and attention you must have required at that horrible time."

"I think, rather, you and I have had similar lives, actually."

The whir of the summer insect population echoed around them. Rolfe raised Jane's hand to his lips and kissed the back of it. Jane could not summon a sound to her mouth.

"Do not fear. I shan't compromise you again—if such a thing is possible. You have my word." He lowered her hand. "I will leave on the morrow for London with the definite intention of not returning. I doubt we will see each other again."

The warm, familiar scent of him curled through her. She rested her cheek against the lapel of the blue superfine coat and closed her eyes. It would be so easy to give in to the secret passion that coursed through her veins. But she would not allow it to happen. Rolfe, while kindhearted in some ways, was the epitome of the domineering male. She would never again allow someone to control her life. But, ah, it was tempting. Too tempting.

Jane felt the traces of his whiskers tease her forehead as a gust of wind poured through the archway. She shivered. Rolfe removed his coat and placed it about her shoulders.

"Thank you for everything you've done, Rolfe."

"Ah, how I have longed to hear my name on your lips, without my forcing you to say it."

Jane looked into his mysterious dark eyes and felt the constricting ache of desire. Tentatively, like a doe stepping into a meadow for the first time, Jane slipped her hands up Rolfe's ruffled shirt to entwine her arms around his neck. Leaning forward, she reached his face and kissed his cheek.

A pent-up breath of air escaped from his lips. "Dearest Jane," he whispered into her hair.

Jane shivered again uncontrollably. "I must go."

He did not respond.

"I believe it is for the best." Jane shrugged off his coat, dismissing his protests that she keep it. She edged up from her cold seat and began walking toward the mansion, surprised that he did not follow her.

The night proved to be her undoing. Not only had her sensibilities attempted an about-face, but the calendar was forcing her to face the stark reality of her future. One year ago, Jane remembered as she paced the floor of her bedchamber, Cutty had lain dying in her arms. An abundant late-summer's-night feast with neighbors had brought on the last attack, which had killed him. It seemed so very long ago and yet on the contrary, it also seemed just a few months ago.

As she heard the clock strike four in the morning, Jane cursed herself for being the most perverse female that ever lived. She was devoted to Harry in a much more fulfilling way than she had been to Cutty. And yet Rolfe provoked different feelings altogether. Two such different gentlemen, two such very different feelings—each justified. And yet when she allowed her heart to overtake her mind, she knew what she must do. She had been writing about love, and yet she had refused to look it in the eye and take it. And then it dawned on her. *He was just like her.* In almost every respect. Was that good or bad? She didn't know. She only knew what he made her feel.

She flung herself onto the bed and groaned. Tomorrow—or rather, today—would be a difficult day indeed. She feared she had not the courage to accomplish what must be done.

Rolfe awoke refreshed for the first time in a long while. He tugged on the bell pull, signaling his desire for a private breakfast. He moved to the porcelain basin and splashed water onto his face as he whistled a military tune. A quarter hour passed before a valet entered the room carrying a tray and polished boots with the scent of wax emanating from them.

"Good morning, my lord."

"Yes, it is a good morning, is it not, Jennings?"

The manservant looked up with a surprised expression on his face. "Yes, sir."

"Are the others up and about?"

"Yes and no, my lord. Your brother is, I believe, still abed.

The doctor has returned early to see Mr. Thompson. Mrs. Lovering has already breakfasted."

"Ah, yes, splendid. Jennings? Please inform my coachman I will be delaying, perhaps even postponing our departure today. I will see him before lunch to give further instructions."

The valet bowed and smoothed out the clothes he had placed on the bed. An aubergine-colored superfine coat, buff riding breeches, a pressed lawn shirt, and a stock lay above the gleaming Hessians on the floor. "Shall I assist you, my lord?"

"No, Jennings. You know my preferences."

"Yes, my lord." The valet departed.

He was hopeful. More hopeful than ever before. She was in a delicate balance. One false move would tip the scales out of his favor. He knew, with a certain clarity, what he would have to do to win her over. He must proceed with caution and care. But for the first time he felt he had a chance. A small chance, to be sure. But it was a chance nonetheless.

Rolfe moved toward the basin to begin his morning ritual. He gulped hot, black coffee between swipes of his face with the razor. He finished the job and combed back his unruly hair, peering at the few gray strands in the small mirror before him. Perhaps he should step aside for that young puppy, Harry. Nah.

A scant twenty minutes later found him searching the house for her. His perusal of the morning dining room and the small sitting room she had occupied the evening prior proved fruitless. The early stages of a crisp, sparkling day peeked through the double doors. A breeze, still stronger than the previous evening's, flowed through the nearby weeping willow tree, forcing the long tendrils to swirl in a mesmerizing brushstroke pattern. Perhaps she had gone to the rose arbor.

As he approached the archway, he noticed several sheets of paper twirling in the grass, engaged in a tug-of-war with gravity and the wind. He retrieved them and entered through the large arch to find still more pages caught in the wells beneath some of the rosebushes. He collected them all and sat on the stone bench. They must be Jane's, as he could see his ring was the ineffective paperweight in a box he found next to him. But where was she? And what were all these papers? Rolfe shuffled through the parchment, righting them and noticing a lack of page numbers. He was about to place the sack in the box when a word on the top page caught his glance—"Rolfe." What the devil? He read on.

> The shadows flanking the hallway hid the figure slumped in a chair. Rolfe raised his head only once during the endless wails permeating the walls.
>
> "God, save me! Please, someone help me . . ." screamed a hidden female, consumed in agony.
>
> A servant crept down the hall, waving a candlestick. The earl raised a staying hand, and the servant shook his head and turned on his heel. Pangs of regret filled him.

"What are you doing?" a female voice asked, breaking his concentration.

Rolfe looked up and encountered Jane's furious visage. He suddenly felt ill at ease, embarrassed and defensive, like a small boy caught with his finger in the pudding.

"How dare you presume the privilege to read my work. You must know it is private, my lord."

"Jane, I was merely sorting your pages, as the wind had thrown them about the garden. Surely you do not doubt my motive?"

She hesitated. "I do. You were not sorting, you were reading," she said, reaching for the pages in his hands.

"Have no fear. I do not indulge in novels. They hold no interest for me." He could tell by the look on her face that his last utterance had perversely weakened his hand.

"And now you insult my manuscript."

"No. Actually it was quite good," he lied, "if you go for such flights of fancy."

A deep flush rose from the modest black lace of her collar. "Flights of fancy, you call it?"

"Yes. Murder, suffering, and the like are all standard novel fare," he replied.

"Ah, yes. And you know all about that, don't you? Murder, I mean." She at least had the decency to look embarrassed.

Rolfe paused, and hardened his heart. "Why, yes, I do. But you know, you have it all wrong. A murderer does not experience 'pangs of regret,' as you described it. It is more of a never forgetting. . . . You remember when you awake in the morning, when you dine, bathe, dress. Even sleep does not provide a surcease, for that is when the nightmares take over."

"So you admit you are a murderer."

"Yes. But an honest one," he said. Now he knew his position was hopeless. At the very least he could use a straightforward offensive instead of the finesse he had hoped to try. Besides, a sort of furious calm had invaded his body. "At least I am not the fraud you are, Jane. You are forcing a man to marry you who does not love you. Something, I can assure you, that will lead to regret. Nor do you love him."

"You seem so sure of my sensibilities. But then again, you have voiced your opinion of my emotions many times."

"Why do you deny your feelings for me? Was last night, here in this very place, just a moment to act out for a future scene in your novel? If so, you are a very good actor."

"And you, sir, have spoken volumes about the violence of your affection, have you not? Let us not forget your romantic proposal, your dealmaking with my father, your passionate letter, oh, yes, and your sense of duty," Jane stood very close to him now. "You do not love me, nor I, you."

"A thought you have made abundantly clear, my dear, on many occasions. However, you are wrong, you know, about my affections. But then, I think you realize that and have decided to ignore the truth. I had hoped you would accept it, rejoice in it, and also, of course, reciprocate in kind. I see now it is a hopeless case. You are resolved to go against your heart. You were right in one aspect. I have refused to accept your decision in the past. I do so now. I wish you happy, Madam." He bowed curtly, turned, and walked off.

An angry good-bye was stuck in her throat. Jane looked down at the forgotten container she held. She opened the top, releasing the delicate purplish butterfly she had caught to please Harry.

Chapter Thirteen

Jane let herself back into the house at the same double doors she had used that morning and the evening before. Once inside, she found a second set of doors in the room leading to the rear of the house. A rare chance of escaping notice from the hawk-eyed servants presented itself as she ascended the rear staircase and almost ran to her chamber.

She should never have thought it might work. The first threads of a new plan had weaved through her mind last night. It was all forgotten now. Yet she knew she must act upon part of last night's resolve. If not for her, then for Harry, the only man who had truly helped her. Well, the one who had gone along with her plans. A puppet, really, she thought with guilt.

With a long glance toward the armoire, Jane moved toward the heavy, dark-paneled furniture. She hadn't had the heart to put aside her mourning when she had risen. Now she did. She opened the doors and looked at her other dress, a delicate old muslin gown of palest blue. Fine lace edged the collar and low neckline. Her father had relented, upon the false news of her engagement to the earl, and had sent her clothes to Pembroke.

She stared at her old day gown. It had been a shade darker and had featured a higher neckline when first created two years before Cutty died. Her father had had the neckline lowered after refusing her plea to wear mourning longer than three months.

When she had last worn it, Billingsley had made ridiculous comments about the color of her eyes and the state of his heart.

With heavy heart, she knew it was time to make the change. If she didn't remove her mourning today, she might put it off forever. She struggled with the buttons on the back of her gown. Before hanging her blacks in the armoire, she reached for the object in the pocket, the ring she kept close to her always, even in her bedclothes. She looked at it and hesitated before placing it on the tray near the basin. She again struggled with the hooks on the blue dress and succeeded before overexertion flooded her cheeks with color. With her hand on the intricate brass doorknob, Jane paused before quitting the room. She looked back and hurried to the washstand to retrieve the ring. She placed it in her pocket, for safekeeping, she reasoned.

Her footsteps lagged as she pondered the enormity of the discussion and task ahead. Like a child avoiding the proverbial woodshed, Jane's breath seemed stuck in her throat as she approached Harry's chamber and knocked on the door.

Harry's voice beckoned her inside, and she found him lying down with his leg elevated in a window seat in the sitting room adjacent to the small bedchamber. The remains of his breakfast and a pile of books lay on a side table. His face lit up with a warm smile as he saw her. Jane's courage nearly failed her.

"Hey ho, now there's a pretty frock. Leaving off mourning, are you? That's a good idea, given we will be married soon enough. Sorry for the mess, but the good doctor said I was not to move from this ridiculous position for a least a day or so."

Jane moved closer and sat on a chaise opposite Harry and reached for his hand. She rested her cheek in the palm of his hand and then moved to kiss it.

"Harry, I am so very sorry."

"It's all right, I guess. I mean, it'll heal soon enough. It's so silly, really. Stupid me for riding that horse. You warned me against it."

"Does it hurt?"

"It's not pounding like the devil as it was yesterday."

Harry looked out the window and touched the draperies. Jane rushed forward into the silence. "Oh, I'm so sorry I've made you go through all of this. It's been a madcap scheme in every sense."

Harry turned to look at her. "It's all right, Duck. You know I would do anything for you. Just give me a day or two and I'm sure the doctor will say we can continue on our way."

Jane paused and released Harry's hand, rising to pace the floorboards. Silence permeated the room save for her footsteps.

"What is it? What is worrying you? Your father finding us? The earl assured me a mere five minutes ago, when he came to bid me farewell, that he had not told anyone he would stop here. You've naught to fear; your father and brother will not find us. In fact, the longer we trespass on Frederick's kindness, the better chance we have of our plans coming to fruition."

"So, he has left for London, then?"

"Yes. He said he had already bid you good day. Looked fairly put out, too."

Jane continued to pace and did not respond.

"If you are not worried about your father, then what is wrong?"

Jane stopped and looked at Harry, meaning to speak, then abruptly resumed her pacing.

Exasperated, Harry continued, "I'm not a carnival mind reader, Jane. Now have out with it. You were never any good at secrets, you know."

Jane tried to modulate the pitch of her trembling voice as she approached the window seat again. "Harry, I'm afraid I'm going to have to beg your forgiveness, and also beg you to release me from our betrothal."

Harry broke out into a grin and guffawed. "Jane, that's a good one! Now, be serious! What are you about? You're not saying this because you're concerned about my ankle, are you? I'll heal fast enough, and we'll see this thing through."

"Harry, I am serious, and it is not as you say. I am troubled by your injury, but that is not the reason I would like to end our engagement." Jane took a deep breath before continuing. "I do not think we would suit one another after all."

"What?" asked Harry. "We drag ourselves halfway through England, ruin your reputation, and now you decide we won't suit? Certainly you can do better than that, Jane. What is this really about?"

"You are not to worry about my reputation. In the last several months I have learned not to hold it too dearly." Jane found she did not have the courage to look into Harry's brown eyes when she told him the truth. She turned and moved toward the other window. "I have found that I do not have the strength of character I thought I had to become your wife."

"What on earth does that mean?"

"It means that my actions as of late have been unpardonable."

"What are you talking about?"

"I am trying but failing miserably to tell you that despite my deep affection for you, I have broken your trust and committed a deplorable sin."

A heavy silence clung to the air of the room. Jane felt it difficult to breathe.

"I suppose I should be furious with you, Jane. But I cannot. Instead I find myself just rather curious and surprised. I suppose you must be talking about something that has happened between you and Lord Graystock."

Jane nodded, still staring at the floorboards. She felt rather like when she had had to go to her mother to confess her many pranks, yet this was worse. Oh, much worse.

"I shall not ask you what, do not worry. Only a fool would not have noticed the tension between you two."

"It is not tension. It is a deep and abiding dislike of one another that you noticed. I do not like him. I do not like myself for what happened between us. In fact, we shall never see one another again."

"Careful, Jane. It is well known that hate and love are first cousins."

"That may be so, but in this case they are distant relatives many times removed."

"So you will not have him? He is too much the gentleman not to have asked for your hand."

Jane turned away, unable to answer.

Harry continued, "Are you with child? Is that it?"

Jane shook her head, unable to speak.

"You have probably let your pride get in the way, if I have any guess, and refused him."

Jane walked toward him. "You are not to be discussing the earl's, um, my behavior. You . . . you are supposed to be furiously angry with me, and calling me names of every color and profanity, and insisting on the instant removal of my person from your sight. And perhaps ordering pistols to deal with him."

"Yes, well, that is difficult to accomplish, given my precarious perch. However, if you wish, 'Get out, and don't come back any more!' "

"Be serious, Harry."

"You know I can't, Duck. But we are in a bit of a coil. Are you sure we shouldn't just stick to the original plan? That is, if you can't see your way to becoming a countess? What were you planning to do if we didn't marry?"

"Oh, Harry, now I know for a fact that you don't truly love me. Don't you see? If you did, you would be threatening to fight a duel with Graystock, or at least thrashing me."

"Well, of course I love you. Would I have agreed to this escapade to Gretna Green if I didn't? And would I be willing to still marry you if I didn't?"

"Well, you may love me. But I love you more, for I won't let you succumb to a marriage based on friendship. That is what I had with Mr. Lovering. And while it was comfortable, it was a bit lopsided. There is a saying in French, 'Il y en a un qui donne la bise et un qui tourne la joue,' which means, 'There is one who does the kissing and one who offers the cheek to be kissed.' I don't ever want to be the one who only offers the cheek again. Harry, I want to find someone I can love as he will love me in return."

"Yes, well, all that passion nonsense. It seems very difficult to find unless you look for it in novels. Are you sure we shouldn't continue with our plan?"

"Very sure. The new plan will find you ultimately on your way to London, where I daresay you might find and join an expedition to some far-flung country if you aren't too late. I shall find my way with Clarissa's help, I am sure. You are not to worry about me ever again."

"Yes, and I shall have to hope your father never sees me again, for I am likely to face a pistol if he does. And I can only imagine what he will do with you," Harry said and shuddered.

Jane left Harry a quarter of an hour later, feeling as alone and insecure as it was possible to feel. Harry had brought up every possible awful situation that could befall her in the aftermath of the broken betrothal. He had reminded her that no man would ever offer again for a widow with a history of not one but two failed engagements, including a few days' dash toward Scotland alone with her fiancé. If ever a reputation was in tatters, hers was a model. She could imagine the laughingstock she would be once her latest escapade reached the beau monde in London. The heat of the summer might force most of the peerage back to their country seats or to Bath, but the power of ink on a page would move the new gossip only farther, faster. She knew without a single doubt that she had sunk below the fringes of society and that a working-class life was her future. It was even doubtful that a member of the haute *ton* would employ her to be a governess. They would fear she might pass her poor morals on to her charges. She would have to hope to find a position as a companion to a lady who was not afraid of wagging tongues. She prayed she would find such a lady of strong backbone in her aunt's new circle of acquaintants. The prospects were daunting.

Jane's abilities to play the gracious guest failed her completely that evening. She knew Harry would be confined to his rooms, which would leave her to dine alone with the earl's libatious brother. It was too much for one horrible day. So with only a modicum of guilt, she retired to her appointed apartments, requested a bath, and pleaded a sick headache, then wrote a letter to Clarissa. Jane recapped the ink bottle after cleaning her quill and prayed that sleep would not evade her and that the earl would not invade her dreams. But that would prove impossible on all counts.

Melancholy. This was what it felt like. As she forced herself toward the washbasin and fresh towels, remembrance of yesterday's events overtook her. For the hundredth time, Jane's thoughts centered on the earl. What was he doing? What was he thinking? Gazing into the small mirror, she saw faint circles under her eyes that looked huge in her pale face. In anger, she tugged a brush through her blond locks and arranged a prim chignon. As she walked toward the armoire, she knew it was time to face the world again as Mrs. Lovering, widow, twice betrothed and twice unengaged. That was what everyone would know and gossip about behind cupped hands and smirking glances.

She walked down to breakfast and prepared for the company of the Honorable Frederick St. James. Maybe a black sheep could teach another black sheep a thing or two, she reasoned. She was not going to let his drunken familiarity disconcert her again.

With a small sigh of relief, she found herself alone with coddled eggs and sausages. She admired the beautiful blue-and-yellow wall hangings and indulged in a second cup of tea before motioning to Wiggins that she had ended her meal.

"Madam, your presence has been requested in the library," the butler said.

A few steps brought her before a liveried footman who opened the heavy oak doors to the library. Jane studied Frederick as he rose to greet her. His clean-shaven face was pale compared to the disheveled, flushed face she knew. His blond hair was neat, the comb's ridges clearly visible and leading to the old-fashioned queue tied with a black ribbon.

With some awkwardness, he sat back down after offering her a chair near his desk. "It is my hope you have been resting comfortably these past two days. I was much distressed to learn that you were suffering a sick headache last evening."

Jane looked up in surprise. His dulcet voice was lacking the usual, overfamiliar, drunken tones. "Thank you. I am much better this morning, sir. And I hope not to trespass too much longer on your kindness."

"That is unnecessary, my dear. You are welcome here for as long as you desire." He paused before continuing, "It is I who am indebted to you, I believe, madam."

"I don't understand."

"Ah, I was unsure. As you are a confidante of my brother, I

assumed you were somehow involved in his decision before he left here so precipitously yesterday morning."

Jane was silent, unsure of how to respond.

Frederick picked up a document and handed it to her. "It is the deed to Seaton, which he signed over to me before dashing away," he said in bewildered tones. "He said nothing, except that he now knew it was wrong for anyone to have to live under the thumb of someone else and that he trusted me to care for the property properly. He also said something about never returning—yes, he said he would 'never return to the devilish southern country again.' " He looked into her eyes. "Now, ma'am, why on earth would my brother behave in such a fashion?"

"I'm sure I have no notion, sir. But I congratulate you on your good fortune."

"As I am certain you did have something to do with it, I must be allowed to return the favor. My dear, it is quite obvious my brother is in love with you. Never has he behaved in the manner I recently witnessed. While I might be a drunk, I am not a fool. And the deference and glances my brother showered on you might not have been obvious to the casual observer. However, I am not a casual observer, and my brother has never shown interest in any female before save one."

"I am sure you are mistaken," she said while looking at her hands.

"I understand your reluctance to confide in me, given you have known me but a short time. However, please do not deny my joy in learning that my brother has regained his heart. You see, I took it from him quite brutally many years ago."

Jane's gaze flew to his face.

"I tell you this so you may understand him better, as he deserves to be understood. And I know you can be trusted with our secrets." Frederick concentrated on his steepled fingers. "He was all but forced to marry Constance because of the circumstances . . . which were my own doing. She loved me, and I was quite besotted with her—but it was a young, foolish sort of love, and I had been promised—nay, formally betrothed—to another for several years." Jane noticed as he paused that he appeared lost in thoughts of the past.

"Late the evening of the harvest festival, we found ourselves alone and quite inebriated with the champagne and cider, and, well, I'm sure you can imagine the rest. Someone had to save her reputation when her condition became known. My father refused to allow me to break off the engagement with the only daughter of his dearest friends and our neighbors, the Baron and Baroness Selsey. Constance was our distant cousin and all, and so Rolfe stepped forward. My father had had plans for a brilliant match for my brother, and he became bitter when Connie's predicament thwarted his desire. Rolfe did everything to shield her from familial insults, without success. He tried to get her to forget and make a life for themselves, but she could not and did not have the strength of character to change her young heart and her vulnerability," he continued while rubbing his hands over his face. "Rolfe always blamed himself for her death, despite all of my family's assurances. He felt he had failed to protect her. And of course I was the last person he would talk to. I was too embarrassed to address him, as her deterioration and death were my real fault in the first place."

Frederick buried his face in his hands and wept. Jane hurried from her seat to his side and placed a comforting hand on his shoulder. "Please, sir, I beseech you. Please, don't torment yourself. You know your brother does not blame you."

Frederick brushed his wet cheeks with his palms and looked up at Jane. "Yes, but she died, and my child along with her." He paused. "And Rolfe was the only one with her when she died, except for a maid. The doctor had not arrived, and no one with any experience in birthing was there to attend her. I forced the maid to tell me everything. Connie was delivered too early of an infant boy so small that there was no chance of his survival. And my brother watched him die for all of an hour, as the baby struggled to breathe. Connie followed soon after. She . . . she bled to death. The maid said she had never seen so much blood in her life and that my brother had worked feverishly to save them." Frederick shuddered and forced himself to continue. "She died a young girl, her heart and spirit lost. Don't you see? I should never have married Marianne. I should have ended the betrothal, despite the consequences of that act, and taken Connie to live in another country. And Rolfe—well, Rolfe refused the pleas of my parents to wed again and produce an heir. But that was before he had to face the bitter rejection of most of the *ton*, whose gossip would have ended any secret hopes he might have harbored. Now do you see the horrendous nature of my guilt?"

"No. I see a lady who while, yes, was desperately unhappy, did not have control over her own death in childbed. And," she continued, "I see two gentlemen who have blamed themselves for far too long. The burden of presumed guilt has been destroying any possibility of happiness for either one of you."

Jane realized the truth of her words as she spoke. The shock of it made her feel as if she had been punched in the stomach. He had not killed his wife. She felt sick trying to recall her actions and words to him yesterday. Had she really accused him of murder? She felt a wave of nausea at the remembrance of her horrible words. She should have known he was incapable of harming his wife. She knew she had just used her fears as an excuse to distance herself from him. But why? Why did she keep pushing him away?

The awful truth came on black tiptoe to the edges of her mind. She distrusted love and anger. Her parents' two dominant personalities had clashed, and one had broken down altogether. She didn't want to lose herself as her mother had in the face of her father's unrelenting ironfisted dominance and need for control. But then, Rolfe's departure and refusal to provoke her further proved he was not at all like her father. The rush of realization made her feel faint.

"Jane, my dear, you must sit down. Your face is drained of all color." Frederick rushed around the polished desk to help her into a padded leather armchair.

Jane peered up at him and saw the restrained, pale look mirrored on his face. "We are quite a pair," she added with a small smile.

"Shall I call for a maid? Some smelling salts? Maybe some spirits will help you?" He moved behind his desk once again.

"No, no. I beg you, no. Although you, sir, might care for a brandy, perhaps, after all this," she ventured.

"No." At his desk, Frederick rested his face on his hand. "At least for today I shall not consume any spirits." Jane knew not what to say. "I have lost my wife, my son, and almost my very life because of the craving."

"What do you mean?" she asked with concern.

"They left a fortnight ago. Marianne will not come back, and she threatened to keep my son away from me unless I stopped." Jane looked at him, hoping he would continue. "But perhaps now, God willing, I will be able to stop. Rolfe's words and trust meant everything to me. I will try to live up to his hopes for me."

Jane reached across the wide desk, offering comfort. He grasped her hand and stared at her. She felt he looked at her from the depths of his soul. "And perhaps you will live up to my hopes for you."

Jane fingered the heavy ring in her pocket as she watched the maid place the last of her personal effects into her trunk. It was warm in her hands and helped steady her nerves for the trip ahead. Her mind wandered as she moved to the window and stared sightlessly out to the manicured lawns before her.

All the inhabitants of Frederick's manor house had spent the last fifteen days cheerfully and peacefully. It seemed to be the first time in weeks she had been able to quiet her mind. She spent long hours lost in her room with her writings. She was almost happy, moving in the dream of a world far, far away from the eerie finality of her new life.

Harry seemed content. He had written to Mr. Melure, his mentor at university, of his change of plans and had received at his earliest expectation the happy news that he would most likely be asked to join an expedition the following late spring. What joy sparkled in his mischievous eyes! He was asked to teach until then to finance his trip. And the long rest finally allowed the fractured ankle to begin the healing process. Of course, the doctor had said it would be at least another month or two before it would be fully mended. But he was restless and eager to escort Jane home before leaving for university.

And Frederick. Jane had urged him to write to his wife. He had and was now quite anxiously awaiting an answer. Jane had taken great comfort in her long walks with Frederick. In so many ways, she knew they stood at similar precipices. He was changing his way of life, his drinking, and was praying that his wife and child would return. He was also clinging to his departed brother's newfound trust.

And Jane had buried her youthful dreams of a life with Harry without regret. Still, she faced the daunting task of rearranging the pieces of her life, with the likely scorn of outsiders. Worst of all, she must face it alone, without hope of a partner. Any shred of hope that Rolfe might return was erased little by little each day. She sighed and shrugged as she contemplated the future. She would fill it with writing and charitable activities between her working hours. She knew from her past life of training horses that she was truly happy when she was busy. And it would keep her mind off of . . . off of the past.

Jane turned to take a last look at the room she had occupied. She smoothed her hand over the worn wood of the escritoire, which had proved to be her good-luck charm. She frowned as she thought of the sheaves of foolscap that had been packed for Clarissa's future inspection before Sir Thomas would send inquiries to a publisher. She was only sad that the ending of her manuscript had proved to be unsatisfactory. The virginal heroine was too virtuous, and the hero was arrogant and unhappy.

Jane thanked each of the servants that she encountered on her way to the jiggling coach with four impatient matched bays fronting it.

"I cannot thank you enough, Frederick, for lending us your coach. It is truly beyond our expectations," Jane said as she and a maid reached the two gentlemen standing nearby.

"Yes, well, Harry's old thing is ready for its final resting place, don't you think?" Frederick answered with a smile.

Harry laughed. "Yes, but it is my family's only 'old thing,' as you put it."

"Don't worry. I shall see that it is returned to Cornwall as soon as it is repaired," Frederick replied.

Jane had the odd feeling that Harry's old conveyance was already fixed but Frederick had wanted them to travel in comfort. He was also sending a maid to lend an air of propriety to the couple.

Jane offered her hand to him shyly. "I don't know what to

say to you, sir. Or how we can ever repay you. You have been so very kind and have helped us immeasurably in our distress."

"My dear, it is you who have helped me." Jane felt almost moved to tears as Frederick brushed aside her hand and made the unusual move of embracing her, almost crushing her to his chest. He whispered to her, "Don't give up hope. Surely he will come back for you."

Jane stiffly moved away from him, avoiding his eyes. "I am sure I do not know what you mean, sir. But please do not worry about me. I am quite looking forward to living with my aunt."

Frederick handed her into the carriage and clapped a hand on Harry's back as he lowered his voice. "Don't forget your promise. You will write to me if things do not turn out properly for her. I could not bear to think of her unsettled."

"You have my word. And keep away from the Kill Devil. Nasty business that was," Harry replied.

Jane watched through the coach door as Frederick roared with laughter and made some unknown promise to Harry, one of his two newest friends. Really, probably the only friends he had, thought Jane. She knew the feeling only too well.

Chapter Fourteen

From the carriage window Jane could see Clarissa flying out the front doors of Pembroke, brushing past the openmouthed footman. Jane smiled, her heart soaring at the sight of her aunt—gone was Clarissa's old maid lace cap. She pushed open the carriage door and jumped into her aunt's waiting arms.

"Oh, I am so glad to see you again!" exclaimed Clarissa. "You know not the anxiety I suffered for you . . . both," she continued, extending her hand to Harry.

"I am sure you worried about me just as much as ever you did for your dear Jane," concluded Harry with a grin.

"To be sure," Clarissa said, with a rare smile for Harry.

"Is Father here?" asked Jane, moving from Clarissa's arms.

"No. Didn't you receive my letter?" She continued after Jane shook her head. "He is in London with your brother. They followed you but lost all traces after the second day. He wrote to inform me he was on to London in hopes of finding you in town before you went on to Gretna."

"Does he know I am here now?" Clarissa shook her head. Harry breathed a long sigh of relief. "Thank you for not telling him. I realize it goes against your grain to hide this from him," Jane said, holding Clarissa's arm. The demure maid who had traveled with the couple descended from the carriage and was whisked away by a footman soon after being introduced.

The threesome walked up the dusty stone steps of Pembroke and continued into the salon, Clarissa stopping to arrange for tea and scones to be brought to the weary couple. Jane sat on the familiar blue brocade chaise her mother had always favored, a place of old comfort and now of some sadness. She proceeded to relate the events that had passed since she had last written to her aunt. She stopped speaking as George entered the room, following a maid who placed the large silver tea tray in front of Clarissa. Jane placed both her hands in George's outstretched ones as he welcomed her home.

"Miss Jane, I am so very glad to see you again."

"As I am you, George," she said, smiling.

He patted her hand. "Miss Jane, I will leave you to your tea with Mr. Thompson and Miss Fairchild. But I would ask for a word with you in the stables when you are well settled." Harry winked at him and rose to shake his hand as he departed.

When the door closed, Harry added, "It sure is great guns to see the old boy again. Don't know how he stands being in London and all, being the joskin he is!"

"Yes, well, my father usually requires George to reside here year-round, as you know. This past season was an aberration, as my father released several servants from our employ. My father might be a difficult sort, but he does know the value of George's abilities concerning the workings of the stables when I am not here. It is, I believe, the only reason he has kept him on, given how much he detests my dear George," replied Jane.

"Dearest, I don't want to alarm you after all the trials you have faced, but I think we must plan to leave for Littlefield within a fortnight. I think it will be for the best. Certainly you do not want to face my brother's rage if he comes galloping back here to confront you, and I must return to prepare for my marriage and close up the cottage. You must know . . ." She hesitated. "Sir Thomas is delighted you will reside with us in Chichester after the wedding. He was quite insistent, in fact, after I wrote to him."

"I am most grateful and relieved to hear this news." Jane paused and gazed wistfully out the front windows. "I have learned to curb my independent, prideful nature, you will be glad to hear. I know that invading the privacy of your new home is an unfortunate necessity, at least for a short while. I must also beg your aid in establishing a post, perhaps as a lady's companion, as soon as possible. I could not tolerate the idea of forcing myself on you and Sir Thomas without the understanding that it will be of a duration temporary in nature."

"Jane, I know your sensibilities very well, dearest. Fear not, we will face all of this when we are settled." She paused to refill her niece's cup. Avoiding Jane's eyes, she continued, "And how did you leave Lord Graystock? Is he faring well?"

Jane felt ill at ease upon the mention of his name. "He was tolerably well. He has gone up to town, as was always his intention."

Harry grinned. "His lordship was madder than a hornet when he took himself off. Jane made a bumble-broth of it, don't you know."

"Harry!" Jane said in shocked tones.

"Well, ain't it the truth? You would never tell old crotchety, er, I mean, your dear Aunt Clarissa if I don't. It is the least I can do after you led me on this merry farce!"

"Harry!"

"What? And you probably won't tell her you refused his offer and then compounded your muttonheaded behavior by calling off our own superior plan. As I told you before, you are addlepated, stubborn as a mule, and determined to ruin every chance that is handed to you on a silver platter!" Harry said. Then he turned to Clarissa. "I hope you are more successful in talking some sense into her."

"Please, Harry, let's not start this again. You will benefit the most from our change of plans, as long as my father doesn't find you!" Jane insisted. She was tired of being forced to endure Harry's lighthearted arguments. "Enough of this. I must go and find out what George needs," she said, rising to her feet.

Clarissa rose as well. "We can discuss all of this later, dear. I'm sure Harry is eager to be on his way to the manse." She turned to him. "I do hope you will not be facing the inquisition there. I must warn you that my brother was most unhappy with your father after you departed. He did not spare him his tongue. He even threatened to remove him from the living, but I don't think he will go through with it now."

"It is quite all right if he does. The earl's brother, a very nice old chap, invited me to ask my father if he would consider accepting the living in Seaton, as the rector there died just one month ago. He rightly guessed what Jane's father would do. Well, I'm on my way now, to face the tears and sermons."

Jane hugged Harry, thanking him for everything he had done for her. Harry brushed off her gratitude and grasped Clarissa's hand in parting. Jane could not meet her aunt's eyes as she too left, mounting the stairs to change into her riding habit.

"I shall see you at dinner, shan't I, Jane, dear? We have much to discuss," Clarissa called after her.

Jane found, after she had been at Pembroke for one day short of a fortnight, that she had little desire to leave again. Oh, it was not that she was avoiding the future. It was just that she loved the clean, crisp sea air, and the sparkling whitewashed walls in the village, and of course her animals—from the horses to the sleek, yowling barn cats guarding the grain in the stables from the scanty mouse population. As she stood at the first of the long rows of stalls in the main barn, she knew it was life surrounded by her animals that she would miss most. Her mother and her mother's mother before her had been the momentum behind everything that happened here.

Her grandfather had built the stables for his wife to indulge her passion for all things equine. And Jane's mother had only furthered the enterprise by encouraging her parents to begin a breeding farm. Her mother had dreamt of emulating her parents' blissful marriage but had been doomed to failure. Losing her head to Edward Fairchild, a man who had ridden brilliantly, neck or nothing, to hounds, had been her first mistake. A dangerous fall, which broke his collarbone, and his courage, along with his love of horses, had been the next step on their road to ruin. Yes, marrying him had been her mother's fatal mistake. But she had not departed this earth without instilling in her daughter the same passion she had shared with her own mother. And Jane felt the better for it.

Looking at the small gray pony munching sweet hay in the first stall, Jane sighed. Sadness engulfed her heart and forced another chilling thought. She would never have a daughter to inspire, as her mother and grandmother had had. The end of the females in her grandmother's line would be Jane. She could almost see an image of her beautiful grandmother, who shared her unusual eyes, shaking her head.

Jane let herself into Snowy's stall and ran her hand over the neck and back of her old first pony. She slid practiced fingers down one of her hind legs and felt the bowed tendon.

"She hasn't suffered much since she bowed it. It only looks bad," George said as he leaned over the lower half of the wooden stall door. "The new head groom should never have put her in with the two-year-olds—all kicks and bites, they are. As I told you, I don't think he will work out, this new man. A bit of a jackass, if you'll pardon me saying so." Jane, intent on her examination, didn't bother to look up.

"It is the cut on her flanks that makes me uneasy. Her days of being ridden are long gone, so the bow won't matter," Jane said as she stood up from her bent position and looked at the person, more friend than servant, whom she had depended on for so many years. "It will be hard to overlook this new offense, George. Let us give the man his papers and have done with it." Jane patted the pony's neck and moved her long forelock to the center of her head. "Sweet Snowy. You mustn't desert me now. I've too few old friends left."

"Well, you still have me, little miss," George said in the darkness of the stall. The sound of munching filled the silence.

"Not for long. We leave in three days. George, I am mortally tired of saying good-bye. I would give my soul to be able to stay and fill up the rest of my life with days spent right here," she replied sadly.

"If there was a way to reconcile with your father, I would suggest it. But you need not waste your breath. I am well aware of the incontractibility of your good father."

Jane unlatched the stall door and let herself out. They agreed to take a look at the group of new foals out with their dams in the far pasture. After they walked side by side in long strides for a good distance, Jane grasped the elder's hand.

"You won't ever leave here, will you?" she asked.

"No. Never fear, miss."

"Do you promise? I couldn't bear the idea of this place going to wrack and ruin."

"I won't break the promise I made to you, nor the one I made to your mother. This place was her world, just as it is now yours. I would have done anything for her, as I would for you."

They reached the wooden gate leading into the pasture and leaned against it. Her heart started pounding as she worked up the courage to ask the question she had tried to push to the subconscious depths of her brain without success.

"George, I know I can depend on you to tell me the truth if you know it." She paused to pick up a rock and worked its edge with her gloved fingers as she concentrated her attention on it. "Theo has some far flung notion that . . . that the gamekeeper didn't accidentally kill my mother, that it was my father," she finished in a rush. "Is it true? Please, I beg of you, tell me the truth."

George looked at her through kindly old eyes and sighed. "It is a bit of a story, really. But I guess it is time for you to know the whole of it." He looked away, and his expression became distant. Jane was aware of his discomfort. "You see, I loved her and she loved me. I would not tell you, as I abhor distressing you, but she asked me to tell you when you were ready to hear it. She left me a letter explaining why she would do what she did, but I'm afraid it did not console me, nor will it help you. In it she explained that she just could not live anymore. She had begun to let fears of your father's rages seep into her bones, and the guilt of our secret was eating her alive. She thought all of us would be better off without her. She thought it would calm your father, and she thought you and Theodore were old enough to be able to continue on without her. How very wrong she was."

"What are you saying? She didn't kill herself, did she? Good God! She would never do that." Jane could see that George's face was filled with the same grief that was consuming her soul. "She wouldn't do it, I tell you. She loved us all too much. She wouldn't have left the farm, her animals, and all of us," cried Jane. A great sob escaped from her throat, and she reached for George. He took her in his arms, and she drew comfort from the familiar, musty warmth of her companion. When he did not respond, she continued to wallow in the jangling shock of it all. Long minutes passed before she could raise her eyes to George's face. "You are quite, quite sure my father didn't do it?"

George nodded his assent. "Your father hushed it up. Even threw the pistol she used into the sea, or so I believe. He hid the truth more for his own lofty aspirations than for you and your brother, I am sure. But I will give him credit for not telling you. I think he feared that you and young master Theodore would blame him if you knew the truth."

"But how did it all start? She loved my father at one point, I think. She had everything to live for."

"It was my fault. I fell in love with her after her father sent me to watch over the estate when the old steward died. I remember the time well." His eyes seemed to glaze over a bit. "It was just before your brother was born. I was bowled over by her beauty, and her spirit. She insisted on getting on and backing the new batch of one-year-olds, laughing off the doctor's warnings a week after Theodore arrived.

"She was filled with joy and light, until the day your father returned from his fortnight in town. He had missed the birth. It seemed as if all the happiness and light were extinguished when he returned. He delighted in antagonizing her, stooping to call her a simple country miss, who couldn't hide her obsession with horses. Said most girls gave up that passion when a husband entered their lives. She never fought back. But over the years she turned to me more for comfort—comfort I was too eager to offer. Until finally, a decade later, she confided her love for me."

"Well, of course she fell in love with you," Jane responded with feeling. "I was blind not to have guessed."

"No, no. Your mother's moral strength and character forbade her to ever indulge in her dreams with me. And so we were stuck. We could never imagine going off together, leaving you and Theodore and her familial home. And we knew we could not take you with us, as he would have followed in a murderous rage until we would have been found. It was an impossible situation." He looked past Jane to the field of horses grazing. "And your father's temper . . . he never knew I had your mother's heart, but he knew it did not belong to him anymore. And so he made her life a misery—with accusations of adultery, even questioning your paternity and sometimes even your brother's! All this, when your dear mother refused to even kiss me. I tell you this not to turn you against him, but for you to be able to understand your mother's state of mind at the end."

Jane straightened George's neckcloth, which she had disturbed in her distress. "I wish you were my father. I think I always did long for it. Maybe that is why I so calmly accepted my first marriage to Cutty. He and you embodied everything I craved in a father."

"I am so happy to hear you realize that now. I was very concerned when you departed with Mr. Harry. He is a fun-loving young buck, but not at all for you, I think. Are you unhappy with the choices you have made?"

"Oh, George, I'm afraid I have made a muddle of things, just as Harry says. Almost as bad as my mother, really. But at least I did not follow through with it. Now all I must face is the shame of it. But Aunt Clarissa will stand by me, as will Sir Thomas. My despair rests in leaving here, and you. At least I will take comfort in knowing you are here to manage everything." She paused before continuing, "And Theo has sworn off gaming, which assures that eventually we will be able to pay off all the debts, even the one to Lord Graystock."

Jane could see concern etched in his wrinkled old face. "Are you quite, quite sure he won't return for you?"

"George, it is an impossibility. I told you earlier I refused him two—no, three—times. No man returns for more abuse of that kind, least of all Lord Graystock."

"And what if you went to him?"

"I could not. Not after all that has happened. And I cannot allow the ugly smear of my past to spread to his name. He has enough demons to contend with. George, really, we would be the most notorious couple in all of England."

"Would that matter to you? You are spouting words so familiar to me. The ones your mother shouted at me all of a decade ago. Learn from her mistakes, Jane."

Jane knew when George dropped the formality of her title

that he was as serious as he ever got, which was as rare as a display of his anger. "I couldn't bear for him to be ostracized further. Moreover, he detests the very sight of me, I assure you. After all the ridiculous things I have done, and the people's lives I have disrupted—his being a prime example—you really can't expect the man to have me. He has lost whatever regard he might have held dear, long ago," she said, avoiding his gaze.

"Maybe, but perhaps not."

"I shall never know. It is a fruitless question. I shall not see him again. It would make both of us wretchedly unhappy."

Jane pushed open the gate, signaling her desire to end the conversation. She looked up and took his hands again in her own. "Thank you for telling me about Mother. It is a relief to know my father did not kill her. But I don't know how I will ever reconcile the anguish of her final action."

"Give it time, my dear. Peace will come as it did for me, years later. I take joy now in the simple things—the turning of the seasons, my circle of friends, and, of course, watching over her home and her children."

Jane smiled and began walking toward a group of young horses nickering and kicking up their heels. "I am certain I have caused you nothing but sleepless nights rather than joy!"

Jane took the small but significant step of instructing her maid to begin packing her things. With a smile, she left her chamber, thinking she really could qualify for a traveling player, given her extensive "here and thereian" habits of late. She entered the small salon content with new resolve.

She was glad to see Clarissa already there, dressed in a lovely soft blue gown that matched her eyes, a gift forwarded to her from her besotted bridegroom, no doubt! Her aunt's attention was focused on a letter as Jane continued toward her. The small measure of comfort she had taken in her resolution left upon spying Clarissa's troubled expression.

"Whatever is it?" Jane asked as she closed the door.

"It seems we are to be detained from leaving. My brother has discovered your whereabouts from Reverend Thompson. I believe his conscience provided only a very small part of the impetus necessary for revealing our little secret. My guess is the reverend truly is anxious about losing the living or, at the very least, a recommendation."

"We must leave at once, then."

"No. There is more. There was a missive for you within my letter." She handed it to Jane, who sank into the small yellow brocade chair next to the empty fireplace. A dark foreboding made the hairs on her neck prickle as she began reading the letter.

Jane,

I am most displeased with your behavior, as well you can imagine. The latest evidence of your vile perversity has exceeded all prior incidences of willful disobedience on your part. I am most heartily ashamed of you. However, that shall be dealt with when I see you.

    I absolutely forbid you to leave Pembroke. Girl, your impetuous manner has caused me all sorts of trials and tribulations, and you at least owe me the courtesy of an interview. I shall ride down to Cornwall on the morrow to discuss your future. Should you dare to depart sans leave-taking this time, I shall horsewhip out of your hide the contrariness you display so righteously, should I find you. Dare not provoke me further, Daughter. We have much to discuss, some of which will make you think twice about choosing an alternative course with your ninny-hammered aunt.

—Yours, &c.

Jane squeezed her eyes shut and placed her hand on her face, deep in thought. Her first impulse was to leave without delay. But really, what did she have to fear? He wanted to talk to her and likely shower recriminations on her. But she had naught to fear, as George would be near enough to intervene should events get out of hand. And she had much to gain. She could bid good-bye to her father, who had brought more pain than pleasure to her life. And she could try and uncover any remaining ghosts and lies from her parents' past. All in all, it was better for her to confront him than to flee like a coward.

Jane lowered the letter. "I think I had better stay—although you must not feel as if you ought to stay with me. You must

want to see Sir Thomas very much. And I shall very likely tread
upon your heels shortly after your departure."

"No, Jane. I will not leave you alone to face the wrath of my
brother. We shall pack our trunks and be ready to leave on an
instant's notice should he turn ugly. After you speak with him,
we shall not spend another night under his roof."

Jane thought for a moment and sighed. "Very well. I will not
belabor the point, as I am too selfish by half. I will take comfort knowing you are here to bolster my courage."

"Jane, you have more courage than any other female I know.
Come, let us go in to dinner now. I daresay we need to fortify
ourselves for the next few days that face us."

Jane forced herself to consume the meal. Her appetite had
been failing her over the course of the last few months, given
the strain. She knew George had been contriving for Cook to
prepare Jane's favorite meals. She smiled grimly and thought
that at least for tonight she would endeavor to bring him a small
degree of joy by doggedly consuming the feast before her.

After checking on the condition of three broodmares, and
discussing with George possible candidates for the newly va-
cant head groom position, Jane rode one of her favorite young
horses past the fields that separated Pembroke from the manse.
She urged her mount into a canter and soared over a stile near
the dairy. A sense of exhilaration assailed her as she moved into
a gallop and jumped a stone wall followed by a simple post and
rail in quick succession. She brought the horse down to a walk
as she patted its neck.

Oh, it would be quite, quite difficult to leave this all behind
with so little to look forward to. The last time it had been different. She had been planning a life with a husband whose very
nature had promised fun and adventure, albeit with more than a
modicum of poverty. Now she tried, with little success, to see a
silver lining to her future.

And how was he feeling? And thinking? Without a doubt, he
did not think of her at all. With his military background and or-
derly mind, he had put her from his thoughts and was glad to be
rid of the acquaintance. His mind was likely occupied with the

vast affairs of his holdings, certainly not with a woman who had refused him and humiliated him on numerous occasions.

She had lost the secret hope she had nursed in the smallest corner of her heart when she had received a letter from Frederick mentioning not a word of his brother. He related to her only his joy in his reconciliation with his wife, as well as his wish for Jane's happiness. Every empty line screamed that the elder brother had forgotten her.

Peals of laughter rang in Jane's ears as she rounded the corner of the manse. The tired maid-of-all-work took the reins of Jane's horse and muttered her greeting. Five or six of the Thompsons, and the ever present petulant houseguest, Miss Dodderidge, poured through the front door at an alarming rate.

"Jane, Jane, come, you simply must join us!" Harry shouted.

"To where, dare I ask?"

"We're off to go fishing. The ladies refused to let William and me go off alone. And now they have had the audacity to make a wager that they will catch more than us. A boastful bunch, to be sure, when at least one of them has never fished in all her life!" he said while eyeing the coy Miss Dodderidge.

"How can you expect us to sit with our embroidery on a beautiful autumn day like today?" Miss Dodderidge responded.

"Will you join us, Jane? It will be like the old days."

"No, no. I must go back and work some of the other horses today." Jane lowered her voice, as the others had moved a few steps away and were sorting through the tackle in the shedhouse. "Harry, I came to warn you that my father is expected in two or three days' time. You should consider making yourself scarce, as he is like to do you harm!"

"Hmmm. Yes, well. As I told you before, we do not need to avoid him any longer. The Honorable Frederick St. James, that is, our good friend Freddie, put his offer into writing in a letter I had from him yesterday. He promised the living at Seaton to my father should yours cut up nasty. So I shall not run away, as we are having far too much fun here. I leave soon enough for the post at university, really, in less than a week. And you? When do you leave with your aunt?"

"Soon, very soon," she said. "As soon as I make one appearance before my father."

"Jane, you can't be serious! Shall I be at your side when he comes? I fear for your safety, Duck."

"No. I have Saint George, who will be standing by to slay the dragon if need be!" Jane whispered the last as Miss Dodderidge appeared behind Harry's shoulder.

"Slaying dragons? I say, Harry, would you do that for me should the need arise?" inquired Miss Dodderidge with cloying sweetness.

Harry took her arm through his and patted her hand. "My dear, you know I am your most ardent admirer and protector. Know that I would save you from all the wild beasts, great and small, to be found in Cornwall's formidable wilderness."

Jane rolled her eyes as Harry grinned. Honestly, how he could stand being in the presence of such a determined flirt she would never know. And when had they discarded formality in favor of their Christian names? Harry shrugged when Jane's eyes met his.

Chapter Fifteen

Lord Fairchild was in no mood to see anyone the day of his arrival at Pembroke. His bones felt jarred from their very joints, given the dry, rutted roads of September. Head pounding, he descended from his plain carriage and waved away the addresses of the servants. He went straight to his library and poured himself a large brandy to wash away the dirt of the roads. He sank into the brown leather chair and cursed at the piles of papers stacked neatly on the nearby desk, no doubt by his redoubtable daughter or that infernal George. How he hated the country, the dirt, the quiet, and the wretched loneliness of it all. It infuriated him to be back just when he had been settling into the hustle-bustle of town. He adored London. Mornings at White's, afternoons spent plotting advances for the reopening of Parliament, evenings at salons full of important personages, and after midnight, everything imaginable for the male palate. It was glorious. It was what he craved. Looking at his dusty boots and creased clothes, he frowned in disgust and rang for a hip bath to be brought to his chambers. He finished the brandy with one long last swallow and hoped that his head would stop aching after a short repose. He was not up to facing Jane yet or, for that matter, his own sister. Females were the bane of his existence. He rubbed his eyes before striding out of the library toward the sanctity of his rooms above.

All in all, he felt a good deal better the following morning, although the early air was never something he coveted. It seemed the household had avoided him at all costs. Both ladies were absent from the breakfast room. So he toasted himself and settled into his ham and eggs with a good deal more relish than the last evening's supper.

"Excuse me, my lord, Miss Jane has requested I inform you she awaits your lordship's presence in the front salon, at your leisure," George said upon entering. The butler bowed and exited as Fairchild acknowledged his words with a slight nod and a wave of his hand. Looking down at his plate, Edward Fairchild thought his breakfast had lost most of its appeal now. He took one last bite, and with a grimace rose to face his task.

Jane paced the room, and then stamped her foot in annoyance, angry with herself for her sense of agitation. She had resolved on remaining calm in the face of the storm. She would not let him take the upper hand. And if he rang a peal over her head, she would insist he desist. Failing that, she would leave. Jane also took comfort in knowing Clarissa and George were in the next room, their chairs drawn close to the door that joined the rooms. She started at the sound of the door opening.

"Good morning, Jane," Lord Fairchild said with coolness.

"Good morning."

"I trust you are well?" he inquired, as a formality.

"Yes, quite. You left my brother in good spirits, too, I hope?" she responded. Her father nodded his assent, and Jane shivered as she anticipated the end of the trivialities.

"Yes, well. I am sure you have surmised the reason of my return to the bowels of Cornwall, a place whose appeal is lost on me."

"Unless it is to banish me again from my birthright, you are wrong, sir, I cannot fathom why you would wish to see me," she said, lifting her chin. "Have no doubt that my trunks are packed, along with my aunt's. We are prepared to depart on a moment's notice. We shan't depend on your charity any longer."

"You are incorrect in your assumptions and are taking great delight in displaying your newly acquired contemptuousness."

"This will not do. I shall not listen to your insults. If you have something of consequence to say to me, say it. Otherwise, I will leave at once," Jane replied quietly.

With a pause and a long sigh, her father seemed to try and rein in his temper. "Not so hasty, my dear. As I said in my letter, I have something of importance to relate to you. I understand your ill ease, as the letter I sent to you was written in a great fury. Since then, I have had time to resolve myself to your impetuous actions of late regarding Mr. Harry Thompson and Lord Graystock. And while I could dearly wish that you had allied our family name with the earl's, I have come to believe that the present resolution will at least bring a measure of peace to our family. And I can at least be glad that you did not marry that noddy parson's son, Harry Thompson!"

Her father's words startled Jane. So prepared was she to accept a severe reproof that his words bespeaking peace threw her into a silence, as her muddled brain could not form the necessary retorts. Of course, he had not been able to resist belittling Harry, but this was as close as he was able to come to offering an olive branch in her direction.

"Ah, I see the cat's got your tongue. Maybe this will loosen it," he continued as he drew a sheaf of foolscap from his breast pocket and handed it to her.

Jane scanned the pages and lowered herself into the nearest chair. She sucked in her breath sharply when she sifted through to the last page and saw the familiar angular signature. She returned to the first page and noticed several references to Pembroke's stables. Her father's words broke into her perusal.

"I shall hasten your understanding of the matter, if you will allow. You can complete your reading at your leisure."

"If you please, sir."

"I had the pleasure of a visit from Graystock soon after my arrival in town. That is, after the folly of chasing you and your bumbling bumpkin throughout the countryside," he harrumphed.

Jane said nothing in her defense, preferring to learn as soon as possible why she held in her hands a document signed by Lord Graystock. Undoubtedly it must concern the colossal amount of money her father owed that gentleman.

Her father continued, "In any case, he came to propose an agreement to resolve our fiscal debt following the ignominy of your elopement. In exchange for granting him the title to—"

"Good God, Father, no! You didn't give him Pembroke, did you? You wouldn't do that! Please, oh, dear God, please tell me you did not?" Jane implored in shock.

"No, I did not, you silly girl! Have patience. In exchange for an even larger financial settlement to the one stated in the marriage contract, I sold to him only that portion of the estate he requested, that being the stables and the breeding stock." Jane closed her eyes in horror but kept silent. "It is for the best, you know. I will be able to concentrate on my life in London and the House of Lords, and it will resolve all our debts. And Theo is delighted. He never shared your enthusiasm for the horses except for fox chasing, of course. He always did prefer the agricultural concerns of the property, which will still be his upon my demise," he said, loosening his cravat.

"Yes. I see how it has all been resolved," Jane said, as a sort of numbness crept into her being. "It is a good thing my mother is not here to see the day her most beloved corner of the world has been sold," she added with great feeling.

Her father exploded with pent-up rage. "Do not go lecturing me, Jane, on your dear mother's emotions. She lost all rights to what became of Pembroke when she died."

Jane forced herself to remain calm. "This is when I bite back at you and defend my mother. But I shall not, because I know the truth."

"Ah, your brother's 'truth'? Or the actual truth?"

"You should not act so smug, Father. I know the simple truth. She . . . she killed herself. But I also know what Theo believes is also partly true—she committed suicide because of the unhappiness in her marriage. Can you deny it?"

"I do not have to deny it. We were all living under the same depressing roof, girl! Do you not think I was not miserable myself? But at least I stuck it out. I stayed here, on this hellish country estate, watching the woman I married become estranged from me, finally detesting the very sight of me. But I stayed. And I didn't leave you and Theo orphans, as she did by half. Even though you are not of my blood, I did not forsake you!" His face was bloodred in anger. Then he stopped and crumpled at her feet, great sobs overtaking his body. "I loved her! I loved you all! But she would not let me in. She would not let me be part of her world and yours. And she would have none of mine in London," he said in a rush.

Jane felt tears course down her cheeks as she urged him to his feet and wrapped her arms around his bulk."

"Oh, Papa, I have waited so long to hear those words. I love you, too, you know. You are a great fool," she said as she closed her eyes and leaned on him. "I loved you, and Theo worshiped the ground you walked on. Why did you not disabuse him of his crazy notions? In my heart I knew his ideas were not true. Even when he spoke of the discharged gun being in your hands. But why didn't you put a stop to his gaming?"

"I could not take the fond memories of your mother from either of you, no matter how much you both hated me. I also presumed you might take her same path if you knew. We all know suicide runs in families. And your brother's ruinous actions proved he might follow her course." He stopped to mop his brow before continuing. "He refused to believe Harstead had fired at a stag. I held the gamekeeper's gun as he went in search of the stag that he thought he had nicked. Instead, Harstead found your mother. I hid her pistol and made a pact with him. But I must have given him back my clean gun instead of his, when Theo appeared."

"Come, Papa, sit beside me on the chaise and let us resolve this. All of it." With bowed head, he accepted Jane's proffered handkerchief as they moved to the blue chaise. He blew his nose loudly into the delicate cloth.

"I know part of all your past bitterness stems from your belief that Theo and I are not yours," Jane said, looking into her father's brown eyes. He refused to acknowledge her statement and instead looked at the floor. "*You are my Papa,*" she insisted. Jane had an idea suddenly and prayed it would provide the necessary proof. "And I will show you, so you will never have to doubt it again, if you will not laugh or take offense."

He nodded and looked quite unable to say anything lest he lose control of his sensibilities again.

Jane began unlacing her left boot, avoiding his face. "I know

I am the very picture of Mama in every respect save one." She then removed her boot and rolled down her stocking to display her foot. "Now, Papa, you must do the same."

He had not quite recovered his usual gruff detachment, and to her surprise he complied with her request without a word. When he had finished the job, he placed his foot next to hers. Slowly, his face broke into a wide grin as he looked at their feet. "Why, they are identical, I do declare, except yours, of course, is smaller. From the pathetic excuse for a little toe down to the peculiar indentation on the top of the big toe!" he exclaimed with great laughter.

Jane chimed in, "And look at the longer second toe, and our square nails! Mother once told me we had similar feet. But I was not sure until I saw yours today. I prayed she was right."

Her father caught her in a great hug and squeezed the breath from her. "It was all my fault, then. I would not believe her denials, and so I drove you all away. Ah, Jane, how can I ever receive your forgiveness, after all I have done?"

"You have but to ask. And seeing you here now, and after everything that has happened, there is no need, as I have much to require forgiveness too. I am sorry to have led you on such a chase and to have ever caused you worry."

"That is nothing to what I have done to you. Allowing Cutty to marry you was of course the worst offense. But forcing you to sell your possessions, and then insisting that you accept Billingsley, were also unforgivable. But you know not the blackest of my crimes."

"I think I do, really," she said, unable to meet his gaze.

"In a drunken state I even considered accepting Lord Wythe's vile proposal. I was only lucky Cutty appeared in time to put a stop to it. What a horrible fool I was. But Jane, I do not expect your forgiveness, only your understanding," he said.

"But you have it. Pray let us not ever dwell on it again."

He kissed her cheek and held her hand as he reached for the document, which had fallen to the floor. "It seems you have a choice, then, my little one, in the question of where you shall reside. You now have before you four choices." Jane looked up at him in surprise. "You may go with your aunt to Chichester, where I understand you have a great desire to become a lady's

companion or some such nonsense, or you may live in this
house, which I know you love more than anything. Of course,
you may also come to reside with me in London, although I assume I have not even the slimmest chance of your wanting to
do that!"

"You are most dear to even consider inviting me! But I am
most curious, Papa. Whyever did you mention four choices?
There are the three you mentioned, and no more. Indeed, I feel
most fortunate that you have offered me the last two. I never
dreamed I would be allowed to remain here," she said shyly.

Lord Fairchild cleared his throat gruffly and reached into his
pocket for his spectacles, which he placed low, near the end of
his nose. He reminded Jane of Saint Nicholas just then, and she
hugged him, filled with the happy knowledge she could now do
so without fear of rejection. She wiggled her toes in delight.

Ruffling the pages, her father continued, "Lord Graystock
apparently acknowledged your superior horsemanship after his
anger had cooled. It says here—yes, in this very part," he said,
hesitating as he scanned the page. "Yes, yes, here it is—'Mrs.
Jane Lovering is to be offered the position of Steward of the
Stables, a post that shall remain open to her for the duration of
her lifetime. Should she accept the position, she would report to
my steward in London, and she and her husband would be allowed the use of the small steward's cottage. In addition, the
stables and breeding operation described herein shall revert to
the ownership of Mrs. Lovering or her offspring upon the event
of my death.'" Her father removed his glasses and rubbed his
eyes. Jane was effectively silenced. "So you see, my child, you
have a plethora of options before you."

She could feel her eyes welling with tears. Caught without a
handkerchief, she wiped her hands against her eyes.

"But, my child, I must make clear to you one point. He made
it very obvious that he had no desire to ever see you or anyone
else in our family again. He purchased the stables purely as an
investment to clear the debt. Graystock included the steward-
ship as your brother pressed him to do so. But understand
this—I don't believe he ever thought for a moment you would
return to Pembroke. He said as much. He agreed to it quickly,

as he was in great haste to conclude the business and be on his way. What do you say? Will you hold him to his offer?"

"I don't think there is any question, Papa," she said with a smile. "I won't leave here if I am to have the choice. I think, though, that I would prefer to stay in the estate house to oversee all, if you will allow it. But when and if Theo ever marries, I shall remove to the cottage so as to not interfere."

"Good girl. I knew you would choose this course. It really is for the best. Now, shall we go and bump the knees and faces of the two eavesdroppers on the other side of that door?" Lord Fairchild said, nodding in the direction of the adjoining door. As they rose, he continued, "I shall be returning to town the day after tomorrow. Right after the bruises have resolved from the journey hither!"

As she sat behind the large, simple pine desk in the main barn, tapping her quill on the blotter, Jane took her decision. She would not go to Littlefield. She would not go to her aunt's wedding. She had withstood the mild rebukes from George, as well as the hesitant suggestion of Papa and, worst of all, the two loving letters from her aunt. Each time Jane examined her resolve, she felt relief. The very thought of encountering Lord Graystock again brought waves of great anxiety. The embarrassment could not be endured. Mostly she would not go because she did not want to cause the earl any further unease. He would heave a great sigh of relief when he arrived at Hesperides and learned of her absence. And so she would not go. Jane had written to her aunt that she would be better able to witness Clarissa and Sir Thomas' connubial bliss if she came for a visit to Chichester sometime in early summer next year instead of a one-day visit to Littlefield this autumn.

She pushed aside the pile of cream-colored paper, frustrated with her manuscript. Clarissa had not fancied it and had suggested a different ending. Try as she might, Jane could not force the characters to behave in the fashion Clarissa had suggested. Instead, she moved forward the schedules she must review and approve. It seemed a much less daunting task.

She had settled quite happily into the role she was born to, that of stable master. Her life was perfect in every way. She could not even have uncomfortable feelings the day Harry had ridden over with Miss Dodderidge to announce his happy news.

"Hey ho, Jane! Wish me happy!"

Laughing, Jane had said, "Ah, you've heard again from Mr. Melure at university, then?"

"No, no. Better yet!"

"We're to be married, Mrs. Lovering," rushed on Miss Dodderidge.

Jane had had to control all of her wits not to dissolve into laughter. The expression on Miss Dodderidge's face bespoke the truth of her words. But when Jane had recovered from the surprise, she was rendered speechless.

Harry had jumped from his saddle and whispered to her, "I knew you wouldn't believe it. But don't hurt her feelings or she might turn frosty. It's like this. I started getting used to the idea of wedlock when we left together. I realized that the idea had many merits."

"Impossible," Jane had giggled while trying to maintain a serious expression.

But it had been possible. She had congratulated them with sincere warmth after inviting them in for tea. It seemed they were off to Scotland with his sister and father to marry without the delay of the banns. Miss Dodderidge had even insisted Harry continue his plans for the expedition later in the term!

Jane brought her attention back to the blacksmith's notes and spring foaling charts. The rumbling of a conveyance in the stable yard broke her concentration. As she stared out the doorway to find her father's carriage in the yard, a feeling of dread swept through her. Father would never return so soon unless a calamity had beset the family again. A great welling of relief poured through her when Theo descended from the carriage.

"Not even bothering to hide the breeches anymore, Jane? You have been rusticating too long!" he said as he embraced her.

Jane laughed with embarrassment. "You've caught me."

"I see life here agrees with you, as it always did." He followed her into the large office and threw himself into the chair opposite her desk. He shook his head after picking up one of the charts and put it down with little interest.

"Be a good sister and give your dear brother a drink, if you please. Father refuses to spare a shilling to refurbish that rattle-box, and the dirt seeps in through every crack. It's a disgrace, I tell you."

Jane smiled and pulled an unlabeled bottle of brandy from one of the drawers as well as two dusty glasses. "Will this do?"

She poured as he nodded. "To sisters who obey their brothers' every command!" he toasted.

"To undemanding brothers," offered up Jane.

"Have you guessed why I'm here?" quizzed Theo after drinking long and deep.

"I cannot guess," she said. "You aren't planning marriage, are you? I don't think I could bear to hear anymore cooing."

"No, but you shall hear spoon-talk all the same. I'm here to take you to our dear Aunt Clarissa's wedding."

Jane held up her hand. "Stop. I am not going. You have added needless time to your trip if that is the purpose of your visit. I have arranged to see the newlyweds next summer. I can't go. I have a mare expected to drop any day now, and her last foaling was difficult. I won't go!"

"Easy, you old thing. Touched a nerve, did I? Well, it won't fadge. You're going, even if I have to bundle up your belongings myself and stuff you into the carriage, fetters and all. And don't think I wouldn't do it! I have it on very good authority that someone here—yes, I do believe his name is George—will help me tie you down if necessary." Theo continued over the frequent interruptions of his sister, "Honestly, my dearest, what are you thinking? How ever can you consider denying our aunt the pleasure of your company on the most anticipated day of her life? The very person who loved you and cared for you like no other these last few months! You once told me I should be ashamed. Well, now I fling it back in your face!" Theo threw up his hands as he left, refusing to listen to any of the shouted excuses following him out into the yard.

She would go. She wasn't comfortable with her decision, but she was packed. And Theo had not had to resort to any of his repeated threats over the course of the last two days. The way Jane envisioned it, she might even be able to go and be in

his presence for a few short hours at most. She and Theo would
stay but one night in Clarissa's small cottage. That was the
promise she had insisted on and secured from her brother. After
the wedding ceremony, they would go the short distance to
Portsmouth and stay at an inn. At the very least, the trip to Littlefield would ease her guilt over denying Clarissa's appeals.

With heavy heart, Jane left. She felt a pang when she noticed
a conspiratorial wink from George to Theo as she entered the
carriage. It seemed everyone thought her reluctance amusing.

"You do realize Lord Graystock said he had no desire to
continue our acquaintance. Why you insist on adding to his discomfort I do not know. But I shall say no more. I am bored with
our discussion already. I hope you do not expect witty conversation this trip, for I am not up to the task."

"A bitter tongue does not suit you, Jane. Come on, shake
hands with me, then. I won fair and square this time. You win
most of the other times. Be a gentleman even though you aren't
wearing those breeches again today. Thank God, I might add!"

Chapter Sixteen

The winds were blowing less now, but the air became chilly as they moved up the eastern coast. The chestnut trees she had seen earlier in the year, lush with foliage, were dropping their matted ceiling of leaves with every rush of wind. The promise of spring was now lost to autumn's killing frost.

Jane clutched her hands in front of her to stave off the slight trembling as they approached Littlefield. As the carriage stopped in front of the grove of trees between the road and Clarissa's cottage, Theo leaned forward and opened the door. After bounding down, he held his hand up to help her. She avoided glancing about her and hurried to the cottage.

Theo laughed. "You are a hen-hearted girl! Fear not. There is not a soul about at this unearthly hour."

Jane turned. "If you are going to continue to tease and needle me, I will return to Portsmouth now! See if I don't!"

Theo relented and whistled a merry tune while walking toward their aunt's door.

Rolfe stood staring out the intricate stained-glass windows, his hands clasped behind him, feeling very relaxed. While it was true he had had only a few hours of sleep the night before, he was fully awake and could smile at the nervous tapping of Sir Thomas' fashionably shod foot beside him.

"Steady there, Gooding. Wouldn't want to appear rickety, would you?" he asked with a smile.

"I suppose you would be calm if we switched places?" Sir Thomas asked as Rolfe patted him on the back.

Rolfe could be relaxed, as he had had a moment the previous evening, when he had arrived, to review the list of people who had accepted invitations to breakfast at Hesperides. *Her* name was not on it; only Theodore was included on the list. Even the father had chosen to stay away, much to Rolfe's relief.

Yet while he could remain steady, there was just the smallest part of him that had shriveled up and died last night. It was the part that had smoldered the past month while he had traveled among his far-flung estates. It had refused to budge despite the hours of tormented reflection he had endured. It was final now. She was lost to him.

The morning sunbeams, streaming into the small church through the arched front doorway, dimmed as a few quiet noises emanated from the back. The pews, filled to capacity, became hushed as a backlit figure moved to the center aisle. Rolfe looked at his friend to see joy fill his face. He looked back at Clarissa to find her looking younger than he remembered, and almost pretty in a cream-colored dress and long gloves.

Another slim figure was beside her, rearranging a flower in her hair. The familiar form slipped into the second-row pew next to her brother.

Rolfe turned toward the old reverend and stood motionless, feeling all the blood rush from his head into his pulsating fingertips. Good God! He wasn't going to faint, was he? No, never that. She had come. He closed his eyes and tried to think. She had come because it was her duty. Her aunt would have begged her to attend during this, the most celebrated day of her life.

He opened his eyes again as he heard Reverend Gurcher's request for the ring. He managed his office without a tremor, all the while keeping his eyes fixed on the couple before him. A loud whirring in his ears would not allow him to hear the rest of the vows. Finally, raucous laughter and good cheer filled the church while everyone filtered out into the yard.

Rolfe was the last to leave the church and the first to enter one of the few carriages in the yard. The vast majority of the villagers had chosen to walk to Hesperides, given the sparkling perfection of the cool day. Rolfe closed the curtains of his carriage to block out the light and any urge he might have to look for her face among the throngs of people. He lay back against the cushions and sighed. She had come after all.

As she trudged through the fallen leaves, up the last hill before the vista that held the entrance to Hesperides Hall, only Theo's strong arm linked with hers kept her moving forward.

He had not looked at her once during the entire ceremony. It did not bode well for her. But then, perhaps she was just of a timorous mind. Viewing the large number of villagers walking before her, she thought there was a good chance she would have to endure only a few minutes before the host, bidding the required number of thank-yous and good days. Before she could form in her mind the words she would say, she found Theo propelling her up the long steps leading to Hesperides Hall, where the doors had been thrown open wide to admit all. She pulled the edges of her pale gray cloak more tightly together as she looked at Theo.

"It will be all right. Don't be such a ninny. It doesn't suit you," he whispered before bowing to the dowager countess.

"So good to see you again, Lady Graystock," Jane murmured as she curtsied. She presented her brother to the older lady.

"My dear, the pleasure is all mine, I am sure. I had such grand hopes you would attend. A pity you could not come earlier for the fall festival this week past. But then, I failed to entice my grandson as well." The matriarch patted Jane's hand. "The weather cooperated, and such a fine time was had. But never mind, you are here now. Come, let me introduce you to the Smiths, and the Kellerys down from London," Lady Graystock said as she motioned the footmen to close the doors.

"You are most kind, Lady Graystock," Theo responded.

"Young man, at my age, one is not kind, just practical!" she responded with a deep chuckle. "Ah, I see Mrs. Gurcher headed our way. Make your escape while you can. I am afraid, my dears, you are going to have to fend for yourselves," she continued while extending a welcoming hand and a false smile to the reverend's loquacious wife.

Theo pulled Jane into the large salon in the rear of the hall. Spanning one end of the mansion to the other, the sunny yellow room was filled with the happy sounds of a celebration. Mounds of sugared confections and exotic fruits were artfully piled on tiered stands upon the large table in the center of the room. The scent of hothouse flowers teased Jane's nostrils as she and Theo advanced toward the largest gathering of people, sure to include the bride and her proud husband. Jane was careful to keep her eyes trained on the floor ahead of her.

"Ah, you are here at last! Theo, Jane, do come stand beside me," Clarissa implored with a radiant expression.

Jane's eyes darted to the tall gentleman standing next to Sir Thomas. Her gaze moved away when she perceived his reserved expression.

"Aunt Clarissa, as I told you this morning, you are a ravishing bride, and Sir Thomas—you are a lucky man!" Theo exclaimed as he clapped his hand on Sir Thomas' shoulder.

"I am indeed. And you both have made my bride very happy with your presence, and so you are in my good favor."

"Thank you, Lord Graystock, for your kind invitation to my sister and to me," Theo continued.

The earl bowed to Theo and Jane. "Where is Mr. Thompson? I am sorry he was not able to be present," Lord Graystock said.

Startled, Jane responded. "Why, he's at university for the start of the term." She turned to Clarissa and Sir Thomas then. "But he did ask me to send you his warmest regards and best wishes on this happy occasion."

Sir Thomas embraced Jane and added, "And now I may finally call you my niece. Doesn't that sound grand? And you may both call me 'Uncle Thomas' instead of that stodgy old title!"

Theo laughed and shook hands with his newest relative as Jane moved again to Clarissa's side, furthest from the earl's penetrating stare. Jane felt all the awkwardness of Lord Graystock's presence and could not make her mind or her mouth function as etiquette dictated.

"And has Mr. Thompson's ankle healed properly, then?" asked Lord Graystock with the minimum of words.

"Yes, quite. When last I saw him, he was walking with the barest limp. The doctor said he would be fully recovered in another few weeks' time," replied Jane without looking at him.

"I am glad to hear it," he replied. A silence fell on the group, all the more noticeable because of the boisterous goings-on all around them. Jane felt deafening pressure to fill the void.

A tall, dark beauty moved toward the group and slipped her arm through Lord Graystock's. "Ah, there you are, my lord. I have been searching quite throughout the Hall for you. Have you forgotten the tour of the portrait gallery you promised me? And of course Mama?" The circle moved back to include the intruder. "But I see I have interrupted you."

"Not at all, Miss Kellery. May I introduce you to our new guests?"

The elegant young lady looked toward Jane and Theo. "Oh, there is no need, I have known Jane forever. We had our come-out in London together, even the same dancing instructor. And of course, I have met her brother. Mr. Fairchild?" she said with a curtsy to Theo and a tilt of her nose toward Jane. "I was so sorry to learn of your unfortunate misadventure with Mr. Billingsley this past spring, Jane. A bit of a muddle, was it not? Whatever happened? The town fairly buzzed with your news, but then you up and disappeared. I am sure I had no idea I would find you here! It has all subsided, you know, what with the *ton*'s attention drawn to newer *on-dits* . . ." she would have prattled on, clearly bent on rattling Jane, had not Graystock intervened.

"Shall we ascend to the gallery now? Perhaps your mother grows weary waiting for us."

"Oh, of course, sir. I would not dream of inconveniencing you, or taking you away from your guests, though," Miss Kellery added with a sparkle in her eyes. She had a very clever way of drawing all the gentlemen's attention to her bubbling form.

"Not at all. It is my pleasure." He escorted her through the maze of people toward the doors.

With Miss Lavinia Kellery and Lord Graystock gone, Jane

regained a small degree of her usual poise and made an effort
to please her aunt with every expression of happiness she could
compose. And it was not difficult, as her aunt had never appeared as radiant or as happy as she did that day. Jane tried
mightily to hide her anguish. Lavinia had, without doubt, cap-
tivated Lord Graystock with her vivacity and charm.

After she consumed the obligatory number of cakes and
fruits, and spoke to the required number of people, Jane took
her leave with a huge sigh of relief. She felt guilty not staying
a bit longer after the urgings of Lady Graystock. She arranged
to meet Clarissa at the cottage before they both departed that
same late afternoon, one toward Portsmouth, the other toward
Chichester. Theo refused to budge from the Hall due to the
pouty charms of the local squire's daughter.

"If you want to return to the cottage for the exciting job of
repacking our few possessions, go right on ahead, Jane. I've
had enough of carting you around!" whispered Theo, thoroughly put out by Jane's repeated requests to leave.

Stung by his words, she turned and walked from the yellow
room, through the Hall, and out the door pulled open by the
lounging footman. She was able to release all the pent-up air in
her lungs only when she had walked a quarter mile past the
tree-lined drive. When she was sure she was out of sight, she
moved behind one of the large oak trees in the field and leaned
against it. She burst into tears and sagged down the length of
the support until she found herself surrounded by tall grasses at
the base of the tree. She tried to stifle her sobs, fearing that
someone, possibly one of the villagers, might come along. But
no, she would be the only fool willing to leave the celebration
this early. But she could not stay. Seeing him was too much.
Her still-raw emotions were ripped open just by the sight of
him. And on top of it, Lavinia was dangling after him. Jane
could not imagine a more exquisite or intelligent lady. And her
brother, Mr. Kellery, had clearly sanctioned the acquaintance.

She had been such a prideful, stubborn fool! Her love for
Harry had been but a transitory affection that barely skated the
thin ice beyond camaraderie. She had fed on the memory of
those immature sensibilities during her marriage and beyond,
imagining her feelings to be tenfold what they were in truth.

The emotions she felt for Rolfe were pure agony and would haunt her every waking moment unless she did something to extinguish them.

With excruciating clarity, she realized she must bolster her courage and swallow her pride . . . *and go back to face him again.* She would never be able to form a future without him if she didn't find the courage to talk to him, to offer herself to him. And if he didn't want her anymore, which in all probability was the case, well, then he would have to tell her, so that she could pick up the mantle of her complete humiliation and go back to Cornwall brokenhearted, perhaps, but at least with a clear mind.

She pushed her soggy handkerchief into her pocket and shivered as she rose from her damp spot. She tried in vain to smooth away all the creases in her dress and shrugged her shoulders. She would return to the party even if her dress was wrinkled and wet in the back. Oh, there would be a few raised eyebrows, to be sure, and many more if she was able to wrest Lord Graystock away from the fawnings of Lavinia and the glorious festivities—all for a moment of privacy. But she didn't care what anyone thought, she was able to convince herself. Almost.

She turned from the old oak tree and stepped through the tangle of summer's spent grasses toward the road. At that moment she heard the pounding of hooves in the distance. She stepped onto the road and began walking back to Hesperides. Just before she rounded the corner onto Hesperides' drive, a man on a dark horse entered the lane. Surprised by Jane's figure, the horse skidded to a halt and reared slightly. Jane remained calm and moved to the edge of the road. When he had gotten the animal under control, she spoke.

"I am most sorry to have startled your horse, my lord."

"You are frequently known to do that."

"I am sorry."

"You have said that already."

A silence intruded, and Rolfe used it as an excuse to dismount.

"May I ask where you are headed?" he asked.

"I-I was returning to Hesperides."

"Ah, I see you recollected you forgot your cloak," he said as he lowered the folded garment from his saddle.

"Yes. It was silly of me to forget it. It is quite chilly. Thank you very much for bringing it to me."

Rolfe shook out the cloak and wrapped it around Jane's shoulders without touching her. "Well, I must return to our guests, but at least you are warm now."

She grasped the cloak's edges and pulled them tightly together. She did not know where to look now that the opportunity to talk to him was present before her. Before she could make her mind function, he was up on his horse again and turning around to bid her good-bye. Her mouth frozen, her hand in midair, she watched his horse start to trot away. Her vision blurred with tears, she tore out an agonized cry. "Rolfe!"

He stopped his horse and turned around. She ran in her soft slippers to him, grabbing his hand, which was full of the reins.

"I am so very sorry for everything I've done. I must tell you this. I am afraid I've made a very gross mistake and I don't know how to fix it. The proper way of telling you this has deserted me. I beg of you to forgive me for all the wretched things I said to you in the past."

Rolfe looked down at her with an unreadable expression. He did not grasp her hand in return. "You have my assurances that I have never sought or expected any apology from you. I thought our last meeting put to rest any questions or answers each of us sought to make clear. You have attained your point and your goal. I am happy for you, as you must be happy for me. It has turned out for the best. I always knew there was never any doubt of your success, and surely you cannot regret what you have done, for it is quite impossible to change it now," he said.

She shivered as embarrassment flooded her. Clearly he was glad to be rid of her, and his feelings toward her had evaporated. And he had referred to her attaining her goal of returning to live at Pembroke. It was another reason to thank him. "Yes, and I must thank you for arranging everything. It was too much, really. I can never thank you enough." Jane stopped. It had turned awkward. He wanted to be on his way. He had told her he was happy for her and asked her to be happy for him. "Will you, then, then . . . marry Lavinia?"

"Lavinia Kellery? I certainly will not!" he replied without pause. "But, rather, what if I did? It is not your affair."

"Forgive me again. I did not think. You are of course right. I wish you very happy, my lord." He was cross. She could see the two angry lines meeting between his brows. "I am so sorry to have taken you away from your party. Pray forgive me."

"Enough of this! All this begging of forgiveness does not suit you. I must be on my way. Good day to you." He rode back without once turning to look at her. She knew this as her feet felt frozen to the ground, unable to propel her forward.

She resisted the urge to call out to him again. She could not humiliate herself a second time. This miserable exchange would have to do for her final encounter. If her heart had not been so full of wretched pain, she would have been furious at herself for bumbling her one chance. She forced herself to turn around and trudge down the lane, filled with such embarrassment at his rebuffs that she was unable to think properly.

It was done. She had packed her belongings and shuttered the cottage for Clarissa, save the one window in the front room. She sat staring out the window, dressed in her modest gray wool traveling clothes, watching the sun fall lower and lower in the sky. She had convinced herself that with each passing minute she would feel less pain, but that had not been the case. She longed to be on her way, anything but this silence in the gloom, but she stayed and waited, praying for fortitude and peace of mind.

At long last a lone figure appeared, walking through the small grove of trees fronting the cottage. She rose to open the door for her brother but then stopped and stared.

It was he. Whyever had he come? More torture? Her body was numb to it now, not hesitating to face further torment. At least she would have one more memory of him to store in her mind for the long days and nights ahead.

She opened the door before he knocked. He walked the few remaining steps and removed his hat from his head.

"May I come in?" he asked hesitantly.

"Of course, my lord." She ushered him into the front room, finding it difficult to meet his eyes.

"I am sorry it is so dark. I've shuttered the place for Clarissa and expect her at any moment."

"Ah, yes. She asked me to carry a message to you. She and Sir Thomas have decided to postpone their trip to Chichester this afternoon. It has been decided that a storm is brewing, and my grandmother is adept at convincing everyone to abide by her wishes, as you know. She is overjoyed by all the gaiety, and has persuaded them to spend their wedding night at Hesperides."

"Thank you for bringing me the message, although I am sure it was unnecessary. My brother will be along shortly, as we are to leave. He could have saved you the trouble of informing me."

"That is the second message I was to relate. Your brother is having—let's see, as he phrased it, 'a bang-up time of it,' and has accepted an invitation to stay at the Hall as well. My grandmother hastened me here to ask you to rejoin the house party as well, as it appears no one will be leaving tonight."

Jane sat down on the edge of the small settee, her back rigid. "I see," she said as she straightened the edges of her cloak. "Please inform Lady Graystock that I am most appreciative of her kind offer. However, I will remain here."

She had every intention of having the carriage brought from the inn's rebuilt stables. Her coachman from Pembroke could drive her to Bosham if they could not reach Portsmouth before any storm broke. In fact, looking out the window at the stillness in the trees, she thought the theory of a storm was a ridiculous notion accepted by willing invitees.

Rolfe lowered himself into the wooden companion chair beside the settee and sighed. "I was quite angry with you when I left Seaton."

Jane looked up from her hands to see Rolfe working the edge of his hat. "Yes. And I have apologized for my behavior. It was very wrong of me. But you have asked me to stop apologizing."

He looked at her with an unreadable expression. "Jane, I

was angry with you because of your blind stubbornness and preconceived notions."

At his words, Jane jumped up and looked toward the door.

"No, wait. Let me finish," he insisted.

She could feel herself stiffen, but lowered herself onto the seat, forcing herself to endure this abject humiliation.

"I am going about this all wrong, I know." He wiped his hand across his brow. "Jane, I had no idea you had not married Harry Thompson until a mere half hour ago. All this time, when I heard mention of 'Mrs. Thompson,' I mistakenly thought it referred to you. I did not know the featherbrained Miss Dodderidge had married Harry. It was only when your aunt said you would be returning to Cornwall that I clarified the matter."

Silence filled the room. She was too embarrassed to meet his eyes again when he continued, "I decided to come here to find out for myself if you are happy with your situation. On the road you said you were unhappy and that you had made a mistake."

"And you, sir, said it has turned out for the best and everything was quite impossible to change now." She looked into his eyes and saw sadness in the dark, raw depths. It lanced her stubborn pride. She swallowed and continued, "I swore to myself, and to George, I would not let pride get in the way of my happiness again. I know it is not proper for a lady to reveal her feelings, but all notions of propriety were lost to me some months ago when I met you." For the life of her, she could not say another word. She hoped it would be enough of an admission.

Rolfe moved to stand in front of her. Grasping her arm, he raised her up to stand before him. He lifted her hand to his mouth, then turned it over and pressed a kiss on the sensitive area on her wrist.

A thread of hope bloomed within her.

"Dearest Jane. Dare I presume to offer for you a third time? Shall you deny me again, or worse yet, rebuke me?" A warm, tender light appeared in his face.

"Oh, Rolfe," she whispered before her throat constricted. Unable to continue, she moved forward to lay her head on his lapel and wound her arms about his neck. His hand gently smoothed her hair. She persevered in holding back her tears in a grand effort to listen to him. It felt so comforting in his arms.

His cologne teased her senses. She stayed there as he told her of all the pent-up feelings he had for her, the feelings he had tried to repress, and the sensibilities that refused to be denied. He also told her of how he had planned to go away, to travel abroad, as he had been unable to keep her from disturbing his thoughts.

After he had told her of all of his regard, Jane confided hers. "I did not love you until after our second meeting when you embarrassed me so hideously."

"How so, my love?"

"You know very well that I thought you were a groom on that runaway beast of yours. When I saw you in church, I wanted to die of mortification!"

"Yes, that was when I knew unconsciously that I should marry you. You did not wither from the confrontation." A rare smile appeared on his full lips.

"How little you know! I tried my best to avoid the tea at the Gurchers', but it was well nigh impossible." Jane laughed and looked up at Rolfe. As she gazed at his impossibly handsome face, it was suddenly as if time stood still.

"You won't scratch my eyes out if I steal a kiss, will you?" His smile grew, revealing a beautiful, heartfelt expression. He didn't wait for an answer as he lowered his lips to hers. Jane felt all the tension leave her body as he deepened the kiss. He was so warm, and the scent of him sank into the depths of her being. His embrace defined the meaning of comfort, and she never wanted to let go. She reveled in the knowledge she would never have to. She hugged him closer and heard him laugh.

"Ah, Jane. How I love you, my dearest, loveliest girl. And how I have longed to say it." He smoothed the top of her head again with his gentle hands. "However, if we stay here another moment, I fear I will not be able to squash the desire I have to take you upstairs and ravish you properly. But you should know that the looks on your brother, aunt, and new uncle's faces as I departed force me to desist. If I am not mistaken, they will descend on this cottage—with a large entourage—within the next quarter hour to make sure we are not at daggers drawn."

Jane smiled to herself and hugged him tighter. She needed just a few more moments to hold him, to enjoy the sheer luxury of feeling his arms around her. "I know. We must share our good news with my family and yours. My family has been very good about not rubbing my nose in the muddle I made—even my father." She then forced herself to lean away from him. Rolfe buttoned up her gray coat and motioned her toward the door.

She asked him, once outside, "Did you walk the entire way?"

"No, no. I left my horse at the smithy. We can have another horse saddled for you there, too." Rolfe's hand found hers, and he brought it to his lips as they walked through the fruit trees.

"If it is all the same to you, I think I would rather ask Smithy for a pillion," Jane said.

Rolfe laughed. "My pleasure, darling. Although, are you sure you trust Atlas to get us back in one piece? He has only recently let the weight of the world drop from his shoulders."

"Is that what you named him? Well, we shall see. If he unseats us, we shall have to walk. All the better for being alone together just a few minutes longer. I fear we will be swallowed up by everyone upon our return."

The horse was soon saddled and bridled. After a few noises of discontent, Atlas settled to the idea of the extra weight.

Jane wound her arms around Rolfe's waist and snuggled against his form, debating whether she had the courage to mention his past or not. Finally she whispered in his ear, "Rolfe, I do so love you. Will you be worried and unhappy if I'm ever with child? Your brother has finally let go of his guilt over your first wife. Will you be able to do the same? I hope the horrible experience with Connie will not stand in the way of our having a child."

She felt Rolfe's body tighten. "I suppose I will have to let it go, as I will have you as my healing balm every day. And I will remind you, daily, that it is quite safe to let someone guide you occasionally, especially one who loves you as I do."

Jane smiled. "I shall work at being a meek wife," she said with the smallest voice she could muster.

He laughed. "I cannot wait to see the transformation."

"I am quite determined to make you happy," she said with a

smile while nuzzling his neck. "And where shall we live? Please do not say London. I couldn't bear it."

"My dearest, we shall face the gossipmongers when we must. With any luck it will be in a little less than two decades' time, when our daughter or son must have a taste of the beau monde. Until then, you can hide in the stables," he said with a laugh.

Jane giggled. "I suppose we shall reside here, then? I dread to think of what will become of Pembroke's stables."

"Why, if you agree, we shall move the horses here to Hesperides." He paused and tried to turn around a bit to see her reaction. "Now, if you really love me you will stop this prattling and tell me again about your feelings. I have always wanted to hear bad poetry from the lips of the woman I love."

"Ah, but you forget my forte. I do not write bad poetry," she said. "Are you trying to ruin our great beginning with insults already?"

"No, never, my dearest." He reached around to pat her leg. A small object nudged his hand. "What is this?"

"Why, it is your ring, and now I can return it to you without rebuke," Jane said.

"We will have to work on your not disobeying me in future. Whyever did you not send it to me when you left Seaton? Did you not know I would have flown to your side in an instant? Had you so little faith in me? I had given you my word."

"Yes, but you were so angry, and I felt very, very guilty and foolish."

As Rolfe opened his mouth to argue further, Jane rushed on, "You are not going to continue to read me a lecture, are you? First insults, then a lecture?"

Rolfe laughed as he pulled Atlas to a halt just before the final turn to Hesperides. He moved as far as he could in the saddle to look at her. She felt a warm, comfortable feeling in her soul. At last everything felt right.

His smile faded as she stared into the depths of his mysterious gray eyes. He kissed her before Atlas burst their afternoon reverie by pawing the ground.

"That gentleman is eager for his oats." Rolfe threw his leg over the front of the saddle and jumped down. He lifted her from the pillion and continued, "However, this gentleman must have one last taste of his sustenance before facing the inquisitive masses."

As he kissed her, Jane felt the final smudges of emptiness, sadness, and pain wash away from her, to be replaced with an unfurling wholeness and happiness. The rustling sounds of the fall leaves still clinging to their branches were joined by the merest whisper of people's voices in the distance.

Jane reluctantly ended their embrace. With a smile lurking at the corner of her lips, she knew now how to change the ending of her original story. Enough with the wilting virgin in her manuscript! She must change her to a willful widow who succumbs to an arrogant earl, only to find true happiness in becoming a docile wife. Yes, that was it!

"What are you thinking, my love? Are you plotting an escape from the crowd that will soon be upon us? You cannot stand facing down the comments and questions that will be asked by the Mrs. Gurchers and the Miss Kellerys on this earth?"

"No. Nothing of the sort," she said, then arched one eyebrow. "But now that you mention it, your rank does give you a natural command of the situation, and perhaps it would be better if I just go around the gatehouse and leave you to it."

"Coward."

A gurgle of laughter escaped her. "Ah, Rolfe. You do not know me at all. I wouldn't dream of deserting you now, at our finest moment. I wouldn't miss it for the world."

A crowd of people poured through the wings of the gate as Rolfe quickly pulled her into his arms, capturing her lips with his own. Some might call him the coward, but he was loath to verbally reveal his emotions to the masses.

Actions spoke louder than words, anyway. He would let the embrace speak his intentions, thereby obliterating the need for a stilted speech about love.

They would be the talk of the town. This would give the gossips something to twitter about for years to come.

He pulled back to look at her. Oh, to hell with it—he was a love-struck fool. She looked so lovely with her sparkling eyes filled with love and laughter; he couldn't stop the words from pouring forth as the crowd surrounded them. "Yes, well, I love her, as you can plainly see. That's the way of it. I hope you will all wish us happy." Not very tender prose—but at least not a hint of poetic drivel.

"Let's have us 'nother kiss, yer lordship," called out Smithy's carrot-topped lad, dressed in his Sunday finery. Jane laughed and looked at Rolfe.

"Hear, hear," said Gooding, grinning as he turned to Clarissa, whose eyes brimmed with tears of joy.

His grandmamma bustled forward. "Yes, do heed the boy's request. No getting out of it now, you know. I see a parson and leg shackles within a fortnight. Glad I am of it, too!"

All thoughts of propriety and verse vanished as he looked at Jane and encountered the fine light in her eyes. "Most happy to oblige," Rolfe murmured as he enveloped Jane in his arms and kissed her, thereby sealing his fate.